STRIKING OUT

By Robert Lamb

THE PERMANENT PRESS
Sag Harbor, NY 11963

Library of Congress Cataloging-in-Publication Data

Lamb, Robert, 1935–
    Striking out / by Robert Lamb.
      p. cm.
    ISBN 1-877946-06-0 : $20.95
    I. Title.
    PS3562.A429S7   1991
    813'.54—dc20   90-42708
                                      CIP

Manufactured in the United States of America

THE PERMANENT PRESS
Noyac Road
Sag Harbor, NY 11963

For My Mother, Hazel

"I've been searchin' for the daughter of the devil himself,
I've been searchin' for an angel in white;
I've been waiting' for a woman who's a little of both,
And I can feel her, but she's nowhere in sight."
—*One of These Nights,* a song by THE EAGLES

Prologue

A place called simply "the Hill" figures prominently in this story. It is a real place. It is a mythic place. Its long shadow fell across my youth.

I lived near the Hill for a long time before I even knew it was there. A friend showed it to me one day, took me up there. The Hill gave me my first look at another world. I found later that I did not much like that particular world, but it wasn't lost on me that there must be other hills, other worlds. I resolved to find my own.

What kind of hill was the Hill? Well, a geologist might say it was just one of the last volcanic hiccups in Georgia's roll from the Blue Ridge Mountains to the sea. At its highest point it stood only 463 feet. It looked taller, though, because the rest of the town spread out beneath it as flat as a Monopoly board. It was steep too; early automobiles had trouble climbing it and often had to be hitched to mules to make it to the top.

But in Augusta, my hometown, the real significance of the Hill had nothing to do with geology—and everything to do with economics. Think of that Monopoly board as having a hill where Boardwalk and Park Place are, and you've got the picture.

Of course every community in America has its Hill. You've seen it. Maybe you even live there. It's that part of town where suddenly you see space, lots of space, between the houses, and the houses are big and well-groomed, not just boxes with a roof for a lid. It is that residential part of town that looks green and clean, comfortable, serene. Shiny new cars tend to flock there. You can't miss it. It's like going in a wink from black-and-white to Technicolor. But just in case, follow the railroad tracks into town, any town, and then turn right. Go way right. Trains don't rumble through the dreams of the rich.

Not every community's Hill is on an actual hill, of course. It just happened to be that way in my town. So, unless you insist, don't read into the story a symbol that doesn't belong there. In these pages, to paraphrase a very perceptive woman, "A hill is a hill is a hill." Instead, look at it, if you can, as I do: life loves its little ironies, and to emphasize with geography what was perfectly clear already must have been one of its favorites.

There. I dislike long prologues. They are nothing anyhow but a verbal dimming of the house lights, stimulating for a moment, tedious beyond. Eliot put it best: "Oh, do not ask, 'What is it' Let us go and make our visit."

—BB

PART 1

Chapter One

1953

Johnny said we couldn't miss.

"Patty is gonna put out, I tell you. I been working on her for days and she's ripe. And if Patty will screw, Austin will too. They're best friends, aren't they? They do everything else together, don't they? Just leave it to ol' John."

Questions thronged in my mind, but they got all tangled up on the way to my tongue. Too, I was afraid of asking a dumb question, so I just shook my head and said, "Yeah."

"We'll drive up to the lock and dam, and park," Johnny said, lowering his voice, though we were alone on that part of the school grounds. "I'll start putting the make on Patty, and when I've got her really steamed—you know what hot pants she's got—I'll suggest that we get out of the car and go sit on the grass. It'll be obvious to Austin we're going to make out, and you two will have the car to yourselves." He gripped my arm, squeezed it, and flashed a lecherous smile. "Ass, man," he said. "Ass!"

He almost had me believing it would work, and for a delicious moment the thought of scoring, of getting the real by-god thing at last, made me dizzy with lust. Sweet carnal pictures danced in my mind—nipples, thighs, cunt—and I could see myself finally getting it: *It*—the great and wondrous, hot and mysterious, moist and magnificent IT. I almost moaned.

Johnny must have known what I was thinking and feel-

3

ing. "We got it made in the shade, Benny boy, made in the shade. Hot damn!" He hooked his arm around my shoulders and shook me, a big grin on his small face.

Johnny was small all over. He just missed being short, but because he was skinny and his legs looked longer than the rest of him, he appeared taller than he was, about five-feet-eight. He walked taller than he really was, too, holding his wiry frame straight and sort of strutting. He wasn't good-looking; there was too much nose and not enough face for that. But he had nice gray eyes and dark brown hair that couldn't seem to decide whether to curl or wave. He was a sharp dresser too.

I forced a smile and tried hard to feel as confident as Johnny did, but I was capable of only short flights of faith where making out—really making out—was concerned. Close but no cigar, that was me. And I could see myself, come Saturday night, fucking up instead of fucking. Johnny would score and I'd fumble on the one-yard line. He'd wind up with pussy and I'd wind up with nutache. A fervent prayer formed in my mind: *Ph-leeze, God, just this once. I'm 18, for Christsake!*

Okay, so it was an awful prayer. A sacrilege, even. But, dammit, didn't I have a point? God was unfair in the distribution of pussy. He let other guys have some; why not me? Why single out Benny Blake to remain a virgin? Surely there was a more merciful way to punish me for my sins. What had I done that was so awful anyhow? I masturbated a lot, sure, but whose fault was that? *You listening, Lord?*

I wondered if Johnny ever masturbated, or for that matter if Protestants even considered it a big deal, the way Catholics did. That sin, that one mortal sin, kept me in the confessional so much that my knees were calloused. And I just knew that the good Jesuit priests of St. Jude were aghast at the number of times I could repeat the same sin. I could just hear Father Boyle saying to Father Brady in that flat Irish twang of his, "I tell you, Father, the self-

4

abuse of the Blake boy surpasses anything in my experience. Any day now he'll be showing up for Confession with his arm in a sling."

But I knew the shame of it all wouldn't stop me. Except for pussy, nothing short of amputation would stop me. So how, I wondered, was God coming out ahead in all this? In the scales of divine justice, didn't unfairness and masturbation outweigh a little piece of ass? It was enough to make me wonder if God wasn't female.

The school bell rang, ending the lunch break, and Johnny and I walked back toward the school, a huge, three-story brick building that was dark and dismal inside at all times, but was especially depressing now that spring had come.

"Hell of a day to be stuck inside," I said, thinking of cutting my last two classes. I knew I could get away with it; graduating seniors could get away with murder in the last few weeks of school.

"Just think about tomorrow night," Johnny suggested.

"Yeah," I said, but with an enthusiasm I did not feel. Johnny was more confident about *every*thing than I was about *any*thing. I didn't believe for a minute that Austin would go all the way, and I had my doubts about Patty. Worse, if Patty did come across and Austin didn't, then I'd look like a wimp to Johnny. I decided to think about Saturday night only when I had to.

We entered the building through a side door next to the lunchroom. The smell of boiled cabbage and dirty dishwater nearly turned my stomach. "Man, I'll be glad to get out of this place. Won't you?"

"Yeah, but I wanna take the memory of Patty Wilson's pussy with me." He nudged my shoulder with his as we walked along the gloomy hallway.

"You sure you can get your dad's car?" I was hoping to find some uncertainty there, but as I knew he would, Johnny said, "Sure. No problem." It was a '52 Ford that still looked and smelled new, and Johnny got to use it all the

5

time. His dad, the story went, had been quite a lady's man in his day and he understood that you had to have wheels, the nicer, the better, to make out.

My stepfather had no such understanding. Our car was a '48 Chevy, a five-year-old crate with worn-out seats that no self-respecting girl wanted to go out in. "What's wrong with that car?" Zeb would demand. "Runs like a charm, and it's paid for." My mother took a loftier tone: "Well, if it's the car the girl is interested in, then she's not the right girl for you anyhow."

We climbed the stairs to the second floor and headed toward the hub of the building, an area near the principal's office and the school's main entrance where two long hallways met. It was the heart of Riverside High, a sort of big crossroads where, if you stood there long enough, you'd see nearly every one of Riverside's 2,000 students. For that reason people thronged there before and after school, and at all changes of class, mostly keeping an eye peeled for some special member of the opposite sex. Jostled by students streaming both ways in our hall, Johnny and I pushed forward.

"There she is!" he hissed in my ear.

I looked about quickly but saw no one of special interest. "Who?"

"Just ahead, coming this way. Dianne Damico. Um, umm."

As soon as he said her name I came wide awake. Dianne Damico was the walking wet dream of every guy in school. A sexy Italian, she was a cheerleader whose prancing little ass had inspired more touchdowns for dear ol' Riverside than all the pep talks Coach Ramsey had ever delivered. And now through a break in the crowd I saw her: dark brown hair, cut in a pageboy, chocolate brown eyes that said, "Don't you wish you could read my mind?" and pouting lips glossy with lipstick as red as the sweater she wore.

"You reckon ol' Tommy Haynes has been gettin' that?" Johnny asked. Tommy Haynes was Dianne's steady. A sen-

6

ior, he was captain of the football team and played forward on the basketball team.

"Lord, I hope not." She didn't know me from Adam's house cat, but I had built many a sexual fantasy around her sultry good looks, and the thought of Tommy Haynes or anybody else getting into her pants—anybody but me, that is—made me ill. She sat directly in front of me in Spanish, where I spent most of each class contemplating her luscious ass. Framed by the open back of her desk chair, it looked like a perfect upside-down heart, a lecher's valentine that jiggled and wriggled and rolled each day before my eyes until I felt seasick with lust. "But I'll still trade places with him," I said as Dianne glided by us, passing so close that I could have leaned over and kissed her. Of course, the odds of my ever kissing Dianne Damico were so remote that she might as well have been in Afghanistan. She could have any guy she wanted.

"Better wait." Johnny said; "I heard they were about to break up. Might've already happened."

"Oh, yeah? What's the problem?"

"Don't know. It was her idea, though."

I frowned. "Well, I didn't think it was his. What guy with walking-around sense would break up with *that?*"

"Ain't it the truth?"

"But where do you hear these things? Nobody tells *me* things like that." It was true, exasperatingly true.

For an answer Johnny gave me a smug smile and peeled off to the right as we reached the hallway intersection. His next class, drafting, lay in that direction, and mine, a study hall, lay straight ahead. "Later," he said, meaning after school. We met every day after school to walk home together.

It was almost time for the bell, so I hurried along to class. But my mind was still on Dianne Damico and the news of her breakup. Maybe I should just lean forward in Spanish class soon and say somthing smooth, like, "Say, Baby, let's you and me conjugate some verbs together, starting with *amore*, you dig?" Maybe she'd turn around and smile and say, "*Si, Senor,* Beeny. And you can split my infinitive anytime you want to." Ha! That'd be the day.

Study hall nearly put me to sleep. The room was quiet except for the steady hum of lowered voices—you were allowed to talk as long as you kept it down—and I sat in a desk by windows that caught the afternoon sun. The weather was warm for mid-April even in Georgia, the windows were open, and something in the spring air made it hard for me to keep my eyes open. I had nodded off when a sharp poke between the shoulders startled me awake.

"What'cha gon' do this summer, Blake?"

It was Bruce Holdenfelt, a tall, rangy senior with ugly carrot-red hair and a long freckled face that seemed set in a permanent sneer. "Johnny Kelly and I are planning a trip to New Orleans," I said over my shoulder. It was a flat-out lie. We were going to the beach in Savannah for a week. But I knew Holdenfelt wouldn't have brought up the subject unless he had a great summer planned. I knew too that he wanted me to ask about it, but I didn't.

"I'm spending the whole summer at Jekyll Island," he soon volunteered.

"That's nice," I said, hiding my envy. Jekyll Island was on the south Georgia coast, near Brunswick. I didn't know that much about the place, but anybody who could spend a whole summer at the beach, any beach, was a lucky SOB in my book.

"Got a job lifeguarding," he said, knowing damn good and well that half the guys at Riverside High, including me, would kill for such a job. He poked me between the shoulders again and leaned forward to whisper. His hot breath bathed the back of my neck, making me feel queasy. "Think of all that poontang, Blake. Friend of mine who was a lifeguard down there last year said he had to quit the job a week early just to rest up. Ain't that a pisser?"

I gave him one side of a sickly smile as visions of suntanned girls in tight, brief swimsuits danced in my head. "Some guys have all the luck."

He fell silent for a minute or two and then leaned toward me again. "What's in New Orleans?" His tone of voice said that he could not imagine why anybody would want to vacation in such a god-forsaken place.

"Jazz. Johnny and I like jazz."

He snorted. "Jazz?" The word sounded nasty in his mouth. "You're a weird sumbitch, Blake. So is Kelly. You two make a good pair."

He snickered and my blood began to simmer, but I didn't say anything. It would delight the bastard to know his needling had gotten to me.

"Say," he added, "are you and Kelly sweet on each other? Ain't New Orleans full of artists and queers?" He snickered again, enjoying himself enormously. "I see you two together all the time. You and Kelly goin' steady, Blake?"

I wanted to turn and hit him in the mouth, but his size made me think better of it. He stood at least six feet tall and must have weighed 175 pounds; I was no more than five-ten and didn't weigh 125. Sarcasm seemed the wiser course. "Actually we're engaged. I really shouldn't be talking to you."

He let out a horselaugh and flailed about in his desk, having a grand old time. I went on trying to ignore him, but he knew he was getting to me. Soon he was back again, prodding me between the shoulders and leaning forward. "Say, Blake, ain't you some kind of artist, too? Miss Johnson is always saying how good your themes are and how you ought to be a writer. I wish I was a teacher's pet, 'specially Miss Johnson's."

Miss Johnson, an attractive woman of about 25, was my English teacher, second period. Holdenfelt was in the same class.

He whispered again. "You gettin' any of that, Blake? She looks like a hot one to me, and some of these teachers like that young stuff, you know—and her single and all."

I turned to face him. "Why don't you shut up?"

He laughed and all but danced in his seat. He had finally gotten a real rise out of me—maybe because at last he had guessed too close to the truth. Not, of course, that there was anything between Miss Johnson and me—that was ridiculous—but heaven knew I had harbored lustful fantasies about her for two years, ever since she had first come to Riverside High. She was a brunette with cool, sky-blue eyes, terrific legs, and lips that seemed swollen with passion, and nothing she wore could hide so ripe a figure. All the guys in school talked about how much they'd like to get in her pants, and it was rumored that Coach Ramsey had walked right up to her in the hallway and offered to eat her pussy. But as guilty as I was of the same lust, I hated to hear her talked about that way, especially by a jerk like Holdenfelt.

"Are those tits real, Blake?" He pretended serious interest and looked quickly about, inviting me to take him into my confidence. "Are they? You can tell your ol' buddy Bruce."

"Ol' buddy Bruce can kiss my ass," I said, finally hot under the collar. Holdenfelt was big, that was true, and I had never been much of a fighter, but I did have a temper that could get the best of me, and when it did I was prone to recklessness.

But Holdenfelt's game was merely to bait me, it seemed. He ignored my remark and said, "Naw, I guess you wouldn't know about Miss Johnson's tits, seein' as how you and Kelly have a crush on each other. Just forget I asked, Blake."

I had started to turn away when he added: "Does Austin Armisted know about you and Kelly, Blake?" He was full of phony concern. "I mean, she's a sweet gal and I'd hate to see her get hurt. How serious are you two anyhow?"

So *that* was it, I thought. The bastard had his eye on Austin. I shouldn't have said anything, should have let him stew in his own jealous juices, but I didn't think fast enough. "Austin and I date—that's all. I have no strings on her and she has none on me."

I saw my mistake right away: he had heard what he wanted to hear, and I had thrown open the door to Austin

10

for him. He said nothing more and I didn't either, but I spent the rest of the period mentally kicking myself. I was not in love with Austin, and she wasn't in love with me. But I hated the thought of that sonofabitch dating her. Austin had gone pretty far with me, and in my more hopeful moments I thought she might, just might, eventually give me some. A rival would screw things up royally.

"Holdenfelt?" Johnny said. "Do I know him?"

We were walking home from school, a distance of a mile or more. We lived two or three blocks from each other, depending on which way you went, in a part of Augusta called Milltown, a sprawling section of small, frame houses built very close together that had grown up around the city's cotton mills. Most of the grown-ups in that part of town, including my mother and stepfather, worked in the mills.

"Big ugly redhead. Face like a horse."

"I know him," Johnny said. "Runs with the Hill Catholics. Rides a motocycle."

"That's him."

Johnny laughed. "Those fellows sure don't like you, do they?" He meant the Hill Catholics.

"They're not fond of you either, Ace."

And then we both laughed. The boys of the Hill Catholic clique hated our guts for the simple reason, it seemed, that we didn't live on the Hill. All of Augusta was divided between those who lived on the Hill and those who didn't—the haves and the have-nots—and Johnny and I belonged among the latter. We were even worse than outsiders; we were Milltown boys, and Milltown people had a reputation for roughness. Nevertheless, for more than a year he and I had been venturing into neighborhoods on the Hill to date Hill girls and to attend their parties. In fact, we had first met at one of those parties, the first he'd ever attended and only my second or third, and ironically it was the Hill Catholic boys who had thrown us together. Two or three of them approached Johnny during the party and offered him a dollar to whip my ass. Johnny told them, "I don't need a dollar that bad."

"The proposition offended me," he told me later. "Did I look so hard-up that I'd do their dirty work for them for a lousy dollar? But it made me curious about you. Who was this guy they hated so much they'd pay to see his ass whipped? So I walked over and introduced myself."

We had been fast friends ever since.

"Maybe I ought to have a word of prayer with Holden-felt," Johnny said. "Maybe he'll be at Harriet Pringle's party tonight. Wanna go?"

Harriet was one of the Hill Catholic girls. Among Riverside High students who lived on the Hill, the Catholics formed one clique and the Protestants another, and they rarely mingled socially. The rest of the students, who by far made up the majority, didn't count, at least in the social scheme of things. If they even gave parties, I didn't know it.

"Yeah," I said, "but I wouldn't start anything if I were you. There are a lot more of them than there are of us." That was the truth, and I hoped it would give Johnny pause, but the deeper truth was that, in spite of being a Milltown boy, I was afraid to fight. It was an unreasonable fear and one that made me feel ashamed, but I had been unable to overcome it, in spite of having been in several fights in which I at least held my own. Besides, fighting seemed stupid to me, and I'd never had the heart to hurt anybody unless I lost my temper. Johnny, on the other hand, acted cocky and tough, more like most of the other guys in Milltown. I had never seen him in a fight, but he was feisty and seemed fearless, and though he was small and weighed less than I did, nobody seemed eager to tangle with him.

"I wouldn't start anything at the party," Johnny said, "but if he wants some of me it can certainly be arranged."

I laughed uneasily. "I don't think it's you he wants; it's me."

"Beat his ass."

12

"Have you seen that sonofabitch? I can't *reach* his ass."

Johnny laughed. "He is a big one, ain't he? But relax. He doesn't want you *or* me; he wants Austin." He kept a straight face, waiting for me to respond to his dig.

"Thanks, buddy."

We both laughed some more.

"Can you get your car?" he asked.

"Maybe. I'll see. Wanna ask Glenn to go?" Glenn McNulty, another senior, often ran around with us, but we weren't as close to him as we were to each other.

"Naw, not if you can get your car. If you can't, then we'll call him." Glenn seemed able to get a car just about anytime.

We had reached the corner in Milltown where our paths separated, but we stopped for a minute to talk. Johnny said, "Forgot. Guess who'll be at the party tonight."

I was stumped. Obviously he meant somebody special. "Not Austin and Patty." It was more a question.

"They weren't invited. Harriet doesn't like Patty. Remember?"

I remembered. "Who then?"

"Dianne Damico."

A lot of good it would do me, I thought, but it was still good news. I could at least look at her. "Good," I said. "You can go after Bruce Holdenfelt's ass while I go after hers."

He scoffed. "You should live so long," he said and started toward home.

"Ain't it the truth?" I said. "Ain't it the truth?"

Getting our family car was not all that difficult, just frustrating. I knew the routine by heart. First came the third degree: Where are you going? Who are you going with? What's the occasion? What time will you be back?

Then came my mother's instructions: Drive carefully; behave yourself; wear a clean shirt; show that you've got some manners; be sure to tell Mrs. What's-her-name (or, if it was a date, Miss What's-her-name) that you had a good time; be sure to lock the door when you come in.

Finally came my stepfather's lecture on the proper use and maintenance of an automobile. He had told me so many times to "be sure to set the handbrake" when parking that I reached for it out of habit everytime I slid into my desk at school.

Oil was his big thing, though. The way he carried on about oil, you would have thought he was a Rockefeller. "Now, Benny," he would prompt, cocking his head and pointing a finger, "whatever else you do, be sure to keep an eye on your oil pressure." Actually, I was always glad to see him do that, because the cocked head and the pointed finger meant that we were finally down to the serious business and that the lecture was almost over. "Oil pressure—that's the thing," he would say. "You run out of gas, all it'll cost you is shoe leather. But you let her run out of oil—" Here he would pause for dramatic effect and then, like a symphony conductor, bring down his hand with a swoop: "—and the engine is gone. Ruined." I never left home in that damned car without visions of mechanical mayhem churning in my mind—and all because Benny Blake had neglected to put oil in the transmission. I could see this internal-combustion engine lying on its deathbed, choking, gasping, tubes running in and out of it, while the doctor looks at me accusingly and says, "Tsk. Tsk. One quart of Quaker State 30 wt.—that's all it would have taken."

Harriet Pringle's house was one of those rambling affairs in which one room seemed to lead to another, and that one to still another, so that people mainly roamed from room to room during the party to make sure they didn't miss out on anything. It was a good arrangement for me and Johnny, because it meant that we weren't trapped in the same room all night, as we often were at such parties, with the Hill Catholic boys glaring at us. It didn't seem to bother Johnny the way it did me, but, hell, they acted like wolves in a pack, milling restlessly among themselves while waiting for the boldest to get impatient enough to lunge at our throats.

"Fuck 'em," Johnny said, and he ignored them without even seeming to ignore them. But their behavior not only made me uneasy, it puzzled me. We had been putting up with that for months, and I couldn't figure out why they never did anything but glare at us. In Milltown, hateful looks counted for nothing in showing anger; if somebody decided he didn't like you he'd crawl your ass right then and there. But this—this was new to me.

"At least they're not all together in the same room here," I said in a low voice to Johnny. We had been at the party for about ten minutes and were leaning against a wall in the living room, surveying the partygoers.

"Screw 'em," Johnny said. "I'm going to dance." He nodded toward the back of the house, from which music could be heard. We had already learned that the den was set aside for dancing, and obviously the den was back that way somewhere. I didn't like the idea of splitting up, but before I could say so, Johnny spotted our hostess as she walked into the room carrying a bowl of peanuts. A pale girl with blue-black hair and perfect white teeth, Harriet was striking rather than pretty and looked as if she could easily get fat. At 17, however, she was still thin enough to be called shapely and was popular with boys, though personally I'd always thought she was a bit stuck-up.

Johnny caught her eye, nodded our way and said, "Come here."

It always surprised me to see him talk to a girl that way, as though ordering her about, but it surprised me even more to see them obey. Harriet smiled as if flattered to her shoe tops, put the bowl on a coffee table and walked straight toward Johnny. Ever on the alert for ways to improve my technique with girls, I had tried Johnny's trick several times, but when I wasn't ignored altogether they shook their heads and said, "*You* come *here*." Maybe the difference was that I never could master his devil-may-care attitude about it all.

"Yes, sir?" Harriet said brightly, stopping in front of Johnny and clasping her hands behind her back. She even made a cute little curtsy.

15

"Kee-rist!" I muttered, turning away to roll my eyes.

"Got on your dancing shoes?" Johnny asked, all non-chalance.

Harriet glanced at the white ballerina slippers on her feet and, blushing, said, "Yes."

"Well, take me into your den so we can show these people how to *really* dance."

Johnny was a good dancer, but, heck, so was I. But if I had tried his routine on some girl, first it would have turned out that she was wearing hobnailed boots and then that she either 1.) had never learned to dance, 2.) had promised the dance to somebody else, or 3.) suddenly remembered that she had a phone call to make.

Johnny and Harriet, holding hands, walked away. Not wanting to seem a tag-along, I stayed where I was, but soon began to feel conspicuous standing by myself against the wall, so I ambled about, stopping here and there to chat briefly with people I knew. I kept moving because I wanted to see who all was there and what was going on, but I was aware too that I had not yet seen Dianne Damico. I concluded that if she were there she must be in the den dancing, but since I had not run across a desirable dance partner I was reluctant to go into the den and appear out of place. Instead I struck out down a hallway, exploring, and soon found myself in a nearly deserted recreation room, hearing as I entered the slam of wood against wood and a girl's voice saying, "I quit. You're too good for me." I looked around just in time to see a girl I did not know walk away from a table-tennis game and come my way. As she passed me on the way out she said over her shoulder to her opponent, "Here's another victim for you. Try him."

Standing at the table's other end was Dianne Damico, a smile of triumph on her face, her hair in fetching disarray and looking damp with sweat. Looking at me, she wagged her ping-pong paddle and said, "Why, I know you. You're in my Spanish class. Third period. Remember?"

Remember? I thought. *Is the Pope Catholic? Does a bear shit in the woods?* But if my mind was racing, my tongue was paralyzed. I managed only a nod.

16

"You play?" she asked. "Grab a paddle." She bounced the ball of her own paddle several times, eager to get going.

I thanked God that indeed I did play, played well, in fact. But one needs mobility to play ping-pong, and so help me Jesus my feet would not move toward the table. A blaring headline flashed into my mind: "Teen Struck Dumb and Lame by Table-Tennis Challenge."

"Well?" she said, making ready to serve.

Somehow I got to my end of the table and picked up the paddle. As soon as I did, a torrid serve sizzling with top-spin streaked across the table, hit my paddle and ricocheted to pop me right between the eyes. My opponent laughed—she couldn't help it, but it still stung worse than the ball had—and I felt my face turning a fiery red.

"I'm sorry; I thought you were ready."

"I thought so too," I lied. "That's some serve you've got."

She smiled. "My brother taught it to me. Ready to play?"

I set myself and nodded, and in the wink of an eye she launched another sizzler, just like the first. This time, though, I managed to get my paddle in front of it and send it looping back over the net. Surprised, she made a feeble return to my right and with a flick of my wrist I sent the ball humming over the net, fast and low, and just out of her reach.

She chased the ball down and returned to the table, giving me a look of reappraisal.

"Luck," I offered. But I saw her teeth bite into her lower lip. Her face set with determination, she said, "One up," and fired a blue darter at me that was nothing more than a blur shooting across the table. It was aimed at my back-hand, and my backhand was the weakest part of my game, but only in the sense that I was reduced mainly to defense with it. The defense was pretty darned good. I flicked the shot back easily, giving the ball bottom spin, and when she closed in on what looked like an easy kill she hit it straight into the net.

She had to strain to retrieve the ball with her paddle from the middle of the table, and as she did, her breasts,

bulging against her white peasant blouse, pushed up and
threatened to spill out on the table. At the same time, bent
over as she was, her ass, the ass that had tormented me so
in Spanish, stuck up into the air and wiggled back and
forth as she struggled to recapture the ball. I lost the next
point and the one after that.

"Three-two, me," she said. "Your serve."

Here I was guilty of showing off, for I had in my bag of
tricks a number of baffling serves. She won not a single
point during that set and wound up down seven to three,
to say nothing of having chased the ball all over the room
while I ogled as she ran, stooped, bent, kneeled, squatted
and stretched. It was wonderful, like having her perform
some private pornographic routine for me and me only,
though it was obvious that she had no awareness of the
effect of all this.

Meanwhile I had both warmed up and measured her
game, and I saw that except for one wicked serve it was
only fair. I let her score a few more points, but won easily.

She was a good sport. "You're good. Very good."

I blushed. "Your brother must be pretty good too."

"He used to be, but his playing days are over, I guess.
He's entered the seminary."

She looked proud and sad at the same time, so I didn't
know whether to congratulate her or to say I was sorry. To
me, becoming a priest was a fate worse than death, but to
many Catholic families it was a badge of honor.

An awkward moment followed as we stood there, the
table between us, saying nothing. At length, inspired by
desperation, I asked, "How're you doing in Spanish?"

She smiled. "*Muy bien, gracias.* And you?"

Around her I was having trouble enough with English.
"All right."

We got quiet again, but soon she knocked the ball toward me. "Let's just hit awhile. I'm tired."

That was fine with me. At least I didn't have to stand
there looking stupid. As we volleyed I remembered that I
hadn't introduced myself. "I'm Benny Blake."

"I know. I'm Di—"

"I know."

We laughed at the awkwardness, and then, just to see what she'd say, I said, "You date Tommy Haynes, don't you?"

"We went out a few times. Nothing serious, if that's what you mean."

"Just making coversation. I don't know Tommy."

"Tommy's all right. Just a little mixed up." Saying that, she hit one hard that zipped by me.

"Aren't we all?" It was more a statement than a question. I chased down the ball and returned to the table. "Going away to college after you graduate?"

"Marymount. It's in New York. Tarrytown."

My heart sank. New York was a long, long way from Georgia.

"You?"

"I don't know," I said, and I really didn't know, a fact that had worried me a lot lately. I wanted to go to the University of Georgia, but my parents couldn't afford it. "Maybe junior college somewhere; maybe the Navy."

"I can see you in the Navy," she said, stopping, smiling. "Cute little sailor suit." She hit the ball again.

Suddenly it dawned on me that she must have a date around somewhere. "Who'd you come with—to the party, I mean?"

"I came by myself. Walked. I live only a few blocks from here." She paused. "Why? Does a girl have to have a date?"

I blushed. "No. But it *is* Friday night. And this *is* a party."

"Then who's your date?"

I blushed more furiously. "You got me," I said. "I don't have a date either. Came with a friend. Johnny Kelly."

She laughed and hit one of her scorchers at me. Off guard, I lunged at it, missed, and fell to one knee. When I got to my feet she was standing beside me, her face showing concern. "You all right?"

"Yeah. I still say that's some serve you've got there." She

19

smiled, and up close her smile was even prettier. "Dazzling" was the word that came to mind. "Say," I said, "do you dance?"

She smiled again and affected a heavy southern drawl. "Why, ah thought you'd never ask."

Lights were low in the den, it was crowded with other couples, and on the record player Kay Starr was singing "Wheel of Fortune" as I moved onto the dance floor with Dianne. For a few moments I actually trembled as we began to slow dance and cursed myself for being so nervous. If ever I had needed to appear cool and suave, this was it. But apparently the trembling went unnoticed, and soon after we began moving Dianne looked up at me, smiled and said, "You dance well too."

"Thank you," I said, and then in a line I thought divinely inspired for smoothness I added, "but the credit rightly belongs to my partner."

She looked up at me again and cocked her head. "That was glib, Benny Blake."

She said it in good humor, but the reproach was there. I decided that this was one angel who was down to earth and that I'd better be too. "It was," I confessed, "but you do dance well."

Actually I wouldn't have cared if she danced like a hog on ice. She felt so good in my arms, and I was so surprised to find her there, that nothing else mattered. She smelled so good—not perfumed, but clean and natural—that it was intoxicating, and the movement of her body against mine, soft here, firm there, did nothing to help clear my head. Only the end of the song did that, and it seemed to come so quickly that I cursed under my breath when it ended. In a matter of seconds, though, another record began playing, "I Believe," by Frankie Laine, and I was flattered when she turned to me and said, "Let's dance again. I like this song."

This time, though it was as nice as the first, I had some wits about me and soon noticed other dancers giving us the once-over. A couple of guys, both Hill Catholics, gave me dirty looks, I thought, and some of the girls looked us up and down as if to say: "What have we here?" But none of that bothered me. With Dianne Damico in my arms, I was above life's petty concerns. Once, when the crowd parted for a moment, I saw Johnny and Harriet over in a corner, not really dancing, but rather swaying to the music, his arms around her waist, hers scissored about his neck. They were looking raptly into each other's eyes. I shook my head in wonder and thought: *Another one bites the dust.* I also thought how sweet life could be, for there was Johnny making time with one of the most popular girls in school, and there I was, well, if not making out, at least dancing with the Sweetheart of Riverside High, the centerpiece of countless erotic fantasies.

I was in such a dream world that I hardly noticed I was getting bumped around. But soon a hard jolt to my shoulder brought me back to reality. Turning to see who had collided with me, I looked into the ugly face of Chuck Conlin, one of the ring leaders of the Hill Catholic boys. A malicious smile playing around his thick rubbery lips, he said softly, for my ears only, "Tommy Haynes wants to see you—outside." Having delivered the message he danced away, but he looked back and nodded his head once while raising his eyebrows, as if to say, "It's true, sucker. Your ass has had it."

Immediately I was flooded with a feeling that I knew all too well and that I despised in myself. It was fear, pure and simple, and it turned my insides to ice. My first thought was to run, just slip out the back door and get gone, but, hell, a guy couldn't do that, no matter how scared he was. He'd be the laughingstock of Riverside High for the rest of his natural days. Next, I thought of Johnny: maybe he could get me out of this, or better still, take up the fight himself. But most of all there was Dianne. The girl seemed to like me. Wasn't that a dream come true? And she seemed to have soured on Haynes. What more did I want? Wasn't this my big chance?

21

The record ended, and Dianne, who had noticed nothing wrong, broke our embrace and turned to speak to a girl at her side who had spoken to her. Getting Dianne's attention, I excused myself "for a moment" and turned to walk away—but not before she caught my arm and said with a smile, "I'll wait right here."

I almost had to will my feet to move, and it all seemed so unreal that later I remembered nothing of the long walk from the den to the front porch. My brain simply went into a stall until I saw Haynes, standing among some pines in the yard, just beyond the range of the porch light. He wasn't that much taller than I was, but he had a muscular build, and I knew that if he could fight at all he could overpower me.

"Over here, Blake," he said.

I went down the steps and walked to where he was, wondering vaguely where he had come from. I was almost sure I hadn't seen him inside during the night.

"I hear you been foolin' 'round with my girl." Anger twisted his blond, blue-eyed good looks into an ugly mask.

I had decided to try to talk my way out of this if I could do it without seeming cowardly, but that hope faded as he spoke, because I saw that he had been drinking. Still I tried. "Never met her before tonight, and we've done nothing but dance."

"Thass not the way I heard it."

"She's inside; ask her yourself."

Either that was the wrong thing to say or he had planned all along to do little talking. With a punch that came whistling out of the dark he hit me flush on the jaw and down I went, light exploding inside my head and then fading, receding. He must have jumped on me after I fell, because the next thing I knew, Johnny and somebody else were pulling him off me as a crowd of people, mostly girls, looked on from the porch.

Then and later, that was the worst of it: the way they looked at me, their faces showing a fine contempt. It was bad enough to be part of a public spectacle, I who hated even to be conspicuous, but there I was, the innocent victim of an ass-kicking, being stared at as if I were a piece of dog shit. It was as if they were thinking: *Oh, it's only Benny Blake; what can you expect of a Milltown boy?* As far as I knew, they didn't even know I was from Milltown. The problem was that *I* knew it and worried all the time that if these Hill people looked at me closely they'd figure it out too. It was silly, I knew, but that humiliation hit me harder than Tommy Haynes had.

I must have swum in and out of full consciousness for a moment or two, for next, without my realizing how she got there, Dianne was kneeling at my side, her face working in anguish. "Oh, Benny," she said, making a quick sign of the cross and putting a hand to my face, "I'm so sorry. Are you hurt?" I didn't feel great—my head felt lopsided—but there was no pain, probably because I was in shock. "I'm okay," I said.

"Thank God!" She lifted my chin so that I was looking her in the eye and tried to explain something. "Benny, I—I mean, Tommy and I—She gave up the effort and looked around the yard. "Where is he?"

I hardly knew where *I* was, let alone Haynes, but I followed her gaze and saw him. He was leaning against a shiny blue Buick in the driveway, facing two or three guys who seemed to be talking to him, trying to reason with him. I devoutly hoped they would succeed.

"Wait right here," Dianne said, rising and walking toward him.

I glanced around and saw that an adult, probably Mrs. Pringle, was herding people back into the house and going inside, herself. I got to my feet and noticed that Johnny was standing behind me and apparently had been there for some time.

"You okay, champ?"

"Some champ," I said, feeling my jaw, working it back and forth. "Son-of-a-bitch coldcocked me. Didn't see it coming." I tried to smile. "Not that it would have made much difference. He hits like a truck."

Johnny stepped up, put his arm around my shoulder and looked at my face. "You'll live," he pronounced.

I nodded my head toward the house. "Did you see the way they all looked at me? Like I was garbage or something lying there."

"Naw," Johnny said. "They were just glad it wasn't them laying there."

"I don't think I want to go back in."

"Fine. I'll say goodnight to Harriet and we'll leave." He looked over to where Dianne and Haynes were standing. We couldn't hear what was said, but she appeared to be giving him hell. He stood here, leaning against the front fender, arms folded, head hanging. "What about her?" Johnny asked.

"She said to wait. I'd like to if you don't mind."

"Be back in a minute." He turned to go inside.

"Apologize to Harriet and her mom for me, will you?"

"Sure."

He left and I moved to the porch and sat on the steps. A minute or two later Haynes got into the car and started the engine. He leaned out the window and said something to Dianne, and then he backed out of the driveway and drove off.

She came over to where I was sitting. "Can you drive me home?"

It was a simple request, but I panicked. Dianne Damico in *my* car? Why, she'd take one look at it and say, "Uh, thanks, but I think I'll walk." But what else could I say? I said, "Sure. Soon as my friend says goodnight to Harriet."

"Thank you. I'll call Harriet later; I don't want to go back inside." About that time Johnny came out and we left.

I burned with shame the whole time I was driving her home, and I couldn't help but think of the shiny new Buick Tommy Haynes was driving. More and more I was noticing that bastards like him seemed to have everything. It didn't make sense to me. Where were the rewards for being a good guy, or at least not a bastard? Was there some law of nature at work here that nobody had told me about, some law that said, "Okay: the bastard gets the new Buick and Dianne Damico; give Benny Blake an old Chevy and a hard time"? If so, I wanted a new deal. I wanted *my* turn as a bastard.

But if Dianne even noticed my car, I couldn't tell it, and in no time we pulled up in front of her house.

"Walk me to the door, Benny," she said, and then to Johnny, "Nice to meet you. Good night." I got out and she slid across the seat to follow.

A brick walkway led to her house through a white picket fence. The house, also white, had two stories and looked, well, homey. A light was on in the living room, and I could see through the window that it was nice inside. It was the kind of house I had seen in so many home-magazine ads: comfortable, nothing fancy, but solid, cozy. I wondered if I would ever live in such a house.

At the door, Dianne took my hand and turned to me. "Benny, I owe you an explanation." I started to protest, but she shushed me with a hand to my lips. "Yes, I do. You wouldn't have gotten involved if it hadn't been for me, and the least I can do is explain—and tell you how sorry I am." Her hand moved to my face, where Tommy had hit me. Touching gently, she asked, "Does it hurt?"

"It'll be all right."

"I'm furious with Tommy about all this. He had no right to attack you, and he's given me his word that he'll apologize first thing Monday at school."

"That's not necessary," I said. But the truth was, I didn't want Tommy Haynes anywhere near me, come Monday. Or Tuesday. Or any other day.

"Let him do it for my sake, Benny, if not for yours. He's got to understand that he has no claim on me, and part of his agreement with me was that he would tell you he was wrong: I'm *not* his girl. And the sooner he gets that through his head, the better."

A tone of urgency had slipped into her voice, and I thought for a moment that she might cry. She got hold of herself, though, and continued. "You see, Benny, I'm nobody's girl, and never will be. I'm going into a convent two weeks after I graduate. I'm going to be a nun."

She could have said, "I'm actually a male," and pulled out a cock, and I would not have been more stunned. Dianne Damico a nun? Impossible. Unthinkable. My heart sank like a rock cast in the sea. "But you said—"

"I lied about college. It's the story I'm telling so people won't—won't think I'm some kind of freak. You do understand, don't you? I know it's wrong to lie, to deceive"— here she quickly crossed herself—"and I've asked God's understanding and forgiveness this one time. This is, after all, a very personal, a very private decision."

There was no doubting her sincerity. She looked me straight in the eye and spoke with conviction. Still I asked, "Are you *sure* this is what you want to do?"

"I've known since sixth grade. And I've never wavered in my decision."

Never? I thought. "What about Tommy?"

"Tommy and I have never been anything but friends." She gave me a knowing look. "I know some people think otherwise. But it's not true."

I rubbed my jaw. "Well, something tells me Tommy didn't get the message."

"He got it, all right; he just doesn't want to accept it. I told him about my plans six months ago, when I saw that he was getting serious. And I thought he understood. Then, as the time got closer, he set in to change my mind. That's when—and why—I stopped dating him."

"Where in hell did he come from tonight?" Suddenly it hit me that I was talking to somebody who was almost a nun. "I meant 'heck.'"

"He followed me there." She threw up her hands. "He's been pulling this kind of stunt for weeks now, following me around, drinking and moping, thinking it'll change my mind. Even if I did change my mind I wouldn't see him anymore—not after all this. It's stupid and childish, but more than anything else it's weak and self-indulgent,

Tommy's grand chance to play the tragic figure." She laughed drily. "He's having the time of his life; he's happier now than he was when he thought he had me."

Sonofagun, I thought. The girl talked with a lot of sense, and my estimation of her was rising by the minute. "One more thing," I said. "How did I get caught in all this?"

She sighed. "I guess he wanted to cause a scene to call attention to himself. It's pretty hard to play the tragic figure if you don't have an audience. The target just happened to be you. He knew he couldn't come to the party. He was not invited and was turned away at the door by Mrs. Pringle when he tried to crash it. I guess he just hung around outside."

It was beginning to come together for me. "So that's why you were back in the rec room. Hiding out. I wondered about that."

"Yes. I saw him coming to the door and I didn't want him to see me. As for the rest, I guess somebody went outside and told him I was dancing with you." She looked at me with those big brown eyes, so soft, so earnest. "Why did you go outside? You hardly know me."

I came within a whisker of saying: *Because I don't have the sense God gave a goat.* But I caught myself and said nothing, just shrugged my shoulders. How could I tell a future nun that her lucious ass was the cause of it all, that I did it because of my towering lust for her pussy, that I had wanted to get into her pants so bad that I'd fight Haynes and six more like him if her panties were the trophy?

"Well," she said, smiling sweetly, "he may be bigger and stronger than you, Benny Blake, but he's not the man you are."

Now I did feel bad. I wasn't a man; I had been scared stiff, to say nothing of being leveled by one punch. Maybe she wasn't so smart, after all.

She moved closer and took my hands in hers. "And I'll tell you something else: If I *weren't* going away, if I weren't going to devote my life to Christ and the Church, I'd want to see a lot more of you." With that, she stood on tiptoes, brushed her lips quickly against mine, whispered, "Good night," and hurried inside before I could say anything. But there wasn't anything to say, and she had known that. With the scent of Dianne Damico in my nostrils and the feel of her hands in mine, her lips on mine, I walked back to the car.

When I slid in under the steering wheel, Johnny leaned over and peered at my face in the darkness. "Gee," he said, "the face is familiar, but it's been so long since—"

"Sorry. She wanted to talk."

"And?"

"Tell you all about it later. What time is it?"

"Let's see: it was April when you left. . . ."

I groaned. "Cut the comedy. What time is it?"

He held his wrist up to catch the streetlight on the face of his watch. "Ten-thirty. Early yet."

"You hungry? Let's go to the Varsity." The Varsity was a drive-in restaurant and the favorite hangout of Riverside students. It was located near the high school, about half-way between the Hill and downtown.

"I got a better idea: Let's look up Tommy Haynes and put a whippin' on him."

I didn't know whether he was joking or serious, but I said, "I've got an even better idea: *You* look up Tommy Haynes and put a whipping on him, and then come down to the Varsity and tell me all about it."

He laughed.

"Fact is," I continued, starting the car and pulling away from the curb, "Haynes is supposed to look *me* up on Monday—and apologize."

I could feel Johnny staring at me. "You know, I could have sworn you said—"

I interrupted. "You heard right, Ace." Playing it grandly, I explained: "Dianne told that chap that he did me a grave injustice, that he was a bully and a blackguard, and should be ashamed of himself, and that if he did not

28

apologize to me at his earliest opportunity, she would cut off his nuts and use them for Christmas-tree ornaments."

"Sure. And he said, 'Why, Miss Dianne, I'm just as sorry as I can be that any act of mine could find disfavor in your eyes. Here, take my riding crop, please, and thrash me soundly about the head and hindquarters'."

We began laughing and couldn't stop. I laughed so hard that my jaw started hurting, so hard that tears rolled down my cheeks and I couldn't see to drive. I knew it was silly, but it felt so good to laugh like that after the evening I'd had. And, what the hell, it beat crying.

When the laughing fit wore off, I said, "Crazy as it seems, there's a measure of truth in what we said just now." I told him all about it as we drove to the Varsity.

Johnny said he still couldn't believe it. "Dianne Damico a nun? Come on."

We had parked at the back of the Varsity's huge lot, turning the car around and backing in so we could watch the other cars as they came and went. Johnny was eating a hamburger and drinking a Coke. I was working on a chili dog and a chocolate shake. We were sharing an order of fries.

Pointing a french fry at Johnny, I said, "Tell you what *I* can't believe: that all this could happen in one evening. I mean, I finally get a chance at Dianne Damico, sweetest little ass this side of heaven, and what happens? God whisks her away to a nunnery. And, for good measure, He sends a guy around to punch me out. All in one evening! Do you think He's trying to tell me something?" I was only half joking.

Johnny sipped on his Coke. "If He's telling you to give up pussy, don't listen to Him."

Wish to God I had some to give up, I said to myself. Then, changing the subject, I asked how things had gone with Harriet Pringle.

"Fine as wine. I'm taking her out next Saturday night.

Why don't you get a date and join us? We could take in a movie and then check out Teen Town. Teen Town was a recreation center run by the city. Located on the Hill, it featured table tennis, a pool room, a snack bar, and dancing, mostly to a jukebox, but sometimes to live bands. It was a popular hangout for Hill teenagers.

"Sounds good," I said. "Now all I need is a date. Harriet and Austin don't get along, you know. Besides, I'd like to date somebody new. I need a fresh start."

"What about Cherry Ashford? She and Harriet are best friends."

I nearly choked on my last bite of chili dog. "Cherry Ashford? You gotta be kidding." Cherry was a pretty girl, very pretty, but, to me at least, she was as unattainable as an "A" in algebra. She was different from the other girls—made of finer stuff, you might say, and she was very shy. Word was she rarely dated, probably because guys saw her as too far out of their league. I knew I saw her that way. The Ashfords, an old Augusta Catholic family, represented not just money, but wealth; not just social position, but breeding. They were the kind of people who summered in the mountains, who wintered in Palm Beach. Hell, Cherry had even been to Paris, France. Spent a whole summer there studying art at the Sorbonne. *Me, date Cherry Ashford?*

"I think she likes you," Johnny said calmly.

I didn't know what to say. He was suggesting the impossible, the inconceivable. I made a show of looking all around the car and then said, "Look, Ace, there's nobody else in the car but me."

"I think she likes you," he repeated. "Harriet hinted at it while we were dancing. That's how girls put out the word. Guys do it too, don't they?"

How could he be so nonchalant about such a thing, I wondered. "What'd she say?" I was all ears.

With a great show of patience, Johnny said, "I asked her for a date. She accepted. Then she said—maybe the girl doesn't trust me alone—'Why don't we double-date?' I said fine; who've you got in mind? And she said, coyly, 'Well, Benny could ask Cherry.' So I put two and two together."

"That's it? That's all?"

"I'm sorry," he said wearily. "Next time I'll get it in writing."

I sat there letting it sink in. "Can you picture me with Cherry Ashford?"

"What the heck," Johnny said, "you tried to put the make on a nun."

"A near-nun," I corrected, feeling another attack of the sillies coming on. "A near-miss with a near-nun, you might say."

"I'd like to get near *that* miss, nun or no nun, and none too soon."

"An attitude like that could lead to bad habits."

"Stuff and nun-sense."

I held up my hands, giving up. "Awright, awright. Let's get serious here."

"Fire away."

"First, I'll call Cherry for a date. The worst that can happen is that her butler can tell me she said no."

"Now you're talking."

"Next, you'll have to get your car. This one is reserved for near-nuns, and our Rolls is in the shop." I could see Cherry, coming out her door, spotting my old heap, and running back inside screaming. No thanks.

"Can do," Johnny said, downing the last of the fries and wiping his fingers with a napkin. "I doubt if she's ever heard of a Ford, but luckily our ermine seat covers just came back from the cleaners."

"We can tell her it's a Cadillac that shrank in the car wash."

"Good show!" he said, trying to sound English. Then in his own voice, he said, "What next?"

I hestitated. What *had* been next? "Oh. Did Holdenfelt show up tonight?"

"Never saw him if he did. Maybe I ought to look him up."

That was what I was afraid of. "Look, we don't need any more fights for awhile. Girls will stop inviting us to their parties and they won't be allowed to go out with us either." I hoped I sounded practical instead of afraid.

Johnny sighed. "You're right. But we may not be able to help ourselves."

"What do you mean?"

Before answering he paused, obviously thinking. "That Hill bunch has wanted to kick our asses back to Milltown since they first laid eyes on us. Up to now, nobody's had the guts to try it. But now that Haynes has tried it—"

"Tried, hell; he knocked me into next week." I didn't want Johnny tiptoeing around my pride; the truth was the truth, as Zeb was always saying.

"He sucker-punched you," Johnny said matter of factly. "Could've happened to anybody. But *they* don't know that. They didn't see it. And Haynes ain't gonna tell 'em."

I saw what he was getting at. "Damn!" I said. "So what do we do?"

He laughed. "Well, there's always prayer."

"No. Get serious." I was getting worried. They could be coming for us right now, and there we were, backed up in the rear of a parking lot with a ten-foot fence on three sides, trapped. I began to pay closer attention to cars driving through the lot.

"Tell you one thing: I'm not going to let them run me off the Hill. Are you?"

I said of course not, but already I was thinking of things I could do around the old neighborhood for awhile until things cooled off. Then a scary thought hit me. "They wouldn't try anything at school, would they?"

"Naw. You know Mr. Thompson; he won't stand for any crap like that." Ed Thompson was principal of Riverside High. He was also an ex-Marine and had brought to the school the same tough discipline that he had learned in the

32

service. "Besides, most of 'em are seniors and they want to graduate too. No. They'll catch us on the Hill, on their home turf, and probably not at a party. After all, they like to get invited to parties too."

"That leaves Teen Town."

"Right."

That made me feel better. All we had to do was to avoid Teen Town. But then I remembered. "And you want to go there Saturday week? With dates?"

"They won't start anything with girls around. They'll be too afraid the fight might not go their way. No, they'll wait and catch us by ourselves.

"Yeah. Probably *me* by *my*self."

"Look, Benny, it's gonna come sooner or later—"

"I'll take later."

"The way to make it later, or never at all, is to show the bastards we're not afraid."

Afraid was not the word. I was plain scared. "You better be right about Saturday; there are a lot of them and only two of us."

"Trust me," Johnny said.

I didn't say anything—I just hoped to God Johnny knew what he was talking about—and for awhile we sat there in silence, watching the activity in the parking lot. It was near midnight now, and though the lot was still full the pace had slowed. Earlier in the evening, when Friday Night Fever was at its peak, one car after another, windows down, radio blaring, had cruised through the lot, its occupants in high spirits, laughing and waving right and left to friends. They were there to see and be seen. Now fewer cars came, and in those the people seemed subdued, as if on a different mission from those who came before. They seemed to be—I couldn't quite put my finger on it—looking for something and not finding it. Some swept through quickly, as if knowing exactly what they were looking for; others drove slowly, stopping now and again, before leaving. It might have been my imagination, but I thought of these latecomers as lonely and I identified with them. I didn't know why. Johnny was sitting right there beside me, but suddenly I felt very lonely.

"I need a girl," I announced out of nowhere.

"Don't we all?" Johnny said.

"No. I mean it: a girl who's all mine, a girl who's—oh, I don't even know."

"What's wrong with Austin? She'd go steady with you if you asked her, I bet."

"Yeah. Steady for maybe two weeks, until somebody else caught her eye."

"She does bat those baby blues, don't she?"

"Yeah." I smiled. "You know, when I first met Austin I thought she was, well, not all there, the way she jerked around, this way and that, and so damn changeable. I said to myself: this girl's got a nervous condition. And the way she bats those eyes . . . Some of her friends call her Blinky, you know. But the more I looked at her, the cuter she got."

Austin *was* cute. About 5-feet-2, she had a nice shape and very pale skin set off by pretty, coal-black hair. She even acted cute: she was fun-loving, laughed easily, even at herself, and said exactly what was on her mind. Still, there was all that jerking around, as if every now and then some of her wiring got crossed and she shorted out.

"You know what Zeb would say about Austin, don't you? He'd say: 'That gal needs a fucking; she's *dying* for it— that's what all that jerkin' around is all about.' He'd tell you to push her over and slip her the meat."

I sighed. That was Zeb up and down, all right. But that was Zeb's advice about every girl, and I wasn't as taken with his philosophy as Johnny was. Maybe that was my problem, I thought: I was dying to get laid, but when girls said no—I figured they must practice saying it in their sleep—I took them at their word. Maybe Zeb was right after all: "Don't *ask* 'em; just push 'em over and fuck 'em."

"Is that what you plan to do with Patty?" I asked it with a smile, but I was angling for advice.

He nodded. "Damn straight. Of course, I hope to use a

lit-tle more finesse. Not throwing off on your step-pa, but the Zeb Carboni School of Seduction is a mite primitive."

Johnny knew I agreed. He knew just how I felt about my stepfather. Zeb had his good points, I guessed, but to me he was crude, even by Milltown standards. He made me feel sorry for my mother, and I was embarrassed that she had married him. Sometimes I got the feeling that she was embarrassed too.

Johnny went on: "Fact is, there's some truth in what ol' Zeb says; he just takes it too far. Some girls do say no and mean it. On the other hand, no—up to a point—is just so much hot air. They don't mean it and they hope you don't think they mean it."

I nodded and said, "Uh huh," as if my own experience had taught me the same wisdom. But the whole procedure was mystifying to me: no meant no except when it meant yes. How in God's name was I supposed to figure that out? What kind of mind did it take to crack the female code, and why, oh why, had I not been given that kind of mind? Why couldn't a girl just say, "Why, yes, don't mind if I do," or better still, "Oh, I'd love to; thanks for asking"? Jesus!

I blinked the lights to let the curb boy know we wanted to pay up and leave, and reached for the key in the ignition. "You ready?" I said to Johnny.

"Might as well; can't dance."

Before pulling off, I cocked my head to catch the light on the side of my face. "How does my face look?"

He leaned over and peered at it. "All I see is a scuff mark and maybe a little swelling. He must have caught you higher on the head than you thought. How does it feel?"

"Not bad, considering. I just don't want a black eye." I eased through the lot, pulled onto Druid Park Avenue and pointed the car toward home.

"Your eye looks fine. Put some ice on that swelling when you get home—and count your blessings."

"What do you mean?"

He smiled. "You can fuck with a swollen jaw, but suppose he'd kicked you in the balls?"

I played it straight. "Why, that might have been even better. Dianne might have pulled down my pants and rubbed them for me."

"Get Austin to rub them for you."

I wouldn't *trust* Austin with my balls, the way she jerks around."

He laughed. "Then get her to jerk you off."

"Know your trouble? All you ever think about is sex. That's not healthy."

"I'm not the one who tried to put the make on a nun."

"Near-nun," I corrected. He laughed and I added, "Can you picture that luscious body of hers hidden away forever under religious robes? Now *that* is what I call a sin."

"All that meat and no potatoes. Um, Um."

"You really think Tommy Haynes was gettin' that? I don't. That's a nice girl. I mean *nice*. Devout too."

"Yeah, but you know what Zeb says about nice girls: 'A nice girl is one who'll put it in for you'."

"I don't care *how* it gets in; I just want to get it there."

"Well, you'll get your chance in less than 24 hours, my boy." In a fit of anticipation, he clapped his hands and stamped his feet. "Hill pussy, get ready!"

Chapter Two

Johnny said it wasn't cool to come right out and ask a girl for a date. If she said no, for whatever reason, you felt bad, and then the girl would go around telling her friends that she'd turned you down, and that certainly wouldn't help your reputation any. So he had worked out a system. I used it the next day in calling Cherry Ashford.

"You busy next Saturday?" I got right down to business after identifying myself.

"Why, no," she said.

"Good. Pick you up at eight."

She said it hesitantly, but she said it: "All right."

I breathed deeply, moving the phone away from my lips. My palm was so sweaty I could hardly hold the phone straight. "Your friend Harriet has a date with my friend Johnny Kelly. We'll double-date. How's that sound?"

"That sounds nice."

I was listening carefully, hoping to detect how she really felt about this date, but she sounded merely pleasant. I told her what the plans were and she said fine, and then I said, "See you Saturday," and hung up the phone. Johnny said it was uncool to talk on until *they* ended the conversation.

"Is that some new way of asking for a date?"

It was my mother's voice and it startled me. She had come into the sitting room from the kitchen, where she had overheard me. She stood there, wiping her hands on her apron, with a look on her face that said: Is this the boy I raised?

I managed a weak smile. "Things have changed since your day, Mother. Nowadays you have to be cool."

She spoke gently. "Good manners never go out of style, Benny. You should ask nicely for a date."

Her disappointment in me stung, but I felt that she just didn't understand. "Yes, ma'am."

She smiled and came closer. "Who's the girl? Is she pretty?"

"Cherry Ashford," I said, reaching out to hug her. "And, yes, she's pretty. But not as pretty as you."

My mother *was* a nice-looking woman, but, oddly, physical characteristics didn't have much to do with it. Her features were regular: hair that was an average brown, hazel eyes that simply saw. She was even of average height, and her shape, though slender, aroused no envy among other women. What made her nice-looking was her gentle nature and a complete willingness to see the good in others while ignoring the bad. Somehow that temperament gave her a physical beauty that nature had denied her.

She had worked hard all her life, but it had not aged her too soon, and at 36—she was only 17 when I was born—she still looked younger than most other cotton-mill workers I knew. Most of them, men and women, looked ravaged and, rightly or wrongly, I figured that the mill did that to them. Secretly I had sworn that I would starve before I'd work in a cotton mill, and I hated that my mother had to work in one.

"Ashford," she said against my chest and then looked at me. "Do I know the Ashfords?"

"We don't exactly move in their circle, Mom."

She backed away to arm's length and gave me that look again. "Another Hill girl, huh?"

I nodded.

She shook her head, the meaning clear; we had been through all this before. "Is she a Catholic girl?"

I told her yes and that seemed to satisfy her somewhat, though she was no longer Catholic. She had left the Church to marry my father, a Baptist, and had never gone

back. Zeb was—I didn't know what Zeb was, but it sure as
hell wasn't Catholic, in spite of his being Italian. Born and
raised in the South, to parents born and raised in the
South, he didn't even know he was Italian; a passionate
baseball fan, he listened to every major league game he
could find on the radio and was forever running down
players like DiMaggio and Berra as "nothing but old wops"
and as "guinea bastards." I told him once that he was
throwing off on his own kind, and he said, "Whadaya-
mean? I'm American."

My mother started back toward the kitchen. "Get
washed up. Supper'll be ready soon." Then she stopped
and turned. "What's wrong with your face? It looks a little
swollen."

It was also bruised and tender, but the bruise was under
the hairline. Apparently Haynes had hit me on the cheekbone and temple. "Johnny and I were horsing around. It's
nothing."

"You be careful," she said. That was her favorite advice:
"You be careful." I was surprised she didn't wake me in the
night to tell me to be careful as I slept. But secretly I liked
it.

Not long after supper, I went into the bathroom to start
getting ready for my date. I hated our bathroom and was
always in a hurry to get out of it, but ever since I could
remember, my mother had drummed into me the virtue
of cleanliness. "Even the poorest man has no excuse for
going dirty," she would say. "Soap is cheap and water is
plentiful."

Still, I wished with all my might that we could have a
bathroom like those I saw in homes on the Hill: bright and
cheerful, with gleaming porcelain, cabinets, closets, thick
towels, pretty soap dishes, and the mingled odors of good
soap, mild disenfectant, and exotic lotions and colognes.
Our bathroom, though clean, had none of those touches.
And worst of all it had no shower. I had not known there
was such a thing as a shower until I got to high school and
took a P.E. course. But every home on the Hill seemed to

have one, and now I looked upon a shower in the home—having one or not having one—as clearly separating the well-to-do from the poor.

Fortunately, the bathrom—and the back porch off which it sat—was the worst feature of our house, which had five rooms and stood on brick pillars a good two feet off the ground. Zeb, who was something of a handyman, had fixed up the rest of the house so that it was at least okay—in fact, not bad at all by Milltown standards. Still, it was pretty shabby compared to houses on the Hill, and I never liked for any of those people to question me too closely about where I lived. I never even told people that I lived in Milltown unless I thought they already knew. I just said, "Downtown," which was nice and vague, and which included some respectable, even genteel, neighborhoods. I hated doing that. I felt that in some way I was disowning my mother. But social class seemed to be everything at Riverside High—until I went there I had not even known there *were* different social classes—and I soon found myself doing anything I could to escape the stigma of Milltown. Even so, my greatest advantage lay in the ignorance of most Hill students about other parts of town. If I said, as I sometimes had to say, that I lived at 1415 Young St., most people from the Hill assumed that it was a respectable address even though they had no idea where Young Street was located. I was more than happy to let them think that. I often wondered if Johnny felt the same way, did the same things, but I was ashamed to ask him.

Ever punctual, Johnny arrived right on time to pick me up for our dates. But before I could get into the car, he hopped out, motioned me toward the rear of the car, scanned the street to see if anyone was watching, and opened the trunk. Pointing to a neatly folded blanket in the trunk compartment, he said, "Look, we'll start off making out in the car, but when things get going pretty good, I'll ease Patty out of the car, get this blanket and walk off into the dark with her, into that little picnic area." I said okay as he reached into the folds of the blanket and pulled out two small, square packets. "Here," he said, handing one to me and putting the other into his pocket, "you'll need one of these."

In the failing light of the evening I examined the printing on the little package. "One Trojan prophylactic," it said. "Sold for the prevention of disease only."

I looked at Johnny in awe. "You didn't go into a drug store for these, did you?" That kind of courage was beyond my imagination.

"My ol' man buys them by the box. He'll never miss 'em."

A little thrill went through me as I fingered the packet. My very own rubber. I'd never had one before. I smiled. "I hope it prevents that strange Hawaiian disease: lack-onookie." But my mind wasn't really on bad jokes. Instead I was marveling at Johnny's meticulous preparations. It was not that they surprised me; Johnny, I was sure, planned even his trips to the bathroom. It was that his approach was so different from mine. Maybe in his careful planning, I thought, the reason for my many failures was staring me in the face: I never did much more for a date than show up. As we drove away from the house, I said, "You think of everything, don't you?"

" 'Success is 90 percent preparation', m' boy, just as they say." Johnny was always quoting old sayings. He liked his knowledge in neat little formulas, I figured.

"What's the other ten percent?"

He laughed. "Luck—and it often outweighs the 90 percent."

I laughed too, but his words troubled me. I could plan if I had to, but I had never been lucky. If getting laid depended on luck, my quest would remain fruitless forever. Johnny *was* lucky, so lucky it was a little disgusting. And he not only knew it, he expected it, took it for granted. Honest to God, he could walk by a candy machine and a Hershey bar would fall out; I could go to that same machine, get nothing and lose my nickel too.

"Expecting luck is the secret to getting it," he had told me once, and now as we sped toward the Hill through an April night so soft it seemed you could reach out and stroke it, he cackled and crowed. "And I feel lucky tonight. Hill pussy, here we come!"

His optimism, his enthusiasm were contagious, and for a moment I caught the fever of certain conquest. But we had not traveled a block before my deeply rooted self-doubt returned, cooling my blood with whispers of remembered failures. *Jesus, sweet Jesus,* I prayed silently, *not tonight. Not again tonight. Be merciful. Take the night off. Slip me a little while the Virgin Mary isn't looking. Are you listening to me, Jesus?*

Of course I got no answer, unless silence itself was the answer, but I searched the sky for a sign anyhow. I saw only a lush and indifferent moon, lazy and uncaring clouds, distant and disinterested stars. Clearly neither God nor the universe gave a tinker's damn whether I ever got any pussy or not, and I found myself wishing I had been born a pagan. Pagan deities were much more reasonable about fucking. No Immaculate Conceptions for them; in fact, the more "maculate," the better, it seemed.

I turned to Johnny. "Do you think fucking is a sin?"

He laughed. "I think not gettin' any is a sin."

The more I learned about Johnny, the better I liked him. "I think about pussy all the time. Do you?"

"Ha! Is the pope a Catholic?"

"The pope frowns upon fucking. Officially, the whole world frowns upon fucking, it seems. Yet the whole world is either doing it or looking forward to doing it. I don't get it." In my mind I added: *In more ways than one I don't get it.*

"Believe me, the biggest frowns are on the faces of those not gettin' it. As I see it, if God hadn't intended me to fuck, He wouldn't have given me a dick and He wouldn't have put girls like Patty Wilson in my path."

"The Church would say He did it to test you."

"Well, if He did, I flunked. But I figure—not throwing off on your religion—that the Church doesn't know what

42

it's talking about. If priests and nuns don't want to fuck, fine. But I'd like to see 'em try a little bit before they set in to tell me how bad it is."

Yep. The more I learned about Johnny, the better I liked him.

I didn't pay much attention to the movie we saw. It was something that Patty and Austin wanted to see, one of those Esther Williams films with little plot and lots of water. I liked all the scenes of girls in swimsuits, but that was about it. My mind was on what would happen later, and I looked forward to it with an odd mixture of desire and dread that felt sort of like driving with your foot on the brakes. And the feeling quickened when, after the movie, Johnny swung the car south instead of west and eased out of town in the direction of the lock and dam.

As it became obvious that we were leaving the city, I heard Patty say softly to Johnny, "Where are we going?" She sat so close to him that in the dark interior of the car they looked like one body with two heads.

"Hush," he said; "you'll find out."

Christ on a crutch, I thought. If I had talked to Austin that way she'd've slugged me. In fact, I was afraid she would turn to me and repeat Patty's question, but she didn't stir. Snuggled against me, under my left arm, she sat so still, her head nestled against my chest, that I began to wonder if she were asleep. But when I craned my neck to try to see her eyes, suddenly they were looking dreamily into mine, and the next thing I knew we were locked in a languid and sultry kiss, a different kind of kiss between Austin and me. Normally we went at each other with a kind of savage but frightened need. This kiss spoke only of need. It felt like a kiss with its mind made up. It even tasted different: hotter and more saline, with a hint of musk.

I didn't look up again during the rest of the ride to the lock and dam, maybe ten minutes. I dimly grew aware that we had arrived when the car stopped rolling and the chirping of cicadas swelled into the night as Johnny

43

switched off the engine. By that time Austin was curled up on the car seat and lying in my arms, on her side, looking like the picture of sweet surrender.

I half-expected her to break our embrace now that we had parked, so as not to get caught off guard should Johnny and Patty turn to say something to us. But she kept right on kissing me and, if anything, grew more relaxed, burrowing deeper into my arms and chest. I'd never seen her that way before—calm and, well, acting normal, not jerking all around. Maybe she *had* decided to give me some, I thought, and the cure was taking effect already. Maybe the Zeb Carboni School of Seduction knew something about women after all.

In the middle of the kiss, I looked up just in time to see Johnny and Patty sink from sight on the front seat amid the rustle of clothing, the groaning of seat springs and a soft, feminine moan. They were little more than silhouettes to me, for we had parked in a dark corner of a picnic area, beneath a stand of weeping willows on the edge of a woods. But it was not completely dark inside the car. The radio was playing softly and the orange glow of its dial served as a tiny nightlight. Also, light from the distant locks leaked through the curtain of willow branches when the wind rippled them.

Austin must have sensed that my mind had wandered, for she pulled me even closer and kissed me harder. Now she had my full attention again. I squeezed her tightly, returned her kiss, and ran my left hand, the only one free for far-ranging maneuvers, down her back, over her hip and beyond, to below the hemline of her dress, which had hiked about halfway up her thighs. When my fingers touched flesh she shuddered. Bringing the hemline with it, my hand then trailed up the side of her thigh, rubbing lightly at first and stopping just below her hip. Leaving her dress up, I moved my hand to her knee, slipped it between her legs and slid it upward until it wedged deep between her thighs. This was farther up Austin's dress than I had ever gotten. She usually cut me off just above the knee. So for a moment I contented myself with the luxury of exploring intimate female flesh. Her thighs felt buttery soft and at the same time firm, and I was seized with a desire to kiss them, to feel them warm and soft under my lips and to nuzzle them with my cheeks. That surprised me. Guys at school made crude jokes about eating pussy: it was perverted and no real man would do such a thing. I had never given the subject much thought, so preoccupied was I with fucking, but now I saw in an instant that they were fools, all fools.

My first goal, though, was to get my hand on it. So after waiting a bit I pried a little and moved it higher, perhaps an inch or two, but she clamped her thighs tighter, stopping my advance, and broke the kiss. Her eyes found mine in the semi-darkness and she nodded toward the front seat as if to remind me that we were not alone.

I removed my hand from under her dress and put it innocently on her hip. She relaxed and started kissing me again, but now my attention was focused on Johnny and Patty as I looked for a sign—some movement, a sound— that might tell me what stage they had reached in their lovemaking. But all was quiet up front.

As I listened, though, a terrible thought bloomed in my mind: What if Austin and Patty got hot at different times, so that Johnny and I couldn't coordinate these seductions?

I recognized the idea as farfetched, anxiety honed on a desperate longing, but mere circumstance had kept me from scoring so damn many times that I had come to see the improbable snafu as likely to happen and the possible snafu as all but certain. In my brief career as a luckless makeout artist I had been denied pussy, or so it seemed, by menstrual periods, little brothers, older brothers, tattletale sisters, sudden seizures of conscience, untimely ejaculations, patrolling policemen, vigilant fathers, and mamas calling—and always, always, it seemed, with diabolical timing.

I began to kiss and stroke Austin again, not with the urgency of before, but with just enough intensity, I hoped,

45

to keep her passion simmering until Patty did heat up. Even with my limited experience I knew it was disastrous to let a girl cool off. A *guy* wouldn't cool off until he'd gotten relief, but girls seemed to come equipped with temperamental thermostats that kicked in when you least expected it and conked out at the worst possible time.

One kiss, however, told me that Austin's passion remained near the boiling point; after a minute or two of restrained kissing, she pressed into me harder and began to grind her lips against mine and make little whimpering sounds that sent an electric current of lust searing down my spine. She wanted no part of reserved lovemaking and seemed determined to fling herself, her passion, against my restraint and break through to a hunger that matched her own.

It did not take her long. Soon my main concern was not to keep her from cooling off, but to keep myself from shooting off. Her kisses seemed to be racing straight from her lips to my groin, as if they were hot-wired together, and every lash of her tongue in my mouth set off vibrations that made my dick quiver like a tuning fork. Making matters worse, my cock stood straight up in my lap, like a periscope of passion, taking a mauling from her body as she writhed against me.

To avoid coming in my pants I shifted slightly in my seat to break contact between my penis and her body. I didn't succeed entirely, managing only to make the massage less direct, less perilous. Consequently I spent the next few minutes trying awkwardly to maintain the embrace with the top half of my body while trying to escape it with the lower half. I felt ridiculous, like a man truly divided against himself, but in a crazy way it seemed fitting: I spent half my time anyhow torn between relentless lust and Catholic guilt.

But even that strategy backfired. Austin, it appeared, mistook my pelvic squirming for passionate writhing and clung all the harder, boring into me fiercely with her body and giving my cock a drubbing that pushed me quickly toward the point of no return.

In panic I broke the kiss and twisted my hips violently to the left to escape the agonizing contact. Teeth clenched, eyes closed, my body so taut it hummed in my ears, I breathed deeply, raggedly, until the crisis passed.

Austin must have thought I was merely overcome with passion, for when I opened my eyes and turned toward her, she gave me a look warm with sympathy and reached up to stroke my face. She was stroking it gently, staring deeply into my eyes, when the car's interior light came on.

"Sorry," Johnny said, halfway out of the car already.

Patty slid across the seat toward the open door and I felt a stab of envy as I watched her get out of the car. Johnny knew how to pick 'em. Patty wasn't prettier than Austin, but she moved with a feline grace that Austin would never possess. She was blonde and wore her hair in a ponytail that swung like a golden pendulum when she walked, her hair switching one way, her hips the other, and all of this accentuating a kind of lazy sexuality. Unlike Austin, she wasn't Catholic. She was a preacher's daughter with the saucy ass of a natural-born sinner and a wild glint in her eye that glasses merely magnified. Johnny could pick 'em, all right.

"See you later," she said in a sing-song voice.

Austin raised up to speak to her, but Patty was gone, the car door closing against questions. In the dark, Austin turned to me. "Where are they going?" She seemed genuinely surprised.

"Beats me," I lied.

She started to relax again, but then sat up straight, sliding off my lap, when she heard the trunk lid being raised. "What *are* they doing?" she asked, looking out the rear window.

"They'll be back."

The trunk lid slammed shut, and a moment later Johnny, the blanket draped over one arm, appeared at the

47

open window on our side of the car. Patty stood a few feet behind him. Leaning down, he said, "Patty and I are going to sit out on the grass. We'll be back after awhile." He nudged me on the shoulder and said to both of us, "Have fun," and walked away holding hands with Patty.

Austin, by now plainly mystified, leaned across me and stuck her head out the window. "Patty," she called.

Patty did not look back. "We won't be far," she sang out and kept on walking. Soon the shadows swallowed them up.

Austin pulled back into the car and flounced down beside me. "Well, I declare," she said, more to herself than to me.

"Maybe they want to be alone," I said pointedly.

"I like to be alone too, sometimes. It just took me by surprise, that's all." She slumped against my side and pouted for a moment, but in no time she scrambled up and leaned across me to peer out the window again. "It's dark as pitch out there."

This was getting to be absurd. Besides, all that jerking around was getting on my nerves. "Maybe they like it that way," I said, an edge of exasperation in my voice.

Austin sat back down beside me, sulking now. "Well, if her mama knew this she'd skin Patty alive."

I wanted to say, "What her mama doesn't know won't hurt her." Instead I said, "Look, I thought you wanted to be alone with me."

"Well, I do," she said slowly, uncertainly, "but I'm afraid. It's creepy here, out there. It's so dark."

"Patty's a big girl. And she's in, uh, good hands. So relax."

She seemed somewhat reassured, though maybe she just figured there was nothing she could do about it. At any rate, I reached out and pulled her closer to me, and a moment later, with her stretched out on the back seat again, we were locked in a tight embrace and she was, if anything, hotter than before. Now her kisses were bruising, punishing, and her whole body was alive. She

48

squirmed and flailed against me, her legs scissoring on the car seat, a series of whimpers and moans escaping her lips. They sang of a need so ferocious it might have been alarming if it hadn't been so flattering. I smiled behind the kisses, congratulating myself, and quickly ran my left hand up between her thighs and, great god almighty, clasped her cunt.

She jumped as if I had zapped her with a cattle prod, but I couldn't tell whether she was moved by alarm or lust. She clamped my hand tightly with her thighs, grabbed it at the wrist with her right hand and said something against my lips that came out, "Mumph!" But she didn't try to break my hold, so I kissed her all the harder, hoping to distract her attention from my hand and get her to relax. Meanwhile I made the most of the precious grip I had gained.

Twisting my hand for room in which to maneuver my fingers, I felt around as best I could, fondling and probing, petting and caressing. I couldn't do much, what with her thighs mashing my fingers together, mauling the knuckles, but for the moment heaven was mine. Never before had I gotten more than a fleeting feel of a girl's cunt—a tantalizing touch ended all too soon by a quick move this way or that, or finally a firm "No." But now I held one in my hand, actually held it in my hand, cupping it as it swelled and rolled against the crotch of her panties, soft, warm, pliable, alive. I could even feel her pulse there, and I wondered wildly if it were nature's Morse code, tapping out an insistent message that said: "Fuck me. Fuck me."

Gradually I was able—I hardly knew how—to free one of my fingers, the middle one, for exploration, and as I raked the point of it along the furrow of her cunt Austin gasped—gasped and shifted ever so slightly. But it was enough to give my hand more room in which to move. I set to work in earnest, pressing, squeezing, massaging, fascinated by the feel of pubic hair against nylon, enchanted by the texture of naked thigh, spellbound by the idea of actually playing with a pussy. I wished with all my heart that I could have one for a pet.

Austin must have liked what I was doing, too, for as I foundled and kneaded she opened her legs wider and shifted her body to give me better access. A moment later all resistance was gone. She lay back in the crook of my arm, breathing shallowly, rapidly, except for little sharp intakes of breath when I touched a particularly sensitive spot.

Her surrender threw me for a moment. I was so used to struggling for every favor I gained from a girl that I hardly knew how to go on against no resistance. Whether by instinct or luck, however, I quickly got my bearings. Pulling aside the crotch of her panties with my index finger, I probed gently with my middle finger, found her moist, velvet center and penetrated it to the first knuckle.

"Unngh," she moaned as a shudder racked her body. Her hips at first recoiled from my touch, but a moment later they relaxed and rolled forward, pushing slightly, seeking. Austin buried her face in my chest and I pushed in further, up to the second knuckle.

Never had I felt anything so soft and warm and wonderful. Deliciously wet, it sucked at the root of my finger and nipped at the tip, moving as if it had a life and mind of its own. In fact, its mobility was to me its most surprising quality. I had envisioned a vagina as little more than a warm, snug hole with hair around it, but here was a truly remarkable mechanism, an awe-inspiring play-pretty that could suck, ripple, spasm and rotate, all at the same time. I was seized with the desire to plunder it.

Removing my hand from Austin's crotch, I hooked my fingers in the waistband of her panties and skinned them halfway down one flank. Startled, she made a feeble grab for them and missed, and then cooperated as much as modesty would allow by lifting her hips as I pulled the panties down her other thigh. The sound of my own heartbeat was deafening to me as next I seized the panties in the middle, pushed them over her knees and shucked them off. Working now like a man possessed, I grabbed the hem of Austin's dress and whisked it up, at least in front, to her waist. In the dim light of the car she lay naked, or all but naked, before me. It was the most beautiful sight I had ever seen, filling me with awe and reverence, and if I did not at that instant become a man I was at least propelled beyond boyhood forever.

Austin, her heart thumping against my chest, now lay very still in my arms, her face burrowed deeper than ever into the pocket of my shoulder. I knew I could do anything to her that I wanted and, though wildly excited, what I wanted most at that moment was to drink my fill of the erotic sight before me.

Lightly, very lightly, I trailed my fingers up the inside of first one thigh and then the other, raking softly through her pubic hair, dark and mysterious, before pausing to press and caress her stomach. Every now and then I would feel for her slit, lay my finger in it and rock my hand back and forth while squeezing it gently. Each time I did that, her cunt felt wetter and seemed to have opened wider. Soon it felt swollen and sucked more urgently at my finger, and in no time at all I had penetrated as far as I could reach and was pushing another finger into her.

Austin grunted softly and pushed her hips forward to meet the fingers. Deep breaths like sobs broke from her lips against my shirt, and she strained as if to engulf my hand. Her writhing, her naked need, whipped my lust into a frenzy, and faster than memory could record the details I scooted from beneath her, kneeled between her legs, unzipped my pants and lowered my body toward hers.

I never did know why at that moment I looked into her face, but I knew right away that I would go to my grave wishing I hadn't. Because when I did I saw, or thought I saw, that she was crying. Moisture around her eyes and on her cheeks glistened briefly in the soft lamplight from the locks. I froze on the point of entry. "Are you crying?" I asked.

She turned her face away, toward the back of the car

seat, and said nothing. But an instant later convulsions racked her body and I heard the sound of muffled sobs.

"Hey," I said softly, pulling up to my hands and knees, "what's wrong? Did I do something wrong?"

She shook her head, but it could have meant anything, and then her hands flew to her face and she began crying hard, really boo-hooing.

I worried for a minute that Johnny and Patty might hear her. I'd look silly as hell, to say nothing of suspicious, if they ran to see what was wrong and found me kneeling over a sobbing, half-naked Austin with my dick hanging out. Besides, I hoped to smooth things over and pick up where I'd left off.

But slowly it dawned on me that she must have been crying for quite awhile before I realized it. Had she been crying the whole time I was fingering her cunt? Had I mistaken misery for pleasure, yielding for surrender? The thought made me feel awful. It also filled me with guilt and concern. I scrambled to perch on the edge of the seat beside her and reached a hesitant hand toward her covered face. "Austin," I said softly.

The sound swamped amid the sobs filling the car. I waited a moment, pulling her dress down over her knees, and tried again. "Austin."

She didn't answer, but the sobs were subsiding.

"I'm sorry, Austin. Please don't cry. It's all right now. I'm sorry." I rubbed and patted her forearms as I spoke, and soon she was merely sniffling. "There, there," I said.

A moment later she spoke through her hands, her words thick with spit, "I couldn't Benny; I just couldn't." She stifled a sob and added, "Nice girls don't."

"I understand, Austin," I said, understanding nothing of the kind. Nice girls did it all the time. All over the world nice girls were doing it at that very moment. Nice girls not only did it, they enjoyed doing it and wanted to do it again and again and again. They just didn't want to do it with me.

"You should have stopped, Benny. You went too far."

I wanted to ask why *she* hadn't stopped. Instead I said, "I'm sorry, Austin; I just got carried away."

She sat up and sniffed. I handed her my handkerchief. "Patty should have stayed in the car," she said.

Yes, and I should have stayed home, I thought.

"They've been gone a long time," she said peevishly. She handed back my handkerchief and felt around the seat.

"They're in the corner," I said, indicating her panties.

She had just gotten them on when we heard Johnny and Patty approaching the car. Johnny's voice was a soft murmur, the words not clear to me, but Patty was laughing, happy—the way a girl ought to sound after a good fucking, I imagined. I was happy for Johnny, but the thought of their frolicking in the woods on a spring night, rolling around naked on a blanket under the stars, fucking and getting fucked while I was striking out only a few yards away, sharpened my misery. This was worse than injustice. Injustice one could blame on forces beyond his control. This was sheer incompetency. I just didn't have it when and where it counted. Some guys did. Some guys didn't. I didn't.

Johnny went first to the trunk of the car to put away the blanket, making plenty of noise to warn me of their presence, and then they sang out, "We're back," just before they opened the door and the light came on.

"Coast is clear," I said cheerily, hoping they wouldn't sense the strain between Austin and me. But I need not have worried. They were in a gay, playful mood and absorbed in each other. They probably didn't even notice, as we drove back to town and up the Hill, that Austin and I spoke not a word to each other. She sat beside me, quiet and still, looking straight ahead or out the window to her left as we drove her home, and she barely said goodnight to Johnny and Patty when we pulled up in front of her house. As I walked her to the door I told her again that I was sorry, but she merely said, "I don't want to talk about it." She slipped quickly inside the house without even looking at me.

Johnny took forever to say goodnight to Patty on her darkened front porch, while I sat in the car feeling sorry for myself and wondering how to join the French Foreign Legion. Nor did it help matters when Johnny got back into the car grinning from ear to ear, obviously pleased as punch with himself.

"Well," he said as we pulled away from the curb, "how was it?"

"Great," I said flatly. "Right up to the point where she started crying and told me that nice girls don't."

"Come on," he said. "You didn't fall for that one."

"'Fraid I did. Sounded real to me."

"Sonofagun. And the whole time I was gone I was sure you were just tearing that stuff up."

I didn't want to talk about it. I changed the subject. "How'd you do?"

He smiled. "In like Flynn."

That made me feel both better and worse. I was glad for him, but his success made my failure all the more bitter. Too, I wondered what he thought of me now, his buddy, The Dud.

"Smooth as silk, Benny—that's how it went. I *knew* she was ready. I just knew it. She nearly ate me up before we got out of the car. And as soon as we got outside on that blanket, I whipped her panties off and really went at it."

"Austin got upset when Patty left the car. She wasn't expecting that." I was hinting that it was all Johnny's fault. It wasn't, of course, but I could still hear him saying, "Just leave it to ol' John," and the memory mocked me. Ol' John had made out like a bandit, and ol' Benny was left with blue balls and a black mood.

"That surprises me," Johnny said, sounding sincere. "Usually, when two girls are best friends, if one puts out, the other will too."

Not if the other one's Catholic, I thought, but I was glad I
hadn't said it, because it probably wasn't true. Besides,
Johnny might have thought I was throwing off on Protestants, when really I knew very little about them. No; I
could have fucked Austin and I hadn't. I had no one to
blame but myself.

"I'm sorry, Benny. They seem such close friends and
all."

"Yeah," I said, feigning nonchalance. "Well, if Austin
won't, I'll just have to find a girl who will."

"Right."

"So tell me about Patty."

He did, in detail, and it made me so horny that I actually
felt ill. I kept seeing myself in Johnny's place, on a blanket
in the woods, between Patty's golden thighs, surging into
her lush and willing body, instead of back in the car playing nursemaid to a damn crybaby, a little cocktease, and
trying to figure out what to do with a disappointed dick.
Just my luck, I thought bitterly, to go out with two girls
and wind up with the one who wouldn't put out. Screwed
again by the fickle finger of fate.

By the time Johnny put me out in front of my house. I
was in the grip of a classic case of nutache. My cock felt
hard enough to crack walnuts and would not go down, and
my balls were so sore and tender that I could hardly walk.
Even the fabric of my pants irritated them, and they
seemed to clang against my thighs every time I moved.
Embarrassed, I stood on the sidewalk, nausea radiating up
from my groin, nearly doubling me over, until Johnny
drove away. Then, taking tiny steps, I inched my way
toward the house. There was no way I could walk up the
doorsteps, so I crawled up them and sat for awhile when I
reached the top. Breathing deeply one moment, doubling
over the next, I cursed Austin for everything I could think
of while waiting for the pain to go away. The last time I
bent over, something popped out of my shirt pocket and
fell on the step at my feet. It was the rubber that Johnny

had given me, still encased in its neat little package, its foil cover shining in the glow of the streetlight. I had forgotten all about it in my eagerness to get into Austin. Still, lying there shiny and new, so obviously unused, it seemed to mock me. Disgusted with myself, I scooped it up, sailed it out into the middle of the street and went inside to bed.

Chapter Three

"I heard about the fight," Glenn said. We were standing around outside St. Jude Church after Mass the next day. The church was a beautiful, gothic building near downtown Augusta, but its main attraction for me was that it held the latest Sunday Mass in town, twelve o'clock, which meant I could sleep late.

"No fight to it," I said; "he hit me and I hit the ground."

"He's big knocker."

"In more ways than one. By the way, why weren't you at the party?"

"No wheels. Perry came home this weekend and took the car. I called you and Johnny, but you were already gone."

Perry was Glenn's older brother, a student at the University of Georgia. In the McNulty family, what Perry wanted Perry got. Glenn didn't seem to mind, but I thought he took a lot a crap from his brother and other people too. Turning the other cheek, which was what he did, was all well and good, but there were people who'd pop that cheek for you too and think nothing of it.

Part of Glenn's trouble, though, was Glenn. I had lived near St. Jude Church before moving to Milltown, and we had met at a neighborhood playground and gotten to be good friends. I didn't know how; we had nothing in common. Maybe it was that everybody picked on Glenn. I didn't like that. Still, a great part of Glenn's trouble was Glenn. He was little, standing no more than five-five, and loud—people were always telling him to be quiet—and he often acted crazy. Well, not exactly crazy, but certainly not normal. Johnny, who could tolerate him for only awhile at a time, said simply, "McNulty's fucked up."

Glenn tugged on my arm. "Come on over to the house." He lived across the street from the rear of the church, the side the rectory was on, in a neighborhood of large and gracious older homes, the kinds of homes owned by people who could have lived on the Hill, but who had remained downtown.

I was hesitant to go. I was still brooding over the events of the night before and preferred to be alone with my muddled thoughts. Besides, Glenn's family made me uncomfortable. His mother was extremely religious and seemed always angry, his father, a tiny man, was loud and obnoxious—Glenn was his daddy made over—and I didn't like Perry worth a damn.

Maybe Glenn read my thoughts, at least about his family. "Come on. Nobody's home but the maid."

I shrugged my shoulders and went along with him. Maybe his company would keep my mind off my troubles.

Glenn's house was an especially nice one. Painted gray and trimmed in white, it had two stories and a big L-shaped front porch shaded by large oak trees. His mother kept it too dark inside, but the way that house was built and furnished gave it an air of permanence that felt solid and good even when you knew it was an illusion. Glenn's house and the others like it were part of an era that was passing. Throughout that part of town stood similar homes that had recently been cut up into apartments and boarding houses or were beginning just to look rundown. Didn't matter; the McNultys would never move unless St. Jude Church moved—at least that was the way I thought of them. They were an old Augusta Catholic family and their lives revolved around that church.

"You still dating Ausin?" Glenn asked. We had not entered the house. The day was sunny and warm, and we sat in rocking chairs on his front porch.

I answered evasively. "Went out last night, with Johnny and Patty Wilson." I didn't want to say any more than that. I knew it was over with Austin and me, but I didn't want to have to explain. And I certainly couldn't tell him about Johnny and Patty. Like his mother, Glenn was very religious, and sex outside of marriage was a mortal sin.

Glenn smiled. "That Johnny knows how to pick 'em, doesn't he?"

If you only knew, I thought.

Glenn added, "Hate to tell you, but I know somebody who's planning to beat your time with Austin."

"Bruce Holdenfelt."

He was surprised. "I didn't think you knew?"

"How'd you find out?" Glenn knew all the Hill Catholics better than I did, and was kin to a lot of them. It was Glenn, in fact, who had taken me to my first parties on the Hill.

"Chuck Conlin told me."

"Why? So you'd tell me? I mean, what business is it of his?"

"Aw, Benny. Chuck ain't so bad."

"No, not if the choice is between Chuck and syphilis." That had always pissed me off about Glenn. He would stand up for somebody, or at least put in a good word for them, when everybody else knew the guy was a prick. I guessed it was Glenn's way of practicing Christian charity, but it didn't make sense to me. What was so Christian about telling a lie to defend a bastard and pissing off people who were simply telling the truth about him? Besides, the Hill Catholic boys didn't like Glenn worth a damn. They picked on him worse than anybody else did. I cooled off and said, "Well, Austin and I don't go steady, you know," and left it at that.

Glenn looked at his watch and jumped to his feet. "Let's go for a ride," he said. "I've got the car this afternoon."

I asked how he'd managed that. He got to use the car a lot, but rarely on Sunday.

"Old Mr. Riley, one of our neighbors, died yesterday

and Mom wanted me to go by the funeral home and say a prayer for the repose of his soul. I said I'd do it if I could have the car for the rest of the afternoon."

It struck me as a bizarre bargain and, I couldn't help it, I laughed. "Real worried about Mr. Riley's soul, weren't you?"

I was only teasing, but I should have known better. Glenn laughed a lot, but he had absolutely no sense of humor. Shaking his head sadly and looking at his feet, he set in gently to shame me, something he did often, for I had a streak of irreverence that troubled him greatly. "You shouldn't make jokes about the dead, Benny. Mr. Riley was a fine old Catholic gentleman, and I'm sure his soul is in Paradise today. He was . . . a guardian of the faith. He . . . he ws a true friend to the Church. A Good Catholic."

Glenn could deliver that kind of speech, none of which sounded like his own thoughts, with a pious air that made me want to snap, "Bullshit, McNulty!" But instead I said, "No offense, Glenn. Forget I said it. Let's go for that ride."

As soon as we got rolling I felt better. In me, despair could saddle up with the best of 'em, but it couldn't ride worth a damn. Soon I was caught up in the sights and sounds of the city—nothing out of the ordinary, but a welcome distraction from my misery. Besides, Glenn and I had rolled down the windows of the '53 Pontiac, and the road wind whipping through spun my thoughts like so many pinwheels. After awhile all of them, good and bad, seemed merely colorful blurs for my amusement. If it hadn't been for Glenn, I might have wound up in a good mood again.

"You're mighty quiet over there," he said at length. "What you thinking about?"

We were riding east on Greene Street, a boulevard lined with old Victorian homes like Glenn's that were slowly giving way to commercial buildings. I hated to see that happen, for Greene Street, named for Nathanael Greene, an American general in the Revolutionary War, must have been at one time one of the most graceful streets in the South. It still was pretty: a wide green strip separated its east-west lanes and was, in effect, a long linear park running beneath the branches of stately oaks. Azaleas, now in bloom, thronged there like children waiting for a parade to pass by, and statues stood on pedestals here and there, keeping solemn watch over the city.

"I was thinking how nice this street is. We seem to be riding through a tunnel of trees."

"You're not brooding over Austin, are you? What I said about Holdenfelt?"

"Austin means nothing to me, Glenn. Brucie-boy is welcome to her. And that's the truth."

We had come to East Boundary, a street marking the eastern edge of the city. Beyond lay a few rundown buildings—mechanics' garages, warehouses, juke joints—and scattered shotgun houses and dirt farms. Past those and a stretch of bottom land lay the Savannah River, altogether about a mile up the road, and across the river lay South Carolina. Glenn turned north on East Boundary, drove two blocks and swung west, putting us onto Broad Street, Augusta's main thoroughfare.

"She's already accepted a date with him."

That bitch, I thought. "Well, I hope they live happily ever after."

"You really don't care?"

I threw up my hands. "Mother of Christ, Glenn! How many times do I have to say it?"

"Well, you're upset about *something.*"

I swirled on the seat to face him. "I'm upset because you keep on about something I've already told you doesn't matter to me. I told you the truth, but you won't accept it. You want an affadavit? An oath signed in blood? Here," I said, slashing a mark on my chest with a finger; "cross my heart and hope to die. Does that satisfy you? Scout's honor. How 'bout that? Now, have I overlooked any oath that you might accept? Oh!" I said extravagantly. "Swear on the Bible." I raised my right hand. "You happy now?"

61

He shook his head. "You're upset about something." With a self-righteous air he added: "And you shouldn't swear."

I thought I'd pop a blood vessel. "You're confused, Glenn," I said, dripping venom. "Swearing as in taking an oath is not the same as swearing as in the use of profanity."

"You said, 'Swear on the Bible'."

"The president of the United States swears on the Bible, Glenn." I spoke as though to a dull child. "He takes his oath of office with his hands on a Bible. He is swearing on the Bible."

"That's different."

"No, it isn't."

"It's different to me."

"That's the sad part, Glenn. That's the sad part."

"What's that supposed to mean?" Agitated now, he shifted about under the steering wheel and darted glances at me and then at the road, at me and then at the road.

Suddenly I felt malicious. His religious feelings didn't matter to me anymore. They were stupid anyhow. "You want to know why I'm upset, Glenn? You really want to know? Austin wouldn't give me any pussy; that's why I'm upset. It's got nothing to do with love or dating or going steady or Holdenfelt—or any of that. It's pussy, plain and simple. I wanted to fuck Austin Armistead and she wouldn't let me. Now do you understand?"

Glenn gaped at me with his mouth open and then slumped behind the wheel. For a full minute he said nothing. He merely drove, looking straight ahead and sighing heavily now and then. We were now moving slowly through the downtown part of Augusta, hitting one stoplight after another, caught up in the lazy rhythm of Sunday in a southern town. Then, just when I thought Glenn wasn't going to respond at all, he said with conviction:

"You need help. I'm going to ask Father Brady to help you."

That really pissed me off. Sweetly I said, "Gee, that would be great, Glenn; I really want to fuck Austin, and if

Father Brady can help, I'll be eternally grateful to you *and* him."

"That's not what I meant," he flared.

I ignored him. "Maybe Father Brady could hold her legs apart while I stick it to her, and if you wanted to help too, you could—"

Glenn stomped on the brakes, stopping the car in the middle of the street, and turned on me. "Damn it, Benny, that's not funny—"

I couldn't resist. In my most earnest and humble tone I said, "You really shouldn't swear, Glenn. And that anger of yours isn't very Christian either."

He laid into me anyhow. "Look who's talking about 'Christian.' What you said—about Father Brady—was blasphemy, Benny, blasphemy." His face was red and severe. "Sex before marriage is a mortal sin, and here you are, trying to seduce good Catholic girls. I fear for your soul, Benny Blake. You're mixed up and you're headed straight for Hell." He turned back to the wheel, suddenly, jerked the car into gear and gunned it forward, speeding for about half a block before hitting another red light and stopping.

Neither of us spoke for awhile, but finally, in an even voice, I said, "Sex is as natural as breathing, Glenn, and the Church's position on it is wrong. What do a bunch of celibates know about it anyhow?"

Glenn snorted. "Who are you to question the Church?"

"I'm me, that's who, and I've got *lots* of questions for the Church."

"Yeah, you're a regular Martin Luther."

"The Church could *use* another Martin Luther. He brought about some badly needed reforms." I didn't know squat about Martin Luther and could not have named a single one of those reforms if my life had depended on it. I said it just to needle Glenn, who thought it was a goddam sin to question anything the Church said or did or stood for.

"He was a maverick priest who got just what he deserved: excommunication. And he's burning in Hell today."

We rode in silence for a moment, and then Glenn said in a finger-wagging tone of voice, "Benny, you sound like a guy who's on the verge of losing his faith. You better talk to Father Brady."

When I made no response, Glenn added: "Is that what's happening? 'Cause if it is, you better get help right away."

I did have my doubts about the Church, about religion in general, for that matter, and even about God, but Glenn McNulty certainly wasn't the person to discuss them with. He had the objectivity of a toothache. "There's nothing wrong with me that a piece of ass wouldn't fix," I said.

"Pray, Benny, pray."

"I do every night—for a piece of ass."

Glenn got hot again. "You better talk to Father Brady."

We were turning right on Thirteenth Street now, heading toward the river, and the turn surprised me. Two blocks ahead lay one of the two bridges that connected Augusta with South Carolina. Glenn caught my surprise and said, "The body's at Pratt's Funeral Home. Mr. Riley's children live in North Augusta."

North Augusta was a small town that seemed to spill down a hill and screech to a halt at the edge of a bluff overlooking the river. It was easy to see from there that most of Augusta lay in a flood plain, and indeed the city had been plagued by floods even after the city fathers built a levee early in the century.

As it did every time I crossed the muddy Savannah, a line from T. S. Eliot came to mind and I said it aloud, just for the taste of it on my tongue: "'. . . I think that the river is a strong brown god—sullen, untamed and intractable . . .'"

Hardly aware that I had spoken out loud, I was surprised to hear Glenn scoff. "What the hell was *that*?" he asked.

"It was poetry, you dumb ass."

"Sounded like mumbo-jumbo to me. You better talk to Father Brady right away."

I wanted to say, "Fuck Father Brady," but instead I said, 'Doesn't it make you wonder that our ancestors, the pride of Augusta, would be so stupid as to settle in a flood plain?"

"What do you mean?" Glenn said, sounding offended.

"Well, think about it. Here were people, wandering in the wilderness, looking for a place to settle. They arrive at this point, this place in the middle of nowhere, and see on one side of the river a flood plain and on the other side high ground. What do they do? They say, 'Hey, let's build on the low side.' To me, that's not quite bright. And if you think about it, it tells you a lot about Augusta."

"Like what?" Glenn was genuinely puzzled.

I rolled my eyes and waved him off. "Forget it," I said, and he seemed willing to, apparently because we had arrived at the funeral home.

From the outside, Pratt's looked more like a bank than a funeral home: dark marble exterior, Grecian columns, wide steps mounting to a long, bare porch. But the moment we stepped inside there was no mistaking the place for anything but what it was. I had always hated the odor of funeral homes, and until I was fourteen or fifteen held my breath every time I went past one, for fear that I might catch a whiff of that sickly smell. Now it hit me full force, enveloping me as we walked through the door, weaving itself into the fabric of my clothes, curling into my nostrils—the mingled odors of hot candle wax, of rooms too long shut up, of flowers sweetly rotting, and for all I knew, the scent of death itself.

"Let's make this quick," I whispered to Glenn. "I don't like funeral homes."

I don't know why I whispered, for nobody else was around, but Glenn whispered too. "Got to say the Rosary."

"The Rosary! We'll be here the rest of the day."

"I promised Mother," he said.

We walked on into the room, which was spacious and thickly carpeted, and paused in front of a sign bearing white plastic letters on black felt. Under an arrow pointing to the right, toward a room with double doors that stood open, were three names, one of which was Riley. We stood there a moment or two, waiting for somebody to come, but when nobody did, Glenn went on into the room and I followed.

This room was long and narrow, and held three open coffins set in semi-circles of flowers and flanked by large burning candles. From where I stood I couldn't see into the coffins, but that was fine with me. I had the notion, silly, I knew, but still forceful, that if I looked too closely at death, it might blink in recognition and say, "Ah, so *there* you are."

Kneeling rails stood in front of each coffin, and when I looked at Glenn again he was kneeling at one, rosary beads in hand, his fingers and lips moving. Looking back as he prayed, he caught my eye and urged me with jerks of his head to join him.

I winced at the idea of kneeling through five decades of "Hail, Mary," but that seemed better than just standing around waiting. That is, it seemed better until a Pratt employee showed up.

We had just finished and were rising when we heard a door open and close. Seconds later a tall, elderly, stoop-shouldered man stood in the doorway looking like a big question mark. He seemed surprised to see us there, but he recovered quickly and stepped forward to shake hands. He nodded toward the coffin and spoke softly. "Are you friends or relatives of Mr. Trowbridge?"

I looked at him, and then at the coffin, and then at Glenn. "Trowbridge?"

"Why, yes," the man said, smiling, not understanding.

Glenn looked sheepish, but he cleared his throat and said with an air of innocence, "We're friends of Mr. Riley. We came to pay our respects."

"Oh, I see," the man said, smiling and nodding. "Well, Mr. Riley's down there." He pointed to the other end of the room, smiled again and left.

Glenn looked at me, and I could read his mind. He was leaning toward saying another rosary, this time at the right coffin. Apparently he could read mine too. But just to be sure, I said very calmly, looking him square in the eye, "At the moment, there are only three corpses in this room . . ."

Glenn looked back at Mr. Riley's coffin, and then at the floor, and then at me. "But I promised my mother."

"You promised your mother you'd go by the funeral home and say the rosary for Mr. Riley. You did that."

"But—"

"But nothing, McNulty!" I could see that he was getting set to do it anyhow, and the stupidity of it all made me angry. And when he actually stepped toward the coffin, I scurried around in front of him to block his path. My hands on his chest to stop him, I said, "Hold on there, Glenn; this is crazy. Do you honestly believe it makes a bit of difference one way or the other?" I pointed with one hand in the general direction of Mr. Riley's coffin. "That man is dead. Dead! Do you hear me? Whatever he did or didn't do in life, it's too goddam late to change things now. When you're dead, that's it. It's too late for prayers. Too late for rosaries. What is it with you, anyhow? Do you think God is so fuckin' dumb that He doesn't know which prayers belong where? My hands moved to grip his shoulders. "You live in a dream world, McNulty; wake up!"

I didn't know what I was saying—not really; I was just babbling in anger and frustration. But Glenn saw in my words proof positive that I was losing my soul to the devil. His shoulders slumped and he gave me a sad, sad look. "We'll leave, Benny—on one condition."

"Name it."

"You promise me that you'll have that talk with Father Brady."

"I'll talk with Jesus and the Twelve Apostles if you'll just get us out of here."

He gripped my forearms. "I'm serious. Promise."

"I promise. Now, let's say grace and blow this place."

Chapter Four

It took Tommy Haynes all week to get around to apologizing to me. Late Friday afternoon, in a crowded hallway during a change of classes, a hand gripped my arm and I heard somebody say breezily, "Sorry, pal." He delivered the apology with the sincerity of a door-to-door salesman and he was gone before I even knew who it was, swept away in the flow of bodies moving in the opposite direction. But that was fine with me; the less contact I had with Tommy Haynes, the better.

For that matter, I had not been eager to see Dianne Damico either, and by going late to Spanish class and either rushing out or hanging back at the bell had managed to avoid her. Once or twice in class she had tried to catch my eye, I thought, but I pretended not to notice.

If my behavior puzzled her, it puzzled me even more. Having gotten to know her a bit, I liked her a lot, but the knowing and the liking made it harder, not easier, for me to approach her. Something in the way she looked at me made me think that she might see me as somebody to pity, an innocent casualty of her problem with Haynes. Well, thanks, but no thanks. I didn't want her pity and I had no desire to play a minor character in The Saga of Dianne and Tommy. I had my own problems—maybe not as bad as hers, but at least I played the lead in them.

I finally asked Johnny about it as we walked home from school Friday afternoon.

"It's simple," he said: "you found out she's not what you thought she was."

I didn't find it that simple. "But I like her even more. And I respect her."

"That's just it. You went from pure and simple lust to 'like' and 'respect.' That complicates things—"

"But I've liked and respected many girls that I wanted to fuck."

"You didn't let me finish. There's something else here: you're a Catholic; she's going to be a nun. Say what you will, that changes how you feel about her."

I thought about that. He was right. No matter how much I liked and respected her, a girl with no interest in sex was a girl of no interest to me. Where Dianne Damico was concerned, Heaven had put out the fires of my lust with holy water. "Yeah. How could you fuck a nun-to-be?"

Johnny scoffed. "Speak for yourself, Jack; I'd fuck her in a flash. I'm *not* a Catholic, and all that nun talk don't signify nohow. You can't listen to what a woman says. They'll say, 'No, please don't,' the whole time they're lining it up so you can slide it in."

I hoped he was right, but it was all very confusing to me. "But what if the girl didn't *really* want you to? What if you simply caught her in a weak moment and later she truly regretted the act?"

"Tough titty! The way I see it, she had a hundred chances to back out, to say no, before it ever got to that point. And what about me? Don't I have some say in this thing, in sex? Is every guy in the world supposed to be at the mercy of women for sex? Heck, they want it and need it as much as we do. I've done a girl no harm by fucking her. Now, in the beginning, yes, it's up to her completely. That's when 'no' might really mean no. But if she says no the whole time one thing's leading to another, and it's obvious that she doesn't want to stop any more than I do, why, I'd be a fool to stop just when I've got it made. Tell you something else: the girl would think I was a fool too."

That hit so close to home that I got quiet. Apparently he wasn't aware of it, but his remarks fit exactly what had happened between me and Austin, and now I felt more like a fool than ever. No wonder she was throwing me over for Bruce Whatshisname. Bruce Anybody could do better than I had done. And I could hear my stepfather's taunt already, if he ever got wind of what had happened: "You didn't give her the meat, boy; you didn't shoot it to her. So she's moving on to somebody who will."

Jesus Christ! I thought: *I'm too stupid to get laid. I don't deserve any pussy. What's wrong with me?* But I already saw what was wrong: I was too damned nice. Yes, that was it: too nice. I wanted to *please* girls, and to me that meant being thoughtful, being considerate, being kind. Austin's tears, for instance, had genuinely moved me; they switched me from passion to *com*passion as easily as a listener changed radio stations. I didn't have the kind of toughness, Johnny's kind, to ignore somebody's tears and push on with no thought but of what I wanted.

Still, I felt that Johnny had the right attitude and I wondered where I had gotten such mixed-up ideas about girls. Again, though, the answer popped right up in my mind as if on cue: Mother. My mother, bless her heart, was all those things that she wanted me to be, and I loved those qualities in her and knew that others admired them too. But, dammit, they weren't suitable for a son, a male. A man's role in life was very different from a woman's, and niceness didn't count for much, with men *or* women, in the world I had seen so far. I decided then and there to be more tough-minded, to be more like Johnny. I'd never go so far as to mess with a girl like Dianne Damico, a girl who was going off to be a nun, I told myself; after all, *something* had to remain sacred. But Cherry Ashford, I resolved, had better look out come Saturday night.

By now, Johnny and I had reached the point, Bailie and Silcox streets, where we parted ways, but we stopped on the corner for a moment to talk.

"What'cha doing tonight?" he said.

"Don't know. I can't get the car. Zeb and Mom are going somewhere."

"I got the same problem: no wheels. We're set for to-morrow night though."

He was referring to our double-date with Harriet and Cherry, and I was glad to hear that there was no problem in getting his car. But at that moment Saturday seemed a long way off, and Friday night was suddenly shaping up as a bust. Friday night in Augusta without a car was almost as bad as finding a pimple on your face right before a big date.

We stood around for awhile looking glum, but then we both had the same idea at the same instant. Snapping fingers and beaming at each other, we even said at the same time: "McNulty!" As far as either of us knew, Glenn had no date for that night.

Making plans as we backpeddled away from each other, I told Johnny, "*You* call him. You can get more out of him than I can."

"Eight o'clock," Johnny said. "If there's any hitch I'll call you. Better yet, why don't you come over to my house around seven? We'll shoot the breeze 'til he gets there."

I waved and we both turned toward home.

Johnny's house was not as nicely furnished as ours was, but in some ways I liked it better. It was less cluttered, simpler, perhaps out of necessity, but I preferred that to my mother's idea of the well-furnished home, which seemed to be that no decorative touch was ever too much. In our living room, for instance, where Mother's decorating art reached its fullest flower, knick-knacks of every description had found a home. Whole flocks of ceramic birds winged along the walls, weaving their way through framed prints, photographs, plaster fruit and frogs, and a plate depicting Jesus in a flowing nightgown at the Last Supper. Beneath all this, in every corner of the room, stood whatnot stands so loaded with gewgaws that some had been moved to the coffee table and elsewhere to start new colonies. And so many doilies, scarves and antimacassars, all white, littered sofa, chairs, tables, and mantelpiece that the room seemed frantically to be signaling surrender. I teased Mother about all this, saying that she

71

loathed a bare spot more than nature abhorred a vacuum, but she took it good-naturedly and went right on adding from time to time a new piece here and there.

In contrast, Johnny's house seemed all but bare, but it was neat and clean, like Johnny himself, and I would have gone there more often if it had not been for Grace, his stepmother, a short, dark woman with the face of an ape, but whose proud bearing saved her from appearing ugly. She was, to me at least, a sour, unfriendly woman who seemed to be nursing a secret disappointment, and I never said anything in her presence that I felt she approved, unless perhaps it was goodbye.

Johnny's father, George, was altogether different. A butcher by trade, he was, like his son, friendly, cocky, quick in movement and thought, a small man with the manner of a bantam rooster. He made good money when he worked, Johnny had told me, but drinking had cost him several jobs and often pushed the family to the edge of real need, which perhaps explained his wife's disposition. I couldn't say, but it must have been bad, for Johnny would not touch alcohol except for an occasional beer.

At any rate, both of Johnny's parents were at home when I arrived, about quarter after seven, and I soon saw that Johnny must have planned it that way. I had hardly said hello to Mr. Kelly, seated on the couch in the living room reading his evening paper, when Mrs. Kelly, washing dishes after supper, appeared suddenly in the doorway and fixed me with a sour look. Johnny was nowhere around, but I heard water running in the bathroom.

"What's this about goin' off to the beach for a week?" she asked after a long moment, leaning now against the door-jamb, wiping her hands on her apron.

Right away her tone of voice put me on the defensive. She made a trip to the beach sound like a conspiracy to hold up a liquor store. I looked at Mr. Kelly, hidden behind his paper, but he merely rattled it and pulled it closer to his face, as though absorbed in some story. Then I glanced toward the hallway leading to the bathroom. No help from that direction. So I tried to act casual and said, "Yes, ma'am. After graduation, you know. We thought it might be fun." Still standing, I looked around as though deciding where to sit were one of life's great puzzles. Suddenly, too, my hands were incredibly inconvenient contraptions, and I was at a loss as to what to do with them.

She let me squirm a bit—she was good at that—before saying, "Fun?"

It had never occurred to me that the word "fun" could be made to sound so trivial, so unworthy of anybody with a sense of common decency. "Yes'm," I said, deciding at last upon a chair across the room from Mr. Kelly, as far away from Mrs. Kelly as I could get. "You know, the beach. Sun. The water. Waves." I was not at my most articulate.

"Whose idea was that?"

The way she said it left no doubt as to whose idea she thought it was, but I feigned forgetfulness and said, "Gee, Mrs. Kelly, I don't remember who thought of it first."

"Um, huh."

Mr. Kelly rattled his paper again, and off in the bathroom the water still ran.

"Your parents gonna let you go off that way?" She still leaned against the doorjamb, though now she was smoking a cigarette, turning every now and then to flick ashes into something in the kitchen behind her.

"Well, yeah. For graduation and all." Actually, I'd had a hell of a time persuading my mother to let me go, and she hadn't consented until Zeb took my side. But I wasn't going to tell Mrs. Kelly that. I also didn't want to ask her if Johnny could go to the beach—obviously it wasn't a good time to ask—but she had me so rattled and looked at me so steadily that I almost asked her anyhow, just to have something to say. Fortunately just at that moment Johnny walked into the room.

"McNulty's coming by at seven-thirty instead of eight," he said. He looked at his watch. "Let's wait outside."

I all but leaped for the door. "Night, Mr. Kelly. Night, Mrs. Kelly."

Mrs. Kelly had stepped back into the kitchen when Johnny came into the room, but now she appeared again in the doorway. "Don't you stay out late," she warned. "You hear me? I got things for you to do tomorrow and I don't wanna have to drag you out of bed and listen to you bellyache all day about bein' tired."

"Yes, ma'am," Johnny said, but it was nearly drowned out by the voice of Mr. Kelly, who lowered his paper with a flourish and barked, "For Christ's sake, Grace, let the boy have some fun."

Mrs. Kelly said nothing more and we hurried on out the door, but not before I saw again that look on her face that said what she thought of fun and of people who wanted to have it.

It was cooler outside than when I had left home, and I wondered if I shouldn't swing back by there and pick up a sweater, but I saw that Johnny, like me, wore a short-sleeve shirt, so I decided against it. We stood for a moment on the steps of the small porch, actually a stoop, and then walked down to wait at the curb. It was seven-twenty five.

"What was all that back there?" I nodded toward the house.

Johnny made a face. "Oh, Grace is on her high horse, bitching about me going to the beach."

"Why?"

"She *says* I ought to get busy finding a job, but that's not the real reason. I think she got pissed off because I asked the old man and not her. She gets like that sometime."

"Well, for Christsake, *work* on her; we don't want this thing to fall through. Not now. It's only, what, five or six weeks away?"

"No sweat."

I raised a hand and addressed the night. " 'No sweat,' he says. You didn't hear her giving me the third degree in there about this trip."

"Yeah, I did."

"What do you mean? You were in the bathroom the whole time. I heard the water running."

He smiled. "You heard the water running—but I was standing in the hallway the whole time. Heard the whole thing."

I looked at him in wonder and then laughed. "You sorry rascal. I *figured* you had set me up for this, but I had no idea you were *that* sneaky. I thought you just wanted me around for moral support when you asked if you could go."

"You don't know Grace; I do. She likes to give me a hard time before coming around. She wants me to think she's got some say over me, but it's really up to the old man."

I gave him a narrow look. "So you figured, 'I'll just let my ol' buddy Benny take the heat this time'."

He smiled. "Well, why not? I take it *all* the time."

"Man, oh, man, I pity you. That woman is tough!"

"Tell me about it. Don't get me wrong, though; she's good to me, in her own way."

"I'll take your word for it. But I hope she's never good to me, if it's got to be in her own way."

Just then, a pair of headlights swung into Johnny's street. A moment later we were piling into Glenn's car, the Pontiac, Johnny riding shotgun, I in the back seat.

"Cathy Collins is giving a party," Glenn said, "and we could always swing by Teen Town, but aside from that, fellows, I've come up dry. What'll it be?"

Cathy Collins was a Catholic girl, a Hill girl, skinny, homely, a bit namby-pamby, but nice—the kind of nice a girl works hard at when she knows that's all she's got going for her. I liked her okay, but I sure didn't like the idea of running into Chuck Conlin and that crowd again anytime soon. Too, I wondered, what if Austin were there?

As Glenn pulled away from the curb, Johnny turned toward the back seat and said, "I know what you're thinking. But we can check it out, and if things don't look right we can leave. After all, it's the only game in town."

"It ain't no game, getting knocked on my can."

"Tommy Haynes won't be there," Glenn said. "Neither will Dianne. That's not Cathy's circle."

"What about Holdenfelt?"

Glenn cleared his throat. "He's got a date tonight—with Austin."

"Good," I said. "That leaves only Chuck Conlin, his brother Paul, Michael O'Grady, Dan Hanlan, Billy O'Connor, Phil Blatt and ten or twelve other guys who'd like to whip my ass."

"Owen Phelps'll be there," Glenn said. "You're friends with him, and he's a big knocker."

"Yeah. Big and friendly—like a watchdog that licks your hand while you steal the silverware."

Glenn shrugged. "Well, let's face it, Benny: you've pissed some people off lately."

"What he means, Johnny, is that I pissed *him* off."

"That's nothing new, McNulty; he pisses me off all the time."

Johnny liked to do that, stir up trouble and confusion by appearing to take the side opposite to what was expected of him. It was his way of having fun at the expense of the gullible, and Glenn fell for it every time.

"I think he needs to see a priest," Glenn said.

Johnny said drily, "I recommended the whole College of Cardinals."

Glenn was slow, but he wasn't hopeless. After a moment he laughed and said, "Aw, Johnny. You too much. Too much."

By this time, Glenn had driven back to Central Avenue, a main drag in Augusta. Left would take us toward the Varsity; right, to the Hill. He sat at the stop sign, waiting, and said, "Well?"

I sighed and sank back against my seat. "Looks like I'm outvoted," I said. "Hang a right."

As he pulled out into traffic Glenn said over his shoulder, "Did you hear me when I said Austin's going out with Holdenfelt tonight?"

Johnny turned and said loudly with a straight face, "Yeah. Did you hear him? Holdenfelt's out with your girl tonight."

I didn't know why, but Glenn could get under my skin

quicker than a splinter. "Whaaat?" I said slowly, as if in shock. "Bruce Holdenfelt out with my sweet Austin?" I leaned forward and pleaded. "Say it ain't so, Glenn; say it ain't so. Oh, desist this very minute. Cease. Whoa. Halt. Stop. The slings, the arrows—I can stand no more. *My* Austin, out with another swain? *My* Desdemona, unfaithful? Oh, does misfortune know no other target?" I grasped Johnny's shoulder. "Please, good friend, mix my hemlock." Then I reeled backward against the seat, the back of my forearm flung across my forehead. "Alas! Alack! Death, where is thy sting?"

After a long moment Glenn turned to Johnny and said with conviction, "He's crazy as hell; you know that?"

"Know it? Why it's all over town. The family won't even be seen in public."

I laughed the rest of the way to Cathy Collins' house.

Entering Cathy Collins' house was a strange experience. It was like walking into two different parties, one with half the people having a good time, and the other half gathered for a lynching. The front room, the living room, was crowded with teenagers, some sitting, some standing, but only the girls were glad to see us. The males, all but one of two of them, merely looked at us with grim faces.

Johnny noticed it too and said softly with exaggeration, "Uh, oh." We were still standing in the doorway behind Glenn, who had started yakking with Cathy as soon as she opened the door and was blocking our way. I said under my breath to Johnny, "'Come into my parlor, said the spider to the fly'."

The Collins' house was typical of a kind built throughout the South in good neighborhoods just before World War II—brick, with hardwood floors, not much of a porch front or back, and pretty much the same floor plan from one house to the next: bedrooms on one side of a narrow hall, and on the other side a living room, then a dining room, and then, at the back, a kitchen.

Often Johnny and I seemed to communicate without speaking, and this was one of those times. We looked at each other, looked beyond the living room into the dining room, and began to move slowly through the crowd in that direction, nudging Glenn along with us and sometimes, when he stopped for too long, giving him a hidden but urgent yank on the sleeve or pants leg. He resisted a couple of times. Glenn loved parties and wanted to linger and chat, and, besides, he had no clue as to what was going on. But in five minutes or so of moving casually through the throng, speaking briefly to this girl and that, we reached the dining room.

It was there that Owen Phelps intercepted us, apparently having come from the living room by way of the hall to avoid notice. Standing in the hall doorway, he caught my eye and nodded for us to come over. Owen and I had never palled around together, but we had always been friendly. He lived near Glenn, and we had often played ball in the St. Jude schoolyard together. So he wasn't one of the Hill Catholic boys anymore than we were. He did, however, play football, offensive guard, on the Riverside High team with many of the guys at that party, and I guessed from the way he was acting that he wanted to stay in their good graces.

When we reached the doorway where he was standing, out of sight of most of those in the living room, Owen said quietly, smiling, sipping on a Coke, "I'd clear out if I were you."

I pretended surprise. I trusted Owen, but like the old World War II poster said: "Loose lips sink ships." "What's up?" I asked.

He looked around before speaking. "Chuck has planned a little surprise for you."

Glenn, still in the dark, said loudly, "A surprise? What kind of surprise?"

Johnny and I both dug elbows into his ribs, smiled like jackasses for the benefit of anybody watching us, and turned to look with unnatural interest at a huge china cabinet that stood on a wall near the hall door. Glenn lowered his voice, but he still wanted to know about the surprise.

78

Owen ignored him and Johnny told him to cool it. Johnny could control him when no one else could.

"They're going to jump you, all of 'em. Or nearly all."

"Who are they after?" Johnny asked.

"Well, you all run around together. They're not fond of either one of you, but mainly, Benny, it's you. Why, I don't know."

"Holy catshit," I said, nodding toward the living room. "There must be ten guys out there."

"Not all of 'em are in on it. You know Buster Rourke, for instance; Buster's not gonna bother anybody unless they bother him first."

I was delighted to hear that. Buster was big as a tree. But that still left enough of them to wind our clocks good and tight. "When?" I asked.

"Sometime tonight," Owen said. "Not here, of course, not inside. But you won't get away without a fight. They've been waiting for you."

By now, Glenn had caught on to what was up, and was full of questions and getting excited. He was also getting angry and wanted to settle it then and there. But for all his courage—and he had a lot for a little guy—I had seen him fight and knew that he couldn't lick a postage stamp.

Johnny had courage too—I was the coward in the crowd—but Johnny could also count, and he didn't like the odds any better than I did. Coolly, he said, "Thanks, Owen."

Owen smiled sheepishly. "Sorry I can't help you out any more than that, but you know how it is."

I *didn't* know how it was, not really, but I nodded. Next minute he had slipped away.

Now I really felt conspicuous. Johnny must have too, for he looked again at the china cabinet and said, "Gee, that thing's big. We could use that at my house as a third bedroom."

I laughed, but not easily, and we started moving again, on toward the kitchen.

Trying to be heard by all around, Johnny said, "Where's Mrs. Collins? I haven't seen that lovely lady in a coon's age." With that, he began to walk briskly toward the kitchen, with me and Glenn in tow.

In truth, Johnny had never laid eyes on Mrs. Collins, but seconds later we found her at her stove taking a sheet of cookies out of the oven. She looked surprised to see us, but flattered too at our attention, and she insisted that we try her cookies.

We each took one, and then Johnny said, pointing toward a small screened porch off the kitchen, "Out here, you clods; don't get crumbs on that lady's kitchen floor."

Mrs. Collins, an attractive brunette who must have wondered a thousand times how a daughter of hers could look so plain, smiled and went back to her cooking. As soon as she did, we ducked out the back door, slipped down the driveway and crept into the car.

"Let's say grace and blow this place," Johnny said.

"Forget prayer; just get rolling," I urged. As we drove away I let out a deep breath and said, "That was close, brother. *Too* close. Those bastards."

"What was that all about?" Glenn asked, still hot under the collar.

Johnny snorted and pointed at me. "It was all about him. That was some *more* people he's pissed off lately. It's ruining my social life."

"What did you do to them, Benny?" Glenn asked.

"Yeah, what *did* I do to them, Johnny?" I was genuinely puzzled.

"You don't have to do anything to guys like that. It's what you are, not what you did. You're an outsider. You don't belong. And, by god, they're lettin' you know it—you, me, all of us. All it takes in a group like that is one guy like Chuck Conlin."

"Yeah," Glenn said, shaking his head. "I don't understand Chuck. I know his parents were killed in a wreck and all that, but he's had a good home, him and his brother. His aunt is one of the finest—"

Knowing it by heart, I finished the sentence for him. ". . . Catholic women you'd ever want to meet."

80

He flared. "Well, she is."

"Yeah, well, before you go getting all teary-eyed over little Chuck Conlin, remember that he's back there waiting to rearrange your face."

When I said that, we all began to laugh.

"I'd like to see *their* faces when they find out we've flown the coop," Johnny said.

"I'd rather *hear* about it," I said; "I want as much distance between them and me as I can get."

"I was glad to hear that Buster Rourke wasn't in on it," Glenn said. "I've always thought he was a good boy."

Johnny and I looked at each other. Glenn's determination to think the best of everybody got to be a bit much at times. I could just hear him saying: "Well, Hitler did kill a few people, but he *thought* he was doing the right thing, and I hear that his mother's friend's second cousin's neighbor was a good Catholic woman."

"I don't know about good," I said, "but Buster's damn sure big. He could rent out his back as a billboard."

"And his head as an unfurnished room," Johnny said, and we all laughed some more. Buster played fullback for the Riverside High Rebels, and if brains were oil Buster would have measured about a quart low. People joked that Coach Ramsey had to diagram his plays in crayon.

"But forget Buster," Johnny said. "Conlin's the problem."

"Not by himself, he isn't," Glenn said. "I've never seen him fight, and I've known him since first grade."

"Yeah, but he's never by himself," Johnny said. Turning to me, he added, "I think Glenn's hit on something. A guy like Conlin will *start* a hundred fights, as long as it's somebody else doing the fighting. And he's a big man only with a bunch of guys around him."

"If you're thinking what I think you're thinking, don't think it," I said. "I've had my fight for April." I was playing it for laughs, but I meant it. It didn't matter a bit to me that Chuck Conlin might be a coward. He couldn't have been more afraid of me than I was of him.

"You're gonna have to fight him sooner or later, or this will never stop," Johnny said.

"Make that later," I said.

"Johnny's right," Glenn said.

"I've got a better idea: why don't you two fight Conlin?" But I already knew the answer.

"It's you he's after," Glenn said.

"It's you he's after," Johnny said.

"Lucky me. And where will you two be while all this is going on?"

"We'll be there," they said.

"Well, if I'm not, just start without me, okay?"

It was still early, too early even to go to the Varsity, so Glenn just drove around on the Hill. But after awhile he suggested going by Melinda Murray's house. "If she's home we'll drop in on her."

I barely knew Melinda. She was a Hill girl, but not a Catholic, the daughter of a dentist, and Glenn had dated her once or twice, but not recently. "We're just friends," he said.

Johnny didn't know her well either. She was more Glenn's type than ours: wholesome. She had a pleasant but plain face, not as plain as Cathy Collins', but still with no claim to beauty, and she was tall and toothy, with long light-brown hair. To me, girls like Melinda had zero sex appeal. They looked well-scrubbed and neat as a pin, which I admired, but if that was all they had going for them, you might as well go out with a steam-iron and a bar of soap, I figured.

At least, that's what I figured until I saw Melinda that night. She was at home alone, her parents having gone out to a movie, and she seemed glad to have company. Soon we were sitting in her den, with Glenn and Johnny and Melinda talking a blue streak on the couch while I sat across the room with my tongue hanging out. From the neck down, Melinda looked smashing, and the longer I stared at that part of her, the better-looking her face got.

Johnny saw it too; while she was talking to Glenn, Johnny caught my eye and made a face that said, "Um, Um."

I had always felt a weakness for girls wearing jumpers, and Melinda had on jumper short-shorts, dark blue, over a tee shirt with bold red and white horizontal stripes. She looked squeaky clean, as usual, but there the similarity to the old Melinda ended, for underneath that jumper and tee shirt was obviously one hell of a body. I began to think that maybe Glenn wasn't so dumb, after all. She had tits that could not be done justice without calling them knockers, a long tapering waist, and an ass that nearly brought tears to my eyes.

Even better, all of this was mounted on the prettiest pair of legs I had seen, with maybe the exception of Miss Johnson's, and they reached all the way from her hips into my deepest erotic fantasy. I sat there the whole time with a raging hard-on.

Apparently Johnny was in the same fix, and when Melinda offered us ice cream and got up to get it, he made such comical faces of desire and frustration at me that I had to look away to keep from laughing out loud.

Still, I made sure not to miss Melinda's move into the kitchen, where she stopped at the refrigerator and took out a huge container of vanilla ice cream. All of us tagged along behind her, but since she and Glenn chatted the whole time, Johnny and I were able to watch her without much danger of getting caught staring. As she moved this way and that, reaching for spoons, bending for napkins, stretching for a dish cloth, I ached with lust and wondered how on earth such a delectable piece of ass had escaped my notice all that time. I vowed then and there to pay closer attention to plain, wholesome girls. And when she went up on tiptoes to fetch bowls from a high cabinet, her shorts riding up to reveal her panties, her tits thrusting up and out, and her legs stretching long and taut, I actualy felt faint.

I had a hard that could've jacked up a sports car, and Johnny was suffering too. He leaned toward me while

Melinda was reaching for the bowls and muttered, "Hubba, hubba."

To hide erections, we had stayed just outside the kitchen door, leaning in to watch, and I wondered what we'd do when it was time to eat the ice cream. We'd look pretty ridiculous standing there facing the wall to eat it, and I could hear us already, trying to explain:

Me: "Oh, this is the way I always eat ice cream. Wouldn't eat it any other way. Makes it, uh, go down easier."

Johnny: "Yeah. I didn't know people ate ice cream any other way. Sure you don't wanna try it?"

Fortunately, Melinda handed us each a bowl of ice cream and then turned to get her own. When she did, Johnny and I hurried back to our seats.

I had thought that the distraction of eating ice cream would make my erection go down, but that was before I saw Melinda eat ice cream. The way she brought the spoon slowly to her mouth, touched it with her tongue to tease her taste buds, and then slipped it in gradually, sucking and savoring the ice cream as it melted, scorched my shorts. And the fact that it looked completely innocent and even dainty made it all the more sexy to me. I glanced at Johnny, and he was watching it too, obviously with the same appreciation. He looked my way and shook his head as if to say, "Mercy!"

Five minutes after we finished the ice cream my cock was still hard, and a few minutes later, when we heard car doors slam near the back of the house and realized that someone was coming in, it was harder still.

"My folks are back," Melinda said, and Johnny and I looked at each other in panic. In the state we were in, there was no way we could stand up for introductions, and certainly not to her mother and father.

Johnny, quick-thinking, plucked a newspaper from a magazine stand at his end of the couch and got on the floor, belly down, to read it. All I could think to do was to scurry over to a chair near the kitchen door, which I did after Melinda went into the kitchen, followed by Glenn, to greet her parents.

Seconds later her father, tall, white-haired and distinguished-looking, entered the room from the kitchen, and when Melinda, behind him, introduced us, I barely lifted out of the chair in a half-crouch and held out my hand. I must have looked deformed, but that was the best I could do. He would have to remember me as a human crab.

Johnny, smoother and more poised, looked up, smiled and waved, and then as Dr. Murray walked toward him rose to his knees and brought the paper up with him. Holding it front of his crotch, he reached out to shake hands.

Mrs. Murray merely looked into the room, smiled, and waved, and won my everlasting gratitude by saying, "Hi, there. Don't get up." Apparently she was busy in the kitchen, and when her husband turned and went in there with her, Johnny and I, still suffering, looked at each other with the same urgent thought: We *must* get the hell out of here.

I hustled back over to my original seat—it was nearer the front door—and Johnny called to Glenn, who was just inside the kitchen, still yakking away, caught his attention and signaled urgently that we wanted to leave. Glenn promptly began to say goodnight and to edge his way into the den, so I stood up, and Johnny, still kneeling in the floor, laid the newspaper on the couch and started to rise. But at that precise moment, all three of the Murrays came through the door to bid us goodnight.

Johnny dropped back to both knees and snatched up the paper again. It was strange behavior for somebody getting ready to leave, but mine, I was sure, looked stranger: I sat back down. Worse than that, I caught the very edge of the seat, slipped off it, and wound up in a squat. Too embarrassed to let on that squatting had not been my intention, I sat there, trying my damndest to look serene and unconcerned, but *knowing*, just knowing, that what I really looked like was a man taking a crap in the woods—or rather right in their den.

I did get glances, especially from Dr. Murray, in which I read the first suspicion of mental illness, but slowly I realized that all three were absorbed in talking to Glenn and were paying little attention to Johnny and me. Dr. and Mrs. Murray, it seemed, had attended the University of Georgia and were telling Glenn, who would go there in the fall, all about it. Better still, they had stopped a third of the way into the room and formed a circle as if something of such interest had come up that they needed to hem it in for a closer look. Slowly I fell forward onto my knees, my hands concealing my crotch, and when I saw my chance, turned and stood, my back to the room. Johnny did the same, and we stood there, studying the wallpaper and snickering, until finally we heard Glenn laugh and say, "Well, goodnight, and thanks again." Turning our heads we saw Glenn and Melinda coming toward us, and Dr. and Mrs. Murray going back into the kitchen. Johnny and I ran into each other in our haste to get to the front door and get out of there.

Glenn wasted no time in telling us how shameful our behavior had been. I thought he hadn't even noticed it, but as soon as we got into the car and drove off he said, "You two are crude."

He was laughing, though, in a good mood. Johnny and I, groaning one minute, laughing like loons the next, tried to apologize, but we sounded about as sincere as we were.

"Lord, McNulty, where have you been keeping her?" Johnny asked. "She gave me terminal nutache."

"You certainly had me fooled, Glenn," I said. "If you dated *that* girl and didn't want some of *her* pussy, then I pronounce you brain-dead."

Glenn laughed. In spite of his pious airs, it tickled him to be seen as a sexy little devil and to think that we envied him. But he couldn't keep it going; his true nature was too strong. "Naw, naw, fellows," he said, grinning. "She *is* a good-lookin' gal, sexy as all get-out, but she's really nice."

"What do you mean, sexy *but* nice?" Johnny said. "Does one rule out the other?"

"Aw, Johnny," he said in an aw-shucks tone of voice, "you know what I mean."

We both knew exactly what he meant; the pity was that *he* didn't know it. Johnny and I exchanged a look that declared him a hopeless case.

Johnny asked what grade she was in. Glenn said junior. And then Johnny said, "Who's she dating now?"

"Paul Conlin."

"Chuck's brother?"

Johnny sounded as surprised as I was. To me, Paul Conlin was a real loser, sort of a twerp, and I couldn't imagine that any girl would find him attractive, least of all Melinda. True, he was a football player, the back-up quarterback to his brother, and I had seen that many girls would swoon over Jo-Jo the Dogface Boy if he wore a football jersey. Still I couldn't see it. For one thing, his face, pale, pinched, weak, didn't match his body, which was muscular and robust, apparently from lifting weights. He reminded me of those photographs snapped at carnival booths where people posed with their heads atop life-size cardboard cutouts of comical figures. Too, his movements were quick and jerky, and he was forever adjusting his glasses by stabbing a finger at the bridge of his nose. Worst of all, he had the kind of big mouth that usually came with a small brain, and his voice sounded like the braying of a jackass. I decided there must be something wrong with Melinda after all if she dated guys like Glenn and Paul Conlin. I could overlook one mistake, but two began to look like a pattern.

"Too bad," I said.

"Yeah," Johnny added; "she sure can pick 'em. But to hell with all that. Let's go to the Varsity."

We got to the Varsity around nine-thirty. An hour later

the place would be thronged, but already things looked pretty lively, with the parking lot about two-thirds full. First, Glenn made a complete circle through the lot, just to see who was there, and then drove to the back, parked near the entrance to the restaurant, and we went inside.

Most Varsity customers never went inside, preferring curb service and, I guessed, the feeling of being in the middle of things, but the small dining room had its advantages too. You could get waited on quickly and through a wall of glass you could survey nearly the whole parking lot more easily than you could from a car.

The dining room was empty as we entered, but a few minutes later Rusty Brown came in with his younger brother, Cagney. We all knew Rusty and liked him, but Glenn and Johnny didn't know Cagney, so I introduced them to him as he and Rusty slid into the booth next to ours and we began to talk. Soon we were telling them about our narrow escape from the ambush at Cathy Collins' house.

Rusty laughed. "Hell, you coulda yelled 'boo' and had that whole bunch shakin'."

Rusty knew every guy at the party. He played on the football team, linebacker, but that was all he had in common with them. He lived in one of the roughest parts of Milltown, a place called Hicks Alley, and I doubted if either he or Cagney had ever even been on the Hill. Too hoity-toity to suit them—especially Cagney, a rough-hewn type who looked slightly subhuman and spoke mostly in disdainful grunts. Rusty, who smiled easily, moved with athletic grace and had a devil-may-care attitude, could have gotten by in any group. But it would have to come to him; he wouldn't go to it. Both the Browns were dark complexioned, of medium height but powerfully built, and known far and wide as boys you didn't want to tangle with.

"Now, I wouldn't wanna get Buster riled," Rusty added, "but the rest of that bunch would mess their britches if you so much as growled at 'em. Chuck don't even want to get hit on the football field. That's why he can't complete a pass. Too worried about gettin' hit. Spends half his time in the huddle givin' somebody hell 'cause they let a man get to him. He's chicken shit." Looking at me he said, "Just knock him on his ass, Benny; there ain't nothin' to him."

I had listened with interest, delighted to hear all that about Chuck, but all it meant to me was that both of us were cowards and that he was the bigger and stronger of the two. Fortunately I didn't have to respond to Rusty, for just then the waiter brought our order: chili dogs, fries and Cokes all around.

The Brown brothers ordered chili dogs too, and when the waiter left, Rusty said, "Where is this damn party? Cagney and I'll go back with you." He smiled. "Sort of even up the odds a little."

The idea was tempting, but neither of us wanted that. If anything happened, it would look too much as if we had started it. Besides, they might not even be there anymore. The Hill crowd often hopped from one party to another. We told Rusty it was probably too late.

That seemed to satisfy him. Cagney merely grunted. But a moment later, Rusty turned sideways on the end of his seat and leaned over to give me some serious advice. In the past, we had run around some together and liked each other. "Benny," he said, "you might have to fight one of 'em. It won't be Chuck—I'd *bet* on that—but whoever it is, make *sure* you hit him first."

That got my complete attention. Hitting first went against everything I believed in, to say nothing of my nature, but I knew I was getting the straight scoop from one of the best scrappers around. Cagney grunted his approval of his brother's advice and Rusty continued. "Hit him first," he said, emphasizing each word, "and hit him with everything you've got." He balled up his fist, turned it toward him and put it near his face. "Listen," he prompted: "Hit him right between the eyes, right on the nose." Cagney grunted his approval again and Rusty went on: "It'll daze him, bring tears to his eyes, temporarily blind him. but most of all it'll take the fight out of 'im."

He shook his head as if to say he had delivered the gospel and I'd better believe it. And I did. Cagney grunted again, and at that point the waiter arrived with their order. Rusty turned back into the booth and the conversation moved to other things. Not much later we paid up and went back to the car.

We stayed about an hour longer, talking, joking, cuttin' the fool and listening to WPDQ, "with the right jive for you." But around eleven we called it a night. Glenn went by Johnny's first, to drop him off, and on impulse I got out with him, telling Glenn I'd walk home from there. I had a lot on my mind and needed to think, and the night air felt good. But after Glenn drove away, Johnny and I got to talking and I forgot about getting off to myself.

"Things like tonight—Chuck Conlin and all that crap—don't bother you, do they?" I didn't know whether the question was my sneaky way of finding out if Johnny was ever afraid too or if I hoped he would give me the secret of his courage. Maybe both. At any rate, his answer surprised me.

"Oh, yes, they do. But it pisses me off and I do something about it. Not against *that* kind of odds," he said, pointing in the general direction of Cathy Collins' house. "But we'll get our chance."

I didn't say so, but I was relieved to hear him say "we." He continued: "Tell you what though: I'd rather have everybody on the Hill after my ass than that Brown boy."

"Everybody on the Hill *is* after *my* ass. But I know what you mean. I've seen Rusty fight, and he can go with the best of 'em."

"Not Rusty," Johnny said. "Well, I wouldn't want to go at it with him either, but I meant his brother."

"Yeah," I said. "Rusty told me once that the only guy in town he's afraid of is Cagney. He laughed when he said it, but I was over at his house once when Cagney got after him with a bottle of Mexi-Pep. Chased him clear out into the street, smiting him smartly, as they say, about the head and shoulders."

90

"Son-of-a-gun looks like that picture in our science book: Cro-Magnon man."

That sparked a crazy, sad thought in me. "You don't suppose, do you, that proof of the Darwin Theory is all around us, right here in Augusta? I mean, think about it: nobody would mistake Cagney Brown—Rusty, either—for a Hill boy. I'm not saying that Chuck Conlin and his kind are any prizes, but they're different from us—you, me, everybody in Milltown—and even a blind man could see it."

"Environment," Johnny said. "That's all it is."

"Well, I'm gonna change *my* environment, Ace, come hell or high water. See if I don't." I had never in my whole life meant any words more than I meant those. I could almost feel them settling into my bones. "Those people up there on the Hill know how to live."

"I'm with you, friend. Did you see that container of ice cream Melinda hauled out of the refrigerator? Outside of an ice cream parlor, I'd never seen that much ice cream at one time in my whole life. Think what it would be like to go to your refrigerator just any ol' time you felt like it and eat all the ice cream you wanted. Why, the refrigerator itself was bigger than our bathroom, and I got a look into that thing when she opened the door. It was bulging with food from top to bottom. That's not the only home I've noticed that in, either. It's all over the Hill, wherever I go, in every kitchen I've been in: full pantries, full pots, full freezers. Hell, at my house I've never even had a Coke that I didn't have to go to the store to get. Those Hill people keep Co'-Cola by the crate, right there in the house. You want a Coke? Why, you just mosey over and get it. Want another? Well, just mosey over again. Plenty of every-thing—that's what *I* like about the Hill."

I had rarely seen Johnny so serious. Food didn't mean that much to me, never had, so I had not thought of the Hill as a kind of horn of plenty. I could see of course that it was, but what I saw more clearly was that Johnny must have been mighty hungry a few times in his life, hungrier than I'd ever been. I wanted to ask him about it, but didn't

91

know whether I should. Besides, the mood had gotten somber, so I kidded him instead. "Do you mean to tell me that all this time I thought you were scouring the Hill for pussy, all you really wanted was a biscuit? Come on."

"Hold on," he prompted: "I said plenty of *every*thing."

"All I've gotten out of the Hill is plenty of trouble."

"That's not true. You're having the time of your life; you just don't realize it."

"I'm having a time all right—but keep telling me that, keep telling me that."

He began to count on his fingers. "You nearly got some of Austin's pussy—and had a good time trying; don't lie. You've got a date tomorrow night with Cherry Ashford, who's tough as tarpaper and rich to boot. You finally got to meet Dianne Damico—"

"Now that's what *I* like about the Hill: the girls."

He kept on counting: "You've got a belly full of chili dog, french fries and Coke, all of it good. And you've got a warm bed to go home to. What more do you want out of life?"

He knew what I was going to say and said it with me: "Pussy!" Then we laughed so loudly that I thought we might wake up the neighbors.

We stood around for awhile after that, swapping comments on Johnny's neighbors, the occasional car that went by—everything in general and nothing in particular. But when we ran out of small talk Johnny looked thoughtful for a moment and then said:

"Know when I first found out about the Hill? I was 13, and working that summer on a Snow's Laundry truck. Our route covered the Hill and took me into lots of homes up there. What a revelation! It was completely different—night from day—from what I was accustomed to. The homes looked bright and cheerful, the people were nice and said, 'Thank you,' and 'How are you?' and nobody seemed worried and unhappy. I realize now that that's just the way it looked to a 13-year-old kid, that the rich have problems too. But I'll still take the problems that go with money over the problems that come with poverty—any day."

"Is that why you go to the Hill now, because it's nice up there, nicer than down here? Is it the food?" I really wanted to know.

"No. I go there because that's where the fun is. How many parties you been to in Milltown?"

"None since I got to high school," I said. "If Milltown's young people even throw parties it's news to me."

"And, of course, I like the girls."

"Yeah. Don't forget *them.*"

"I've been criticized for it, by girls around here, even by Grace, my stepmother. 'Ain't Milltown girls good enough for you?' they say. Well, I didn't tell them this, but, no, they ain't. There are some nice girls, cute girls in Milltown, but you know as well as I do that they're not in the same league with Hill girls."

"No argument there. Of course, Milltown girls haven't had the privileges, the same opportunities."

"Right!" he said. "But that ain't *my* fault. And there's nothing I can do about it. They'll have to get out of Milltown, those who have sense enough, on their own, just as I plan to do, just as you plan to do. In the meantime, I'm gonna go right on dating the kind of girls named Melinda, Claire, Ashlyn and Marcella, instead of girls named Thelma, Geneva, Gertrude, Clara, Pearl and Opal. Show me an Opal and I'll show you an ugly gal."

I laughed and he did too. We both knew he was exaggerating, but there was enough truth in what he said to make the point. "What *are* you gonna do after graduation?" I asked. "Decided yet?"

"Well, can't go off to college. Folks can't afford it. I'll probably get out and get a job. What about you?"

"I'm in the same fix, for now. But one way or another, I'm gonna get a college degree. As I see it, that's the only train out of Milltown—for me, anyhow."

He clasped my shoulder with his hand and squeezed. "Save a seat on that train for me, friend. I might have a different ticket, but I'm sure as hell gonna ride."

Chapter Five

"Under the circumstances," Johnny said, "maybe we'd better skip Teen Town tonight." It was just past seven-thirty and we were on our way up the Hill to pick up Harriet and Cherry. "That all right with you?"

"All right? Lean over here and I'll kiss you." I had brooded all day about going to Teen Town that night. We'd be sure to run into some of the gang that had been at Cathy Collins' party, maybe even all of them.

"I don't think they'd start anything while we were with dates," Johnny said, "but it doesn't hurt to be cautious. Besides, I've had enough of them for one weekend."

"Me and thee. So what *do* we do?"

He smiled a sneaky smile. "Let's skip the movie too. Let's take 'em slummin'."

"Slumming?"

There was that smile again. "Yeah. Let's show 'em a side of Augusta they've never seen before. I'm in just enough of a bad-ass mood to do it. If they don't like it they can lump it. What'cha say?"

I had to admit that it had possibilities. Anything that avoided Teen Town and the Hill had posssibilities.

He added, "Let's show 'em how the other half lives—"

"Now, Johnny," I chided, "you know the Milltown Tour of Homes ain't till next week."

"I'm serious. Give 'em a taste of what it's like on the other side of the tracks. We'll make it up as we go. The Shamrock, maybe. You *know* they've never been in a pool hall. Deason's. Best hotdogs and hamburgers anywhere. Maybe even the Barnyard. Bet they've never been to a real square dance. What'cha think?"

I nodded slowly and gave him an appraising look. "I think it's brilliant." Johnny did have flair and imagination. "But what if they figure out *we* ain't exactly slummin'?"

"I don't care what they figure out. In their hearts they probably already think they're slumming to go out with us. Remind me to tell you something later. Here," he said, offering me a stick of gum. Johnny *loved* Dentyne chewing gum. But when I started to toss the wrapper out the window, he stopped me. "Don't throw it out here; wait till we get on the Hill." I gave him a funny look and he gave me a funny smile. "Told you I was in a bad-ass mood," he said.

I leaned back in my seat, savoring the gum. "Well, one thing's for sure: they won't be able to say we didn't come up with something different to do on a date."

We cackled and Johnny gunned the Ford on up the Hill.

When Johnny went to the door to get Harriet, and she came out dressed to kill, I had some second thoughts about our scheme, and when we got to Cherry's house my second thoughts became cold feet. Could we really do that to girls like these, I wondered, especially to one like Cherry?

What cast the most doubt in my mind was the Ashford's house. Oh, I had seen it many times in passing, had even been to a party there once—not in the main house, but out back in a garage, a garage, I noted, that was bigger and better-looking than my house. But walking up to the front door of that house was different from just knowing about it. The house inspired respect. Two stories high and built of brick, it sat atop a small rise, flanked by old oaks and magnolias, and seemed to gaze with queenly dignity down its lush, sloping lawn at the quiet, tree-lined street, Lakeshore Drive. If that house had had a sign over the door, it could not have said more clearly: "Be Advised:

People of Good Breeding Live Here." My mother would have taken one look at that house and said the same thing, except that she would have added—head cocked, that look in her eye—"And don't you forget it."

I rang the door bell fully expecting a butler to answer. Door bells were still new to me. They were another sign, like venetian blinds, that on the Hill I was in a neighborhood that was several rungs up the ladder from Milltown. In Milltown people *knocked* on doors or, in some cases, rapped on the porch and yelled. I wondered if a yell had ever disturbed the dignity of Cherry Ashford's neighborhood, which lay in a corner at the back of the Hill, like a cove into which Augusta's truly rich had withdrawn.

Cherry's mother answered the door. A slender woman, she had black hair streaked with white and appeared dressed to go out for the evening: a black dress trimmed in gray, black high-heel shoes, pearls, make-up. She also wore, or so it seemed to me, a faint smile stained with disfavor. Her eyes, gray and alert, swept me from top to bottom and I felt that I could read in them her cat-quick appraisal of me: weighed, found wanting.

She waved me in and told me to "wait in the study," a room directly to my left, off the foyer. For some crazy reason, I immediately thought of the study as The James Fenimore Cooper Room. Leather was everywhere. Couch and chairs were done in a rich burgandy, touches of the material decorated tables and lamps, and row after row of leather-bound books stood in floor-to-ceiling bookcases along three walls. The room looked very cozy, even snug, and the lighting, soft and mellow, made it look all the more inviting, but I stood in it for several moments feeling like an intruder. That room, which was after all merely four walls and a ceiling, looked richer with all its leather and brass than I would ever be. It made me feel somehow defeated. The distance from Milltown to the kind of living that room represented could be measured only in light years, I thought, and I stood there feeling like a tin cup might feel among silver chalices.

Eventually I sat down on the couch, startled at first and then embarrassed by the rush of air from the cushion as it deflated under my weight. But as usual my timing was poor, for as soon as my rear end hit bottom, Cherry appeared at the door, and I had to hurry to my feet again.

My heart sank as I saw that she was dressed even nicer than Harriet was—in fact worse, considering what we had in mind. Cherry, wearing a navy-blue dress of light wool trimmed in white at the sleeves and collar, looked more stylish than Harriet did. Cherry had kept it simple, while Harriet had gone overboard: an off-white dress with a full, ruffled skirt, and a lace shawl pulled around her shoulders. I knew right away that in any of the places Johnny had named, Harriet would look merely over-dressed, but that Cherry would look like a hundred-dollar bill in a pocket of small change. It didn't help matters, either, that Johnny and I wore simple slacks and sport shirts.

When we got into the car, I tried my damndest to signal to Johnny in some way that we ought to change our plan for the evening. While everybody was getting settled in and swapping greetings, I made such a to-do over how they were dressed—"They sure are dressed nicely, aren't they, Johnny? Yes, sir, they are *dressed*. Don't you like the way they're *dressed*, Johnny?"—that finally they all looked at me strangely.

Not willing to give up, I then tried to signal to Johnny by cutting my eyes and nodding sharply toward Cherry, to my right, hoping he would wake up and see what I thought was perfectly obvious: that she was dressed much too nicely for an evening of slumming. I didn't know if under the dim glow of the car's dome-light he could even see my eyes, but just when my efforts reached their most urgent and I was actually mugging, I realized that Harriet was staring at me, probably wondering if I had lost my mind. It was embarrassing as hell to be caught making faces like that for no apparent reason, so I went into an elaborate act, pretending that something was in my eye. Mugging

like crazy now, I whipped out a handkerchief and wiped at
my eye for awhile, and then pretended that all was okay,
that whatever it was was gone. By then Johnny had driven
off, so I settled back and prepared for the worst.

Johnny's first stop surprised even me. We were heading
down Broad Street, only four or five blocks from the heart
of downtown Augusta, when he suddenly turned into a
dark side street and parked. Pointing to an old brick building across the street, he said to Harriet and Cherry, "Somebody there I want you to meet." He opened the door and
got out.

The girls stirred, a bit uneasily, I thought, but they said
nothing. To avoid meeting their eyes, though, I looked
across the street to where Johnny had pointed and could
now see a darkened door in an otherwise blank wall. At
first it appeared to be merely the back entrance to a building fronting on Broad, but when I looked higher I saw
windows in the second story and realized that I had been
there before. Johnny's Aunt Jenine, the woman who had
raised him until his father married Grace, lived there in a
two-room apartment upstairs over a feed-and-seed store.

Suddenly I felt sick. Johnny's aunt was as poor as a
churchmouse, and I remembered her apartment as looking tired and worn and cheap. Surely Cherry and Harriet
had never visited in such a home, and I doubted that they
had ever known anyone like Jenine, unless of course it was
their maid or washwoman. This was more than I had
bargained for in an evening of slumming. It was one thing
to show the girls how the other half lived; it was another
to introduce the other half as your relatives.

It bothered my conscience to feel that way, for there was
nothing wrong with Jenine. She was simply a jolly, loud,
salt-of-the-earth woman with apparently no inkling that
she might strike others as coarse. Big-hearted and completely unself-conscious, she took you just as you came and
seemed to take for granted that you did the same by her.

Nevertheless, Jesus went to Golgotha with a lighter heart than I went to Jenine's door.

Moments later, as we walked up a steep flight of dark stairs lit at the top by a faint light from an open door, Johnny sang out, "This is a raid; don't anybody move."

Quickly a large woman appeared on the landing above us. "Raid?" she said, scoffing, hands on hips. "I'll show *you* a raid. Get your little tail up here and give me a hug."

At the top of the stairs Johnny glided into her arms and seemed almost to disappear. His aunt was taller than either of us and was big. Not fat. Big. She all but lifted Johnny off the floor in a crushing embrace. "And who do we have here?" she asked, turning him loose and looking at us.

Johnny reminded her that she had met me before and then introduced her to Cherry and Harriet. I was relieved to see Cherry step forward smartly, smile, and shake the woman's hand. Harriet shook her hand too, but she did it a bit stiffly and with a smile that never quite got to her eyes.

Telling us to call her Jenine, Johnny's aunt shooed us through the door into her apartment, talking a mile a minute, saying in one breath how pretty the girls were— "too pretty for the likes of you, Johnny Kelly"—and in the next breath scolding Johnny for not coming to see her more often. "Go on to the kitchen," she told Johnny, who was leading the way. "I'll pour y'all a nice glass of iced tea. And if you're hungry, why, there's a pot of black-eyed peas on the stove—cooked with hamhock—and a hoecake of cornbread in the oven, still warm."

As much as I liked black-eyed peas and cornbread, I winced at the idea of Jenine serving up such food to Cherry and Harriet. I had no idea what kind of food they were used to, but something told me that it was a lot finer than peas and cornbread.

My concern about food faded quickly, though, as we passed through the room, on the way to the kitchen. It was both her bedroom and her parlor, and it was even shabbier than I remembered. It helped a little that the room was dimly lit, but there was no mistaking that Jenine lived near the raw edge of poverty. In one corner stood a tall iron bed with a sagging mattress. In another, a large old chifforobe with one door missing leaned badly off center. And on the wall ahead of us sat a couch of imitation leather that had been patched in several places with electrical tape. I felt sorry for Jenine and at the same time embarrassed for her, but she seemed not the slightest bit self-conscious, saying merrily, "It ain't much, but it's home." Cherry seemed not to notice the room and went on into the kitchen, chatting with Johnny. But Harriet cast quick little glances here and there, and seemed to be wondering what she had gotten herself into.

In the kitchen, nobody but Johnny accepted food, but Jenine poured four glasses of tea and we all sat down around her table.

"Never known Johnny Kelly to pass up food," Jenine said, looking fondly at Johnny, who sat perched on a kitchen stool at the end of the table, opposite his aunt.

"And you never will, as long as you're the cook," he said.

She beamed and began to ply the girls with questions about themselves. Cherry, who sat to Jenine's right, daintily sipping tea, answered easily and asked questions of her own. But Harriet, who sat on a bench with me, to Jenine's left, said only enough to appear civil. I wondered if Johnny had noticed her behavior and if he regretted having brought her there. But he seemed perfectly at ease.

I wished I could say the same for myself. Never in my wildest dream had I imagined finding myself with Cherry Ashford in such surroundings. The kitchen, lit by a bare bulb hanging by a long cord from the ceiling, didn't look as forlorn as the other room did; still it was drab. An old wood stove jutted out into the room, and firewood lay in stacks behind it. A sink stuck out from one wall and seemed just to hang there supported by nothing but pipes. And the wooden table we sat at was rough and scarred, covered diagonally with red-and-white checked oilcloth that gave off a peculiar, slightly unpleasant odor.

I sat there sipping tea, sneaking peeks at my watch and saying little, and it occurred to me that my behavior was not much better than Harriet's, even if the reasons were very different. I sensed in her a wounded dignity, a feeling that all of this was beneath her and that no one with a proper regard for her would have subjected her to it. My problem was embarrassment, pure and simple, at the thought that Cherry—Harriet too—might associate me with all this. And it helped not a bit that I knew they had every right to do so. It was true that my home was nicer than Jenine's, but to girls from the Hill, I felt, any home in Milltown was just another outpost of poverty. As for Jenine herself, she was no different, except in personality, from my own mother or grandmother, or any of the women I knew in Milltown.

Worse, though, was my guilt about my embarrassment. Johnny adored his Aunt Jenine, and she was a good woman and he was my friend. What was more, I could not help the circumstances into which I had been born. We were all children of chance, and Harriet and Cherry should be able to figure that out too. In another place and time, Jenine might be standing in Harriet's shoes, and Harriet in hers. Harriet and Cherry had simply been born better off.

I told myself all that and believed it. But it didn't help much. And when Johnny finished eating, drained the last of his tea, and announced that we had to leave, I sprang up ready to go. When Harriet did too, I looked at her tea glass. It had not been touched.

Next, Johnny drove to the middle of downtown, between Seventh and Eighth streets, and parked near the Confederate Monument. "Let's take a walk," he said.

We ambled east on Broad, stopping here and there to look in shop windows or just to study for a moment something that had caught our eye. The short block we were on, between Seventh and Monument streets, was Augusta's main bus stop and a good place for people-watching, so we were in no hurry. Besides, the night, milder even than the night before, was perfect for walking, and many people were out.

Before long, though, we reached Seventh Street, heading east, and I was surprised to see that Johnny intended to cross and go on. Broad Street, from Seventh to Fifth, was sleazy and rough, a kind of urban lower intestine favored by good-time men and women, and soldiers from Camp Gordon, an Army post outside of town. It contained clip joints, notorious saloons, cheap hotels, tattoo parlors, and fast-buck stores hawking gaudy goods, and respectable people did not go there. To them, lower Broad was all razzle-dazzle aimed at separating the weak of mind from their wallets and the innocent from their virtue. It wasn't Augusta's skidrow. That was at the other end of the downtown district, on Thirteenth Street, a stone's throw from where Jenine lived. Still, people who hung out on lower Broad were generally thought to be at the top of a slide that would land them on skidrow soon enough. I doubted that Cherry and Harriet had ever even heard of the area, but I knew damn good and well they shouldn't be walking in it. To me, this went beyond slumming, and I expected at any second that the girls would balk and want to turn back.

I was wrong again. Both girls were fascinated, though each in a different way, and showed no reluctance to go on. Harriet, walking ahead with Johnny, seemed attracted and repelled at the same time, like somebody unable to turn away from a scary scene. "Look!" she kept saying to Cherry, and to Johnny and me, and she turned around so often to come and whisper something to Cherry that she reminded me of a target in a shooting gallery. Cherry's behavior was more restrained, but her curiosity was obvious. At times, she seemed to be studying the whole scene as though trying to commit it to memory.

Johnny and I pretended that this was all old hat to us, but it *was* a lively scene, and from time to time I caught myself staring at it like an idiot absorbed in a piece of colored glass. People either in high spirits or merely gawking seemed everywhere around us, milling about, coming and going, or clustered here and there, talking loudly, laughing louder. The stores appeared to be doing a brisk trade, the saloons were packed, and even some cars parked at the curb, doors standing open, radios blaring, were filled with men and women having a high old time. The impression was that life here was so boisterous that it had simply spilled out of the buildings into the street, but except for the automobiles it reminded me more of a carnival midway: neon and other signs all but screamed for attention, music and noise gusted at us from every direction, and occasionally a hard-looking man or woman leaned out from a doorway to mutter words I couldn't make out, but which all the same sounded obscene.

We drew some curious stares ourselves, and though most of them seemed directed at Cherry and Harriet, it occurred to me that maybe I didn't look as much a part of all this as I had thought. I had never spent time hanging around lower Broad, but the people there, except for the soldiers, were the kind I'd been around all my life: common men and women—mill workers, farmers, craftsmen of all skills—to whom any appearance of refinement signaled that you were not one of them. I knew of course that they might be jumping to conclusions about me from looking at Cherry, who stood out from her surroundings like a crocus in a snowbank; still it made me feel strange, happy and at the same time sad. I didn't *want* to be one of them—wanted in fact with every fiber of my being to escape my low-life origins; but neither did I want to be rejected by them. I was, after all, one of them and I felt in spite of my desire to escape that way of life a tender affection for them and a great sympathy that life had cast them in such lowly roles. I understood that they did not think of themselves as lowly and that they would spit on my sympathy as an insult to their fierce pride. But that only made their situation sadder to me: how would they ever get *out* if they never faced the truth about being *in*?

At Fifth Street we crossed Broad to walk back to the car, and that's when I found out how shy Cherry was. That side of Broad, a very wide street—"second in width only to Canal Street in New Orleans," Augustans liked to boast—was quiet, with most of the stores shut down for the weekend, so finally we began to talk. Or at least *I* talked; Cherry, for the most part, merely turned six shades of red while saying as little as possible. Not even direct questions got much out of her.

"Looking forward to graduation?"

"Yes."

"Got a big summer planned?"

"Sort of."

Feeling a bit desperate, I waved my hand to indicate the strip. "That was really something, wasn't it? What did you think?"

She blushed, cut her eyes at me, started to speak, stopped, and then finally said, "It appealed to the painter in me." Turning even redder in the face, she said, "I should have brought my sketchbook."

Seizing on that, I tried to get her to talk about her painting, but all she would say was that she dabbled at it and wasn't "good enough to call myself a painter." And when I asked her about her study of art in France, she said the main thing she learned was that she was no artist.

I couldn't get over this girl. To my way of thinking, money and self-assurance came in the same package. Besides, she had seemed perfectly poised and confident with Jenine. Had she never been on a date before?

Johnny and Harriet, walking a few steps ahead, were now holding hands, so I took Cherry's and we strolled along for awhile saying nothing, which seemed to suit her fine. If I hadn't been so taken with her, I might have thought she was dim-witted, but I knew from her reputation as a straight-A student that she had to be pretty smart. I began to wonder, though, how I could possibly make out with a girl so shy. If she got red and tongue-tied just talking to me, she'd probably turn purple and faint if I ran my hand up her legs.

I told that to Johnny when the two girls pulled loose

from our hands to go look in the window of an antique store, and in typical fashion for him he said, "If she faints, fuck her, you fool. Even Cranston could tell you that."

Cranston Boswell was the mentally retarded son of a Milltown family. About the same age as I, he practically lived on a bicycle, was a fixture in the neighborhood, and for reasons known only to Cranston, if even to him, he delighted in singing out over and over whenever he saw me: "Here comes Benny with the pasteboard weinie."

Johnny added: "Stop worrying about *her* feelings and think about yours. My dad says there are some women who won't lift a finger to help you fuck 'em even when they're dying for it. He once screwed a gal who pretended to be asleep the whole time. Humped him like crazy, he said, right there on the couch in her folks' living room, moaning and groaning and grinding the whole time. Sat up a few minutes later, blinking and rubbing her eyes, and said, 'Oh, I must have dozed off. What time is it?' 'Time I left,' he said, 'though it seems like I just came'."

I laughed, but mainly the story added to my confusion about women. What strange creatures they were! They said no when they meant yes; they said stop when they meant go; they said, "I'm not that kind of girl," when that was exactly the kind of girl they were. Jesus Christ! Who in his right mind could figure out what they *did* mean? And why was I the only male who could not decipher their messages? Did I have to be Sherlock Holmes to get a piece of ass?

Johnny and I had walked on ahead, stopping to wait at the doorway of the next store. Soon we saw the girls coming toward us, but before they got close enough to hear, Johnny nudged me with a finger and said, "Look, the girl's all tongue-tied because she likes you. Make the most of it. What do you care if she turns purple? Purple or pink, pussy's pussy."

"Yeah," I said, feeling my whole outlook on Cherry Ashford change for the better. "You really think that's it— that she likes me?"

"Well, look at her. She doesn't look tongue-tied to me."

The girls had stopped for one last look at the antiques and were talking up a blue streak.

"And she wasn't tongue-tied with Jenine," Johnny added.

"You're right. I'm gonna let *her* worry about *me* for awhile."

"Now you're talking. And she *is* worried. Bet you a quarter they're talking about us and not about antiques."

I laughed. "If you've got a quarter, you either borrowed it or stole it. But something tells me you're right."

We got back to the car, climbed in, and Johnny headed out of town. Soon I knew he was going to The Barnyard, a nightclub about five miles out of town on Highway 1 that featured square dancing to live music and was not particular to whom it served beer. The Barnyard wasn't exactly a rough place. Many couples took teen-age children there and let them roam about while they danced and had fun. But it wasn't the country club either. On the whole, it attracted people who, though of the same class, were more respectable than those who favored lower Broad. But it still got its share of rough-and-tumble men and women whose tempers flared easily, especially when soaked in alcohol. I'd been there only three or four times, usually with Zeb and my mother, but each time had brought its tense moments, with a few licks passed before big, tough-looking bouncers could break it up.

When Harriet saw the place, I could read in her face that she didn't want to go in, that Johnny had finally gone too far. And it did look forlorn. A big wooden building of crude construction, it sat on a rise of red clay overlooking a rain-ravaged parking lot jammed with cars parked every which way. Cherry, however, took one look at the building and marched right up to it, so Harriet went along, but not without casting disapproving looks here and there, I thought, as we entered and found a vacant booth.

A few minutes later Harriet seemed more at ease. We all

moved onto the dance floor, first for a slow dance and then for a rousing square dance, and when we went back to the booth both girls, puffing and perspiring a bit, were laughing. A waitress took our order, beers for Johnny and me, Cokes for the girls, and then we sat back to rest and watch the crowd.

"You've square danced before," I said to Cherry.

She blushed as if I'd said, "You've fucked before," but now I saw her shyness in a new light. It was merely a tribute to my devastating charm. So I just waited coolly for her response. Finally she said, "Yes. In the mountains."

When she didn't elaborate I tried teasing. "You know, your trouble is, you talk too much. Nobody likes a blabbermouth."

This time her blush all but lit up the booth, and I wondered if I had gone too far. But no; she began to try harder. Every summer, she explained, she spent time in Cashiers, North Carolina, with her aunt, and there she had learned to square dance.

I knew nothing about Cashiers, learning only later that it was a mountain resort for the rich. But right away I wanted to know if she'd go there again this summer. I had my own plans for her summer.

Haltingly she told me that she would go again and in fact would leave the day after graduation. She didn't know when she would be back. "But you could write me," she said softly, lowering her eyes.

"Sure," I said, thinking disgustedly that that was all I needed: long-distance love.

"I could give you her address," she said even more softly.

My lips said, "You do that," but my spirit, curdling with disappointment, said, "No. No. That would make it too easy for me, and God wouldn't like that. Let me send my letters out unaddressed. That way, like my cock, they will never land in your box. They will seek but never find. They will come back stamped Return to Sender, just like everything else I've offered to girls, and God and all His

107

Heavenly Host can sing out in a joyful chorus, 'There goes Benny with the pasteboard weinie; wants it bad, but he can't have any.'" I was so awash in self-pity that I barely felt her hand, soft and warm, sneak over mine, resting on my right thigh, and give a little squeeze as she leaned close and said, "Besides, we still have some time until graduation."

The way she said it and then looked into my eyes, just for a second when I whipped my head around, sent a shock of recognition through me. I could be awfully dense sometimes, but unless I was hopelessly stupid, her tone, her hand, her eyes said: "Don't give up so easily; I know what you want and I want it too."

The thought made my head swim, and suddenly I was the one whose tongue was tied. I ransacked my tumbled thoughts for a suave reply, but just as I was about to give up and say something as brilliant as "You're right," I heard Johnny say, "Uh, oh! Trouble."

On the far side of the dance floor, nearly as wide as a football field, a scuffle had broken out, and as we watched, it grew in seconds from a shoving match to a fistfight, and then to a brawl. I thought at first that the dance floor had caved in, for among the dancing couples men and women began lurching and falling in an ever-widening circle as if toppling into a hole. But I soon saw that two men, then three, and then four and more were locked in a violent struggle and hurtling first one way and then another through the crowded dancers, mowing them down as a cannon ball might. I had never seen a brawl before, and one of my first thoughts, ridiculous when I looked back on it, was that they must be doing it all wrong, because it certainly wasn't like the brawls I'd seen in the movies. For one thing, it was all sight and no sound. Either we were too far away or the big room simply swallowed up the noise. Adding to the unreality of it all, the band played on, a slow number sung by a nasal redhead in a cowgirl outfit, as if none of this were happening. In far reaches of the dance floor couples even continued dancing.

But not for long. Soon others, even a woman or two, joined in the fight, while the rest on that side of the room dodged this way and that to keep out of harm's way, and then hurried toward the exit when the brawl lurched once more in the opposite direction.

I kept thinking that at any minute the fight would break up. Where the hell were the bouncers? But every time the crowd parted and I could see what was going on, more arms seemed to be flailing, and now, with fewer people in the room, the sounds of the struggle, fists striking flesh, shoe leather scuffling, grunting, groaning, grew clear and sharp. I quickly measured the distance to the door and glanced at Harriet and Cherry. Their faces white, their bodies still, they looked like rabbits so tense with fear that they could not move. I looked back toward the brawl just in time to see a knot of men go hurtling toward a booth and smash it. *Wham!* It was gone. They scrambled to their feet, tore at each other again, and demolished still another booth. I looked quickly at Johnny and we read each other's mind.

Nudging Harriet, who sat on the outside, her back to him, he said, "Come on." She rose quickly, but still did not take her eyes off the brawl. Clearly she could not believe what she was seeing.

I jumped up to let Cherry out, but in a wild misunderstanding she grabbed my arm and said, meaning the fight, "Don't you go out there!"

I froze in disbelief. Don't go out there? Where did women get these insane ideas? Go out *there*? Hell, my mama hadn't raised no crazy children. A 20-mule team could not have dragged me out there. Still, I didn't miss the fact that she obviously thought I possessed the courage of a lion, and I certainly wasn't going to tell her any different. I looked at Johnny and he looked at me. Smiling like an imp, he said, "Oh, go on."

"No!" Harriet cried.

"No!" Cherry pleaded.

Playing it for all it was worth now, I sighed and said grandly to Johnny, "The safety of the girls comes first. Let's get out of here."

Outside, we stood in the parking lot and watched the door with others. The only ones still inside the dance hall, it seemed, were those fighting and those trying to break it up, and after a few minutes the peacemakers seemed to be succeeding. Men and a couple of women staggered out, clothes torn, the marks of battle shining on face and arms in the brightly lit doorway, and more than once a body shot out the door head-first, as if flung like dirty laundry. They all seemed much the worse for wear, but if anyone was badly hurt I could not see it.

They were still coming out, rats fleeing through too small a hole, when Cherry clutched my arm and said, "Oh! I left my pocketbook inside."

I had no choice. I went back in to get it, picking my opening and dashing inside. As it turned out, I was not in the slightest danger. The fight was now over and the last of the brawlers, under the watchful eyes of bouncers, were looking through the wreckage for items lost in the fight. But you would have thought I was a returning war hero or something when I came back out with Cherry's pocketbook. She beamed and carried on as if I had braved 10,000 savages to rescue her child, and all the way back to town she couldn't keep her hands—or her lips—off me.

Harriet, on the other hand, sat on her side of the front seat and went on and on about "that kind of place" and "our miraculous escape" from it. She "had never" this, "had never" that, and "never would again," she said, rattling on, and in every one of her "nevers" she implied what she thought of the evening and of the kind of date who would take her to "such places."

To his credit, Johnny didn't say a word. Nor did he let on in any way I could detect that he was p.o.'d. But I wasn't surprised when he took Harriet home first. And when he walked her to her door and came straight back to the car, I knew that he had sent her into her house without so much as a "Kiss my ass." He was cool that way.

At Cherry's house I lingered at the front door long enough to kiss her again and to feel her tits, which she not only didn't mind, but seemed to like and encourage, pushing hard against my hand and moaning. But a moment later the front-porch light came on and we broke the embrace.

"Mother," she explained, stepping back, looking disappointed.

I nodded. "Next Friday?"

She nodded yes and smiled.

"I'll call."

"Call tomorrow," she said.

"I will." I turned to leave.

"And the next day."

"I will."

"And the next."

Later, I didn't remember walking back to the car.

"That's a nice girl there," Johnny said, meaning Cherry. We were cruising down Walton Way, down the Hill, headed for home.

I knew he was feeling bad about this date, so I didn't want to carry on too much about how great mine had turned out. I tried for humor. "Not *too* nice, I hope."

"Oh, I didn't mean *that* kind of nice. I meant that she has good manners, class."

I wanted to make him feel better. "Maybe Harriet is just too delicate for a night of slumming."

"Delicate! In a pig's eye. Harriet's a friggin' snob, and there's nothing delicate about a snob. Did you see the way she acted at Jenine's? She took one look at Jenine, and that nose of hers went up in the air like somebody had farted. No, sir, snobs aren't delicate; they're hard and mean little bastards. Or bitches, as the case may be."

"But she seemed okay after that, sort of, until the fight broke out," I said.

"Know why? Because Cherry kept showing her up, and Cherry is everything that Harriet would like to be: rich, top of the social ladder. Oh, the Pringles must be doing all right, but the Ashfords—now *that's* money. But what Harriet doesn't understand is that even with money and a big house, an asshole is still an asshole and sooner or later will *act* like an asshole. Hell, she's so fucked up she probably thinks that's what money is all about: a license to act like an asshole. I'll bet you a dollar Harriet believes that Cherry, in her heart of hearts, agreed with her about tonight, but was too nice to say anything."

I had a sinking feeling. "What if she's right?"

"No way. Harriet's a snob and Cherry isn't."

"I hope you're right."

"Well, look at tonight: Cherry Ashford rubbed elbows with a bunch of people her daddy could buy with a fifty-dollar bill and get change, yet she acted like a perfect lady. Am I right or wrong?"

"You're right."

"As for Harriet, remember earlier this evening when I told you to remind me to tell you something later?"

"Yeah, but you haven't stopped talking since I got back in the car."

"Well, anyhow this is what it was: After I got the date with Harriet, Helen McIver told me something about Harriet that *really* pissed me off."

I groaned. "Oh, Helen McIver—"

"I know: Helen's got a big mouth. She talks too much. But I've never caught her in a lie, and she's told me plenty."

"I didn't even know you talked to Helen McIver." I couldn't stand talking to Helen. She *loved* to get you away from everybody else for long heart-to-heart talks that always wound up being about Helen.

"Well, I do. She's my buddy. Pay her a little attention, give her a little soft soap, and she'll tell you about every one of the Hill girls. Catholics, at least. And she knows, 'cause she's one of 'em."

"Well, she ain't exactly the pick of the litter," I said. She

112

was a sad-eyed brunette on whom nature had played a dirty trick. After creating a pretty face, it stuck a nose in the middle of it that made the creation look ridiculous, pathetic.

"I'm not talking about looks; I'm talking about information. The real poop. The straight stuff."

"So what did she tell you?"

"Hell, after all that, I've forgotten."

"You haven't forgotten," I said.

"Hell, no, I haven't forgotten. Harriet told her, has told all the girls—it's no secret, except from the boys, I guess— that she's going to marry a doctor."

"Dr. who?"

Johnny squirmed in exasperation. "Not Dr. who—just a doctor. Not somebody she already knows—just somebody, *any*body, who's a doctor. Doesn't matter who."

"Did I miss something? What do you care who she marries?"

"I don't care *who*, but I do care *why*. She wants to marry a doctor because doctors make lots of money."

"She actually said that?"

"Her exact words, according to Helen, were: 'I'm saving myself for a man with money, and doctors are a sure thing'."

"Gee," I said, "that's crappy even for Harriet. You reckon she never heard of marrying for love?"

"Oh, it'll *be* for love," Johnny said elaborately, giving me a wide-eyed glance. "Harriet loves money." He shook his head. "She's a bitch. I hope she marries a doctor with a three-inch dick. I'd've broken the date if you'd had wheels of your own tonight."

I could almost feel a light bulb blink on over my head. "So *that's* why we took 'em slummin'."

"Damn straight! I wanted to rub that bitch's snobby little nose in it. And the more she bitched and bellyached about it, the better I liked it. It scalded my ass to know that I was good enough to date, good enough to spend money on her—money earned by a butcher, mind you, money

earned by a man who thinks M.D. stands for Meat Department—but not good enough for anything else. I can see it
now: 'I love you, Charles—or Fred or Wendell—but, you
see, you don't have an M.D., and try as I might my little ol'
cash-register heart just keeps ringing up No Sale.' M.D.!
I've got an M.D. for her: My Dick, right up her snooty
nose."

I didn't say anything for awhile. One reason was that we
had reached the point where Walton Way plunged sharply
down the Hill, and I had always liked that view of the town
below, especially at night, when it looked like a big black
box laced with ribbons of light. But another reason was
that I was thinking, thinking and getting depressed.
Johnny's story had stirred up a nest of doubts in me and
they were buzzing all around inside. Finally I said, "Maybe
we ought to leave Hill girls alone. Maybe we don't belong
up there."

He laughed. "That ain't exactly a revelation, is it?"

"No. But I may be having one. It's been nagging at me
off and on all evening."

"Well, let's have it," he said.

"I don't know where to start. But aren't you tired of
never measuring up with these Hill people? I am."

"What do you mean? We're just as good as they are."

"Not in *their* eyes. And never will be."

"To hell with 'em."

"My thought exactly. So what are we doing up here?"

"That's simple: tryin' to get some Hill pussy. And have a
good time."

"Yeah? Well, I been thinking about that too. I'm not
having all that good a time, and I ain't overstocked with
pussy either. On top of that, half of those people want to
whip my ass. Isn't the message pretty clear: o-u-t spells
out?"

"I can't figure you," Johnny said. "Less than thirty minutes ago you had Cherry Ashford eating out of your hand,
and I *know* you were happier than a hog in slop."

"You have a delicate way of putting things. Anybody ever told you that?"

"Don't change the subject."

"All right: I was happy. But that was before you told me about Harriet. Hell, if it'll take a doctor to get Harriet, what do you figure it'll take to get Cherry? A president? A prince?"

"I told you: Harriet and Cherry are two very different girls. Besides, you ain't thinkin' matrimony already, are you?" He laughed.

"'Course not," I said, "but I'm like you: no use wasting time on a gal who's saving it for somebody or something I'll never be—which brings me back to my point, my revelation, so to speak. I worried all night what Harriet thought of this, that, and the other. Cherry too. I worried so much that I got ashamed of myself. Harriet, Miss Hoity-Toity, ought to have her ass kicked. But, dammit, I ought to have mine kicked too."

"Why?"

I hesitated. I couldn't tell Johnny that I had been so embarrassed at his Aunt Jenine's that I had wanted to crawl into a hole and pull it in behind me. I was too ashamed to say that I had been just as uncomfortable there as Harriet was. I wasn't even sure any more that my reasons were all that different from hers. What I *was* sure of was that I didn't like feeling that way, not one little bit.

"Why?" Johnny asked again.

I sighed. "Because, to quote that great philosopher Popeye, 'I am what I am, and that's all that I am'."

Johnny laughed. "What the hell does *that* mean?"

"I don't know," I said, throwing up my hands, feeling helpless to explain. "Those Hill people make me feel ashamed of myself, of who and what I am, and I don't like it. Hell, they're not better than we are; they're just better off. Oh, sure, they can be nice. Who couldn't be, with everything *they've* got? Would't *you* feel nice living in a nice, big house, with a nice, new car, nice clothes, nice college education all paid for you by your nice father, whose nice wife, your nice mother, had nothing to do but stay at home being nice and find nice ways to make nice things even nicer? Let 'em swap places with Jenine and see how nice they feel, how nice they act."

Johnny laughed. "Wait a minute. Aren't you the guy who told me just last night that those people on the Hill really know how to live?"

"Yeah," I admitted, feeling disgusted. Hell, I didn't know *what* I thought anymore. "And in a way, they do. But it's a way I'll never be. Or don't *want* to be—thinking I'm better than everybody else. I really don't like that. I don't want to get out of Milltown so I can look down my nose at poor people."

"They're not all like Harriet."

"Yeah? Couldn't prove it by me." We pulled up in front of my house. Johnny left the engine running.

"Well, what about Cherry? Gonna pass that up?"

"Are you outa your mind? I like her. Besides, I think she wants to give me some."

He laughed. "Well, I'm glad to see you haven't lost sight of the important things in life. Stroke it one time for me."

"Sorry, Ace, but friendship goes only so far. If I get into her pants, you'll be the farthest thing from my mind."

"You can do it."

"Lord, I hope so."

PART 2

Chapter Six

Miss Johnson was doing it again and it was driving me crazy. Every day, it seemed, near the end of her lecture, she'd move around to the front of her desk, ease up on it, and then sit there crossing and re-crossing those beautiful legs of hers as she summarized the lesson and gave the homework assignment.

I often wondered if she had any idea how that affected me and the other males in the class. Probably not. Girls, I had noticed, seemed for the most part unaware of the effect they had on guys. They'd wear tight skirts or tight sweaters or tight shorts and then act pissed off if you let on that you appreciated what you saw. Didn't make sense to me. If I were a girl and showing off my tits in a tight sweater, I'd certainly know I was doing it and wouldn't get mad if some guy let on that he liked what he saw. Did the fisherman get mad at the catfish for taking his bait?

But it wasn't tits with Miss Johnson that drove me slap crazy. She had nice ones, all right—almost as nice as Dianne Damico's—and in fact Miss Johnson was nice all over. But her legs were the prettiest I'd ever seen, all long and shapely and smooth-looking, and she wore nylon stockings that made a sexy little rasping sound when her legs rubbed together.

I tried not to stare at her legs, but I really couldn't help it. My desk, the front one in the middle row, was right in front of hers, and every time I looked up, there they were, so close that I could see the little muscles flex and watch the light play along her stockings. Besides, if I did manage to look away for awhile, the slightest whisper of those nylons rubbing together brought my attention right back to her knees. I felt sometimes as if my eyes were controlled by her leg muscles. Hell, in a way they were.

Made me feel like a creep sometimes. But I knew I wasn't the only male in class who enjoyed the show. Guys who hadn't been paying a bit of attention came wide awake when Miss Johnson got up to write on the blackboard. And when she moved around to the front of her desk, they sat straight up and grinned.

They talked about her too. Boy, did they ever! They loved to stand around in groups on the school grounds, spitting, rattling their rods, watching the girls go by, and make cracks about Miss Johnson like: "That woman makes my dick sit up and beg like a dog"; "Yeah, I'd like to bury my bone between *those* legs"; and "Dog or no dog, I'd like to bite that woman on the ass."

I didn't like that kind of thing. I thought it was crude to stand around in public fondling your crotch and talk about girls that way. True, my thoughts were crude too, but at least I kept them to myself or told only Johnny. Besides, all that spitting turned my stomach.

Anyhow, that's where my mind was—between Miss Johnson's legs, so to speak—when I heard the bustle of activity that meant the bell would ring soon, looked up, and realized that Miss Johnson was looking straight at me.

I thought at first that she had caught me staring at her legs and maybe read my mind, but all she said, just as the bell rang, was to see her after class.

We sat where we were until the others filed out of the room. Then she smiled and said, "Benny, I read your term paper last night. It's good. *Very* good. A-plus. A-plus-plus."

I broke into a grin. English was my favorite subject and I had worked hard on the paper: "An Analysis of Style in Sherwood Anderson's *Winesburg, Ohio.*"

"You're going on to college, aren't you?" I could tell that she took it for granted that I was, but when I hesitated and then said, "Well, I *want* to," she looked surprised. "You mean you haven't applied yet?" Her tone told me that I should have applied weeks ago.

"No, ma'am. I mean, yes, ma'am; I haven't applied."

"May I ask why?"

I hated to say my parents couldn't afford to send me. It was the same as saying they were too poor. But Miss Johnson had been awfully nice to me and deserved an honest answer. "My parents can't afford it," I said.

"I see," she said, and then a minute later added: "Well, what about a part-time job? If your parents could help you at all, you—"

"No, ma'am," I said quickly, wishing she would leave my parents out of this.

She stared out the window for a moment. Then, as if thinking out loud, she said, "It's too bad your grades aren't good enough for a scholarship of some kind."

I must have blushed, because she added quickly, "Not that they're bad. They aren't. But they're not the kind that win scholarships either. Sort of uneven, you know."

"Yes, ma'am." Lord, was *that* the truth! I had always done well in English and history and subjects like that, but anything having to do with science gave me fits, and math was worst of all. I had made C's in geometry and trig, but still had no idea what they were about, and algebra, especially word problems, made me feel like a complete ignoramus: "If A can dig a six-foot hole in three hours and B is wearing a red shirt that he borrowed from C, who is 5-feet-10, how long will it be before a) the moon comes over the mountain, b) Hell freezes over, c) Brazil surpasses Argentina in the shipment of wool, and d) per capita income in France reaches the square root of three? Je-*sus*!

Miss Johnson eased off the desk to her feet. "Well, Benny, you'll just have to find another way, won't you?"

I nodded, standing up too and noticing that Miss Johnson, with her high-heels on, was nearly as tall as I was.

"You *will* do that, won't you? It would be a shame for writing talent like yours to go to waste."

121

I said yes, ma'am, but I had no idea how to go about finding a way. Besides, my mind was on what she'd said about talent, and I couldn't resist asking, "You really think I have talent?"

She put her hand on my shoulder, looked at me with those sky-blue eyes, smiled and said, "I not only *think* it, Benny Blake; I *know* it."

I grinned like a jack-o-lantern. It was one thing to *think* I could write; it was another to be told it, especially in the way she was telling me. It made me feel special, like I had something after all that set me apart, something that was all mine, something that came from within and could not be taken away. My first thought was to hurry off and tell somebody—maybe Cherry—but my next thought, one I liked even better, was to keep it to myself. Some things just felt better when you didn't go around blabbing them. But I had to do something, so I hugged Miss Johnson. Surprised the hell out of her. Embarrassed her too. But she liked it, I could tell. In fact, she looked so pleased and so pretty and so flustered that I had a crazy impulse to apologize for all those times I'd tried to look up her dress. I didn't, of course, but it was a close call, and I was relieved when she started talking again.

"You know, Benny, there's always the G.I. Bill."

I had heard of the G.I. Bill, of course, but I had only a vague idea of what it was and how it worked.

She explained. "After you serve your time in the military, the government pays you to go to school, any school. I don't know the details, but any recruiting office could give them to you."

"Yeah?" I said. The military had about as much appeal to me as a trip to the dentist, and it lasted a lot longer. Still, as my mother was always saying, "Beggars can't be choosers."

"It's worth looking into, Benny. Many people have gone to college that way, people who couldn't have gone any other way."

I told her I'd look into it. What the heck. I had nothing
to lose and I was going to have to do *some*thing.

"Now," she said, "you'd better run along. I'm on a break
next period, but you've got a class to get to."

I thanked her and started to leave, but she stopped me
halfway to the door with another question. "Have you got
a girl, Benny?"

"Yeah, sort of," I said, blushing. Cherry wasn't exactly
my girl, but we'd been dating since that night at the Barnyard, and not seeing anybody else. Too, we were together
at school every chance we got and we talked on the phone
nearly every night. "There's this girl I *like* a lot," I added,
realizing as I said it that I really did like her. More and
more.

"Good," Miss Johnson said. "You need a girl."

I certainly didn't know what to say to that, so I didn't say
anything.

Miss Johnson smiled like an imp. "And for your sake,
Benny, I hope she has nice legs."

I must have turned beet red. Even my ears felt hot. And
now I couldn't have said anything if my life depended on
it. My mind was just spinning its wheels and going nowhere, like a car stuck in sand, and my tongue felt paralyzed. I just smiled like an idiot and headed for the door,
which seemed a mile away.

But I couldn't even make a graceful exit. Coming in as I
was going out was Coach Ramsey, and I ran smack into him
with a loud "Umph." I didn't even stop. I bounced off him,
muttered, "Sorry," and kept right on going, not even realizing who it was until I heard him say, "Ready, Hon?"

That *really* surprised me, and I almost looked back. Lot's
wife could not have been more tempted to look back. But,
one, I was afraid they'd see me, and, two, I was afraid I'd
see them. Coach had stopped right at the door, I thought,
and Miss Johnson might be there too, and I just didn't
want to see them together—not nice, sweet, sexy Miss
Johnson, my favorite teacher, the leading lady in so many

of my sexual fantasies, with that crude sonofabitch of a jock. It was just too much. *Christ on a crutch!* I thought. Could that sweet, refined, intelligent woman actually be attracted to *that*? "Bet your ass," said a smart-alecky little voice inside me. And could he be humpin' that? Banging away at *my* Miss Johnson, easing between those beautiful legs every night as if he owned them? "What do *you* think?" the little voice said. Jesus, I thought, I'd just never understand women. Or sex. Or sex appeal. Or any of it. The Mystery of the Blessed Trinity was nothing compared to the mystery of girls and sex. I made it to history just as Mr. Blodgett was calling my name. With a heavy heart I answered, "Here."

Johnny knew I was falling for Cherry even before I did. "I just put two and two together," he said. "Every time I see you around school, you're together, off in your own little world. And she's looking at you with cow eyes, and you look like the cat that swallowed the canary."

"I *do* like her," I said. It was lunchtime and we were sitting on the front steps of the school, watching people come and go, and enjoying the warm sunshine. Other people were around—the steps were a favorite meeting place—but we were sort of off to ourselves.

"Yeah, but are you gettin' any?" Johnny said.

The question offended me—not a lot, but the fact that it bothered me at all told me that maybe I *was* falling for Cherry. Any other time, I would have paid no mind to a question like that, at least from Johnny; now it struck me as crude and none of his business. I thought I hid it well though. I just smiled and said, "I'm working on it, I'm working on it."

And I *was* working on it—not only working on it, but making headway. I had now been alone with Cherry five or six times, counting dates and a couple of times when she was babysitting for a neighbor, and each time she had let me go a bit farther. But I hadn't told Johnny about it, and

124

I wasn't going to, though I didn't know exactly why. Maybe she was too nice to talk about that way, not at all a dingbat like Austin. Maybe I just felt that she trusted me to keep certain things to myself. All I knew was that the more we were together, the more protective I felt toward her. She *was* trusting. And sensitive. And kind of naive—the kind that said she hadn't been around much, the kind that said you could easily hurt her. And even if she was one of the richest girls in Augusta, she wasn't at all stuck on herself or the least bit snobbish. I suffered forty hells of shame the first time I picked her up in our old Chevy, but if she even noticed that it wasn't a Cadillac I couldn't tell it. Johnny had been right: the girl had class.

"Where is she, by the way?" he asked. "You're usually together during lunch."

"She's taking a makeup test in French. Supposed to meet me here later."

"So *that's* why you're honoring me with your presence. It's getting so I need an appointment to see you anymore."

He was joking, but there was some truth to it. We still walked home from school together, but I spent every minute I could with Cherry. But that wasn't the whole story, so I said, "I hadn't noticed that you were hurting for company."

He smiled. "You mean Patty. Yeah, we been goin' at it pretty hot and heavy, I guess."

"You guess?" They were together about as much as Cherry and I were.

"Well, Ace, I tell you," he said, like a man forced against his will to brag, "some pussies are part-time pussies. Hit it a lick now and then, is all it takes. But Patty's got a fulltime pussy. That thing just never gets enough. It's tough on me, but what's a fellow to do?"

Before he even finished I started going through the motions of shoveling. "Gettin' deep around here," I said.

He laughed. "No kiddin', though: she's hotter than a Franklin stove, and, like Campbell soup, it's mmm, mmm, good."

125

"You lucky devil," I said, meaning it with all my heart.

But Johnny was no longer listening. "Speaking of good, look who's coming here," he said.

Following his gaze, I saw Dianne Damico coming up the steps with a girl I did not know. The steps were long and very wide, and they were walking up on the side away from us, looking straight ahead, so it was doubtful that Dianne even saw us. In fact, she seemed to be listening so closely to her friend that she saw no one.

But they saw her. Guys chattering away with friends only seconds before fell silent as she approached. They tried to act nonchalant in stealing sidelong looks at her, but they were as obvious as a wart on the nose. And once she was past, they watched her like dogs eyeing a piece of red meat. "Hubba, hubba," said a big ol' boy in a group not far from us, shaking his right hand as if to cool burned fingers. Another in the group, a tall, skinny kid with buck teeth, cried out like a child, "I want my mama!" And from somewhere behind us I heard, followed by gales of laughter, "Who's the guy with Dianne?" Actually, the girl was right attractive, but next to Dianne she looked like a weed sprung up beside a rose.

Johnny watched her, too, until she was no longer in sight, and then turned to me. "Have you talked to her since that night we took her home?"

"Just to say hello in passing."

He looked thoughtful for a moment. "I think you ought to ask her for a date."

"Thanks, but no thanks."

"Because of Haynes? He finally got the message, I hear."

"No. Because she's too religious." Cherry was another reason, but I didn't want to say so.

"Ummm," Johnny said, cocking his head to show doubt, "I don't know about that."

"She's gonna be a nun, for Christsake. You know that."

He shook his head. "No, I *don't* know that. All I *know* is what she said. Wait a minute! I don't even know that, 'cause I got it from you."

"Sure," I said, throwing up my hands. "I made the whole thing up."

"I'm not saying that; I'm just sayin' I don't *know*. And I'm wondering if *she* knows."

"What do you mean? I told you what she said."

"People *say* lots of things, Benny. But look at the girl: she don't dress like a nun, she don't walk like a nun, she don't act like a nun, and she damn sure don't look like a nun. If she's nun material, then I'm St. Peter."

I didn't like to admit it, but he had a point. Being built like a brick shithouse was one thing, but dressing to show it off the way she did was another. Same with being naturally good-looking. There were all kinds of good looks, from wholesome to hot mama; why had she chosen sexpot? But then I remembered how sincere she had sounded. That couldn't have been an act. "Maybe she doesn't know any better," I said. "Girls do seem to be awfully naive about these things."

He looked at me as if to say, "Yeah? Now tell me another." But instead he said, "My old man is always saying, 'I hear what you say, but I watch what you do.' And the more I think about our Miss Damico, the more I wonder."

I still wasn't convinced, but the truth was, I didn't want to be. "You think it's all an act, this nun business?"

"I wouldn't go *that* far," he said. "At least I wouldn't say it's deliberate. But something's not quite right there. Besides, she wouldn't be the first girl to have some cockeyed notion like being a nun, and then one day never give it another thought. Cousin of mine—not bad-lookin' either—got real religious when she was about fourteen. Carried a bible everywhere she went. Read it too. Went to church *all* the time. If the church doors opened, Cassie was there. Pain in the ass, is what she was. I once showed her a picture of two people fucking; told me I was goin' to Hell. Anyhow, this went on for a couple of years, maybe longer. But today you couldn't *drag* that girl to church. When she turned seventeen or eighteen—she's twenty-one now—she threw down that bible and went hog-wild."

"What changed her?"

"Damned if I know. Maybe she's just nuts. Maybe she just outgrew it. Maybe she got her first taste of cock. Guy I know who banged her said it was the best he ever had. Said she was a real tiger. I don't doubt it, if she goes at fucking the way she went at religion."

"She from here?"

"No. Macon. But she's in Germany now. Married a guy in the Air Force last Christmas and went overseas with him."

"Sounds like a lucky guy." I meant it. Nutty or not, a real tiger in bed sounded good to me.

"I don't know about that, but I know this step I'm sitting on ain't getting any softer."

He stood rubbing his bottom and leaned against the railing, and just then Owen Phelps walked up, a big grin on his face. I hadn't seen him since the night of Cathy Collins' party. He was a junior and we moved in different circles.

"Well, well," he said. "Now you see 'em and now you don't. That was some disappearing act."

I laughed. "That was no act, brother; that was the real thing. I couldn't get out of there fast enough."

"I call it a strategic withdrawal," Johnny said.

"I call it running to save my ass," I said.

"Whatever you call it," Owen said, "it was funny. Even Chuck and them laughed about it."

"What did they say?" I asked.

He shrugged. "Nothin'. They knew you'd of been crazy to stay against those odds."

I hated to ask, but I had to know. "They still layin' for us?"

"Haven't heard another word," Owen said. "Chuck's like that, though: mean as hell one minute, nice as pie the next. Just likes to stir up trouble. Doesn't mean anything by it."

"Good ol' nice-as-pie Chuck," I said drily.

"What is it between you two, anyway, Benny?" Owen asked. "He sure doesn't like you."

I said with a straight face, "He's just a poor judge of character, that's all."

"Oh, ho!" Johnny scoffed.

"Shee-it!" said Owen, holding his nose and laughing.

"And, obviously, he's not the only one," I said.

Then they really did let me have it, groaning and gagging, pretending to throw up, waving hands in front of their faces as if to chase away a bad smell.

I pretended to ignore them. "And, of course, I'm so damn much better-looking than he is."

They hooted, and just at that moment I sensed rather than heard somebody behind me. I turned my head to look and it was Cherry, standing three or four steps above me. She was smiling, waiting—too shy to come on down. "Gotta go," I said, rising. "Good to see you, Owen. Later, Johnny."

When Johnny and I saw Dianne Damico coming up the school steps, she must have been on her way to the office then to get the news. Her brother, studying in some seminary up north to be a priest, had been killed, electrocuted in a freak accident. Glenn told me about it later that day when he came by the house after supper, wanting me to go for a ride with him. We were just about to leave, but my mother and Zeb had heard us talking in the sitting room and looked in from the kitchen to ask Glenn more about it.

"Who's that you say got killed?" Zeb asked, stopping in the doorway.

"Colin Damico," Glenn said. "Brother of a girl we know at school."

"And what happened?" said my mother, all concern, drying her hands on her apron as she came on into the room.

"All I heard was that he was on kitchen duty—he was in the seminary in Boston studying to be a priest. Anyhow, he was washing dishes, and a radio there by the sink fell into the water."

"My heavens!" mother said.

129

"Fried his ass, eh?" Zeb said.

Glenn gave me a funny look. He didn't know what to say to Zeb's remark. I just raised my eyebrows as if to say, "What do you expect from a man like Zeb?" He had the sensitivity of a turnip.

Glenn looked at mother and me. "They say Dianne's taking it real hard." Then, to mother, he added, "That's the sister, the girl we know at school."

"Well, it'll be in the paper tomorrow, I guess. I'll read about it then," said Zeb, unconcerned. He went back into the kitchen.

"Well, you tell your friend that I'll remember her and her brother in my prayers," Mother said. Then she added, "Don't you boys stay out late. School tomorrow, you know."

Glenn and I left.

"So where're we going?" I asked as Glenn pulled away from the house.

"Nowhere special. I just, uh, needed to get out of the house for awhile."

"Trouble?"

"No," he said quickly, too quickly, I thought.

"Wanna talk about it?"

"Nothing to talk about," he said. I waited and he added: "Really, it's no big deal." Then he laughed drily and said, "Mom's on the warpath with Dad. She gets that way if Dad takes a little drink and she finds it out. Gives him T-total hell. I'd heard enough. I just grabbed the car keys off the hook and said I was going out."

There didn't seem to be much I could say to that, so I said, "Too bad about Dianne's brother."

"Yeah."

Then a thought hit me. "You wouldn't think God would let that happen to somebody studying to be a priest, would you? I mean, is that any way to run a universe?"

I realized too late that that was just the kind of remark that always set Glenn off. But this time he merely sighed and said, "God works in mysterious ways, Benny, and it's not our place to question His plan. He has His reasons and when He calls, we go."

I didn't say anything, but I sure had some thoughts on the subject. If He called me I'd have plenty of questions: "Uh, God, sir, can't we talk this over? I mean, I know You've got Your Plan and all, but plans can be changed, can't they? What's a few more years to You anyhow, give or take a decade? Besides, I've got a big date this coming Saturday. And baseball season is not far off. Then, of course, there's football. Worse yet, I'm still a virgin—hint, hint. Tell You what: why not think this over and get back to me on it in, say, the year 2,000? I don't have a *thing* planned for that year. Better yet, why don't *I* call *You?*"

"I know what," Glenn said. "Let's go to Teen Town and play some ping-pong."

I had my doubts. We'd be sure to run into some of the Hill gang there, and I said so.

"Aw, that's all over," he said. "If they'd really wanted us they'd have done something by now. Besides, I'm not scared of 'em, are you?"

The true answer was yes, but I said, "I just don't want trouble." Still, I loved to play ping-pong, and the best players hung out at Teen Town. I remembered too what Owen had said, so finally I said, "Let's go."

That was a big mistake. I seemed to be making one big one after another lately. We hadn't been playing five minutes when I noticed that one after another of that gang was drifting into the room, standing shoulder to shoulder at Glenn's end of the table, watching. When five or six of them had gathered, one of them, Don Connell, a fairly short guy with powerful-looking shoulders and arms, said with a silly smile, "I know somebody who's looking for you, Blake."

My stomach felt like I'd swallowed a pitcher of ice and suddenly I felt strangely stiff, as if I had no coordination at all. It took a real effort to keep playing the game. Still I managed to go on hitting the ball back and to say with some show of ease, "Well, here I am."

"He don't like you, Blake, but then I don't either," he said, still wearing that silly smile. "Fact, nobody here likes you. We took a vote and you didn't get a single one."

"Who counted 'em for you?"

He stopped smiling then and stepped forward. "I offered to jump your ass for him, but he said it was personal. He wants to do it himself."

I thought he meant Chuck Conlin, but just then Chuck came into the room and just stood there, looking at me and smiling. I tried to think of a smart reply to Connell, but curiosity got the better of me. "What did I ever do to you? Or to any of you?"

He was smiling again. "I just don't like your looks." He turned to the others. "Do ya'll like his looks?"

They all said no. Chuck added, "I don't like anything about him, and I think he ought to stay downtown where he belongs."

"You think you could do that, Blake? Stay downtown where you belong?"

My mouth felt full of cotton, but I said weakly, "Free country, ain't it?" I wasn't exactly firing off zingers.

"Aw, why don't you leave him alone?" Glenn said to Connell, catching the ball in his hand, giving up all pretense of continuing the game.

"When we want something out of you, Peanut, we'll rattle your shell," Connell said.

Glenn bristled. "I'm not afraid of you, Connell." But I told him, "Stay out of this, Glenn. It's me they're after." I could see I wasn't going to get out without a fight. No need for Glenn to get beat up too.

"Well, you're not all gonna jump him," Glenn told Connell, banging the table with his paddle for emphasis. "A fair fight's one thing, but this—" He motioned toward the group and let his unfinished sentence hang there, his meaning clear.

"It won't take but one of us," Connell said, looking toward the door, "and here he comes now."

Paul Conlin swept into the room and glared across the

table at me. Chuck put his hand on his brother's shoulder, and right away I remembered Rusty Brown's prediction: *It won't be Chuck. He's chickenshit. It'll be somebody he puts up to it.* Still I was surprised. What had I done to rile Paul Conlin?

"What do you mean, trying to make time with my girl?" he demanded.

Now I was really in the dark. Who the hell was his girl? "I don't even know who your girl is."

"Melinda Murray. You went by to see her. She told me all about it."

"Gee whiz!" Glenn said, showing disbelief. "*I* took him by there. He didn't even know Melinda. Besides, nothing happened."

Conlin didn't even look at him, but kept his eyes fixed on me. "That ain't the way I heard it. Are you calling my girl a liar?" He stabbed a finger between his eyes to reposition his glasses.

"I hardly know the girl," I said. "And I didn't know she was your girl or anybody else's girl."

He ignored what I said. "You want it in here or outside?" He took off his glasses and handed them to his brother.

"Outside," I said, putting down my paddle and heading for the hallway that led to the front door, Conlin right behind me, the rest of them following him. I was surprised that my legs would even move, and all I could think of was that the dreaded moment had arrived and that I was trapped. Oddly that seemed to relieve some of the tension. I moved as if caught in a bad dream, but I knew it was real and that I'd simply have to take what was coming and hope for the best. But I sure as hell wasn't going to take it lying down, and the moment I made up my mind to that, more of Rusty's words came back to me: *Hit him first, Benny, and give it all you've got. Try to sock him right in the nose and just keep on hittin' him.*

Later, much of the fight was a complete blank to me, and I realized that those who'd been in a fight and told about it blow for blow either lied or were a whole lot cooler under pressure than I'd ever be. I did things that were as much a surprise to me as they could have been to any onlooker. In fact, my mind seemed to be a mere onlooker too, watching in disbelief as my fists flew this way and that. But its greatest surprise came when I pushed through the front screen door, took one step to the ground, and turned and hit Paul Conlin flush in the face as hard as I could.

The fight didn't end there, but Rusty had been right. That one punch took something crucial out of Conlin, and I could tell it the minute he pushed through my flailing fists and grabbed me and tried to wrestle. Though about my height, he was muscular from all that weight-lifting and obviously stronger than I was, but the full strength of anger and determination just wasn't there in his hold. I broke the hold, stepped back and popped him again in the face, this time with a left to the cheek. And when he stopped, dropped his guard and stared at me as if re-thinking what he was up against, I hit him again.

I felt that he would have stopped then if the circle of spectators around us, all of whom seemed to be on his side, hadn't egged him on. But they were whooping it up pretty good, and when I heard Chuck's voice above the rest, saying, "Get him, Paul! Beat his ass!" I knew he would fight some more.

It was dusk and I couldn't see the faces around us all that clearly even when I caught a glimpse of them. But one face, just over Conlin's shoulder, startled me so that I did a double-take. It was Austin. She was standing next to a smiling Bruce Holdenfelt, looking at Paul, and her face was an excited, twisted, ugly mask as she yelled, "Kill him, Paul! Knock his block off."

I didn't give a damn about Austin, but her obvious hatred toward me struck me as outrageously unfair, unjust, and I wished bitterly that I had laughed at her tears and fucked her into the next week. But more than that it pissed me off, and when Conlin charged at me again, I slipped in another left to the cheek and followed with a roundhouse right to the head that I wished Austin could feel.

The punch stopped Conlin again, but not for long. Looking frustrated, he lunged again, and in trying to avoid his grasp I slipped and fell to one knee. When that happened, the crowd really did start to scream. I heard one lonely voice pulling for me. "Get up, Benny!" Glenn yelled.

Conlin could have had me then. All he had to do was rush me, fall on me, pin me down and beat the daylights out of me. But he knew even less about brawling than I did and tried to kick me instead. I blocked the kick with a forearm and scrambled to my feet.

Not quickly enough, though, to escape his next charge, and that time he got a pretty good hold, grabbing me around the neck with his left arm and pinning me to his body. Then, with his right hand, he began to punch at my face.

He managed only to hit me on the forehead, but it hurt like hell, much worse than you'd expect, and that's when I noticed for the first time that he had a handkerchief folded into a band and wrapped around his knuckles. And with the next whap on the noggin, I realized what was under that handkerchief: brass knuckles.

Again my temper, my outraged sense of fairness, saved me. With a surge of power I twisted free of his hold, stepped back and pointed to his right hand. "You're wearing brass knuckles, you sonofabitch," I said, my chest heaving for air. I was as mad as I'd ever been. "Why don't you fight me fair? You're bigger than I am and you've got all your buddies here to help you. Why don't you fight me fair?"

He looked at me with pure hatred, this guy to whom I'd never done anything before that night. But he slipped his right hand into his pocket as if to hide it, turned and walked away.

Except for Glenn and a couple of people I did not know,

the crowd followed him back into Teen Town. But not before I called to Chuck, who was bringing up the rear: "How 'bout you, Chuck? You like fights, don't you? Like to start 'em—as long as it's somebody else doin' the fightin'?"

This was sheer lunacy, and I recognized it as such before I even opened my mouth. But I couldn't stop myself. One part of me was scared to death that he'd take up my challenge, make me eat my words, but the rest of me was a me I'd never seen before, a reckless, fearless, don't-give-a-damn-anymore Benny Blake. But Chuck merely looked at me and spit on the ground as if to say, "There, that's what I think of you," and went on inside.

I was glad to see him go, but it wasn't lost on me that he had walked away, just like his brother. Of course, I couldn't say that I'd won the fight. The knots that were now swelling and throbbing on my forehead told me that Paul Conlin, whatever his condition, had whacked me a few good ones. But I knew damn good and well that I hadn't lost the fight either.

More than that, my fear of those bastards was gone and it was a great feeling. Oh, I realized that some of them could beat me in a fight any day of the week. But I was also realizing that even if guys *could* whip you, they thought twice about trying it if they knew you'd fight back. Fear didn't protect you from trouble; it invited it. And letting fear rule your life was just plain stupid and no way to live.

"You okay, Benny?"

It was Glenn. He was standing beside me, looking a bit anxious but smiling. "Yeah," I said. "Let's get out of here."

As soon as we got rolling, Glenn said, "Gee, Benny, I feel like all this was my fault. If I hadn't taken you by Melinda's—"

"Forget it. They were just looking for an excuse to start something."

"Boy, you cold-cocked him with that first punch. I was right behind him and saw it. Surprised the heck out of me *and* him."

"I got news for you: it surprised me too. But it worked, and I can thank Rusty Brown for that."

"Yeah," he said. "Well, ol' Rusty ought to know. He can go with the best of 'em."

I said I was so dry I could drink a gallon of Coke, so Glenn headed for the Varsity. When we got there I told him to park under a light and tell me how my face looked. I could feel three knots on my head and they were sore to the touch.

We gave our order, and when the boy went away, Glenn peered at my forehead and said, "Looks all right to me. I see some swelling, but no cuts or anything."

"Sonofabitch did that with those brass knuckles. Did you see 'em?"

He looked surprised.

"Under the handkerchief," I said. "Brass knuckles." I still couldn't get over that. To me, brass knuckles and stuff like that belonged to the world of gangsters.

"Naw," Glenn said. "He wouldn't do that. I saw the handkerchief, or at least something white around his hand. But he wouldn't do that. You must've been imagining things."

I couldn't believe this guy. "Didn't you hear me say, 'You're wearing brass knuckles'? That's when he quit. He slipped 'em into his pocket and walked away. Tell me, am I imagining these knots on my head, too?"

Glenn laughed. "Aw, Benny, Paul may be a hothead, but he's not a—" He wagged his hand to say he was searching for the right word, but he gave up. "Naw. You licked him, Benny; let it go at that."

That made me so mad I could have fought again. Glenn had the most infuriating way of disagreeing that I had ever come across. In the first place, nothing could get past a belief of his, and he was the most wrong-headed guy I had ever known. Show Glenn any set of circumstances and he just naturally came to the wrong goddam conclusion. But worse than that, when you tried to tell him he was wrong,

137

he'd laugh at you in that smug you-can't-fool-me way of his and go right on being dead wrong. Reminded me of Zeb in that way. To both of them, facts were just sly, little devils out to pull the wool over their eyes, and reason was most dangerous when it was most reasonable. Put the brain of either one of 'em in the ass of a hummingbird, and the bird would fly backwards. But I was learning about such people. I changed the subject. "You say Dianne took it hard—her brother's death, I mean?"

"Yeah. I heard they had to take her home, put her to bed and give her a shot to calm her down. She idolized him, they say. Poor girl."

"Yeah, that's rough." But I didn't want to talk about that either. "What you know about the G.I. Bill?"

"Nothing much. Why?"

"Miss Johnson says it'll pay your way to school after you get out of the army."

"Yeah, I knew that. But it doesn't have to be the army. Any of the services will do."

"Well, speaking of the service," I said, "won't they draft me anyhow if I don't go to college?" Like every other guy I knew, I had had to register for the draft when I turned eighteen.

"Yeah, sooner or later I guess they would. They can even draft you out of college."

"Then I don't have much choice," I said, not happy to see that, but thankful at least for the G.I. Bill.

"Well," Glenn said, "you do have a choice. I joined the Naval Reserve last month so that at least the army couldn't get me. You oughta join too."

All of that was news to me, but the navy sounded a lot better than the army and all that damned marching, so I asked Glenn to tell me about it. I could join the reserve, he said, and then if I got drafted I had my pick: army or navy. Better still, I could serve in the navy for two years instead of the four you had to sign up for if you just went down and joined. That sounded good to me, and he agreed to take me with him to his next reserve meeting.

After that, we sat awhile saying nothing, just eating the ice left over from our Cokes and watching the cars come and go. When I saw a brunette in an Olds, though, it reminded me of Austin, and I said to Glenn, "Did you see Austin in that crowd at the fight? She was yelling for Conlin to kill me, the bitch."

"Now, Benny," Glenn drawled, "you can't blame her too much, can you?"

"That's right," I snapped; "no amount of blame would be too much."

"What do you expect after what you did to her?"

"What I did to her was nothing. She wouldn't let me."

He turned toward me, sliding one knee up on the seat. "But you tried, Benny, you tried. You tried to lure her into mortal sin."

"I tried to lure her into a mortal fuck."

He threw up his hands. "Benny. Benny. How can I make you see? Have you talked to Father Brady yet? No. And you promised. You gave me your solemn word."

"I didn't say when."

"Benny," he tried again, clasping his hands in front of him as if about to pray. "Austin Armisted is a good Catholic girl from a fine Catholic family. Who are you to lure her from the, uh, from the—"

"Path of righteousness," I sang out like a gospel preacher, raising both hands in the air and shaking them.

"That's right!" he said, nodding his head emphatically.

I'd had about all I could stomach. I went into an act. "You're right, Brother Glenn, you're right. Great God Almighty, how right you are! The Devil got hold of me there for a minute and I plumb lost my head. But I now see the evil of my evil ways. Yes, Austin Armisted is an angel. Even better, a Catholic angel."

"Benny," Glenn said wearily.

But I wasn't through. This was fun. "In fact," I said, "she's going to Heaven right after graduation. Chuck Conlin too. He's another fine Catholic, remember? They're going on a flaming chariot, body by Fisher, fluid drive, white sidewall wheels—"

"Benny," he said again, shaking his head.

I lowered my voice. "Nobody's supposed to know that, though. I gave God my word on it. He dropped by to see me last night to ask if I minded, seeing as how both Austin and Chuck have been so important in my life. 'Why, hell, no, Your Lordship,' I said. 'Nobody with the sense God gave a goat could blame You for wanting both of those lovely creatures up there in Heaven with You, playin' around Your throne and all, right where You could look upon their shining faces, peer into their hearts of gold, hear their lilting voices—'"

"Benny." His voice this time said enough was enough.

Still I went on. "'They've got some friends You'd like too, Your Grace. Tell You what: why not take the whole damn bunch? They don't do anything here on Earth anyhow except make the rest of us feel bad that we can't be as wonderful as they are'."

"Benny!" This time he shouted.

Still I added: "By the way, Glenn; God said to say howdy."

Glenn turned back under the steering wheel. "You have *got* to talk to Father Brady; that's all there is to it."

"I'll check it out with God," I said. "He's coming by again tonight. But I don't think He wants me talking with any small-fry priests. He likes me to come directly to Him."

Very softly Glenn said, "Benny, sins of the flesh are one thing, but blasphemy is another, a much worse sin."

"Look," I said reasonably, "I'll swap blasphemy for a nice, juicy sin of the flesh any ol' day."

"Well, I'm still gonna hold you to your promise to talk to Father Brady. You are one mixed-up boy."

The "mixed-up" part got me hot under the collar, probably because it was true, though not in the way Glenn thought. "Yeah? And what about you? If anybody even says 'pussy' around you, you drop to your knees, whip out your Rosary, and start prayin' 90 miles an hour. What is it with you and sex? You seem to think a girl's legs are some two-lane highway to Hell. What's wrong with fucking? That's how you got here, how we all got here. We were *designed* for fucking. Or haven't you noticed? Jesus, Glenn! If people didn't like fucking there wouldn't be so many people."

"The bible says man is born in sin—"

"Then relax and enjoy it," I snapped. He shook his head and I went on. "Whether you know it or not, Glenn McNulty, the world is not divided up into nice Catholic virgins who want to go to Heaven and the rest of us, all whoopin' it up in an orgy aboard a southbound freight for Hell. That's ridiculous. Where'd you ever get such a notion? Nice Catholics like sex too. And they don't just tear off a piece of ass every time they want another young'n. They actually enjoy it, Glenn. You hear me? They *enjoy* it. And for every nice Catholic virgin who won't, there are ten more who can hardly wait. I'm just one of that ten. So don't make me out to be some hopelessly lost soul just because I want a piece of ass."

"Rail all you want to," he said matter-of-factly; "it's still a sin until you're married."

I sighed and gave up. I'd never change his mind. He didn't have a mind to change. His beliefs came neatly packaged: God told the Pope, the Pope told the Church, and the Church told Glenn. Catholics didn't have to think about a thing. In fact, thinking was dangerous. Theirs was a god who said, "Just do as I tell you, Pea-brain, or I'll zap your ass into Hell so fast it'll make your nose bleed."

"Let's call it a night," I said. "I'm bushed."

Chapter Seven

The fight was all over school the next day, or so it seemed, but nobody said much to me about it. Two or three guys I knew said things in passing like "Hey, Slugger!" and crap like that, but mostly I got a lot of curious looks and saw some whispering and pointing. Besides, they had Dianne Damico to talk about too. Still, I didn't like being talked about at all and was glad it was Friday; by Monday maybe they'd have new things to talk about.

Cherry, of course, said something about it, but at least she didn't make a to-do over it or carry on for the benefit of others, like a lot of girls would have. She simply caught me coming out of my first class, pulled me aside in the hallway, and said, "I heard! Are you all right?"

I looked into her eyes. She was really concerned, but not acting dippy about it. I liked that. And the more I looked at her brown, brown eyes, the more I liked them. "Do you realize," I said, staring, squinting, "that there are these little flecks of yellow in your eyes that make the brown that much prettier?" She thought I was teasing and blushed, but I was serious.

"Oh, is that all you've got to say?" She was acting put out, but she wasn't. "If you knew how I practically ran down here to catch you, how concerned I was, you'd, you'd—"

"I'd be pleased. And I am. But I'm fine, as you can see. I can even keep our date tonight—if you'll promise to go easy on me."

She blushed again, but she was getting used to my

teasing. "I'll *try*," she said, sighing heavily, "but after all I'm only human."

I liked that. "Come on," I said; "I'll walk you to class."

And of course I had to tell Johnny all about it, but we didn't have time until we were walking home from school.

"Those bastards!" Johnny said. "Wish I'd been there."

"Take my place next time. I'm tired of gettin' beat on."

"He looks worse than you do. He's in my study hall, you know." He looked at me closely. "In fact, you don't have a scratch." He looked again. "Well, maybe a scuff mark here and there, and a knot or two on your head. You say that's from brass knuckles?"

"Kid you not. Glenn didn't believe it. Said Conlin's not that kind of boy."

"'Course not," Johnny said.

And then we said together in a tired, sing-song voice, "He comes from a fine Catholic family," and laughed for nearly half a block.

But I didn't *feel* all that jolly. All day I'd been dreading what my mother would say when she saw my face. I had avoided her the night before, going straight to bed when I got home. And she and Zeb got up so early during the week to go to work that I rarely saw her in the morning. But she'd be sure to see it at supper if not before. Woman had hawkeyes where I was concerned. Could spot a fever blister at 50 yards and a fever itself at 30 paces. You couldn't hide even a heartache from those searching eyes. I could be feeling not good, but not bad either, maybe a little blue, when suddenly she'd swoop down on me, fix me with those probing, caring eyes and say, "You sure you're all right? Here, let me feel your forehead. When's the last time you had a bowel movement? You sure you're not coming down with something? You look a little peaked to me." Lord, what *would* she say to scuff marks and knots?

"Fighting?" my mother said, putting down her fork to give this her full attention, her face showing disbelief.

"Benny," she added in a voice that spoke all at once of disappointment, surprise, concern. She was still in her work clothes, and lint from the mill still clung to her hair.

"It was no big deal, Mother."

Mother looked at Zeb, who was looking at me. "Marks on his face, knots on his head, but no big deal," she said, meaning of course that she'd raised a son who clearly had not a lick of sense.

"Oh, he's all right, Janie," Zeb said. "Where's the salt?" He was still in work clothes too—overalls over a blue work-shirt—and I could smell the cotton dust on him.

She found the salt without even looking for it and handed it to him, peering across the table at me the whole time as if she could see through skin and skull. Heck, she probably could. "Well, I want you to stay away from that Teen Town." She said "Teen Town" as if it were Sodom or Gomorrah. "You hear me?"

"Yes ma'am."

"And I think you ought to stay in your own part of town. What's the big attraction up there anyhow?" She jerked her head in the direction of the Hill.

Zeb leaned over quickly and whispered in my ear: "Don't say poontang."

Mother ignored him and I did too. "My girl lives up there," I said, my tone of voice saying, "Be reasonable."

"What's wrong with Milltown girls?" she said grumpily.

I almost told her, but it hit me as I was about to speak that she was a Milltown girl herself. "Nothing," I said.

She picked up her fork and, still upset, stabbed it into a piece of pork chop. "What's wrong with Inez Crowe? She's a nice girl and she asks about you every time I see her."

I almost groaned. Inez Crowe was the kind of Milltown girl that every Milltown mother tried to palm off on her son: sweet, polite, always minding her p's and q's, es-pecially around adults, very grown-up. Cute, too, if you liked 'em prim and proper. And, I had to admit, a cut above the average Milltown girl. But her every waking moment seemed to be devoted to being nice, or to being *thought* nice. Nobody mentioned her without using the word "nice," as if it were part of her name. And, oh, that *name*. Sounded like dry twigs rubbing together. "There's nothing wrong with Inez, Mother," I lied, "but my girl is Cherry Ashford, and she happens to live on the Hill."

"And happens to be a rich girl, I hear." She was looking down at her plate, but I could tell she was listening very carefully.

I kept eating the whole time, but I felt like I was chewing paper. Only the sweet potato had any flavor at all to me. "She can't help it if her folks have money," I said.

"Hell," Zeb said around a mouthful of biscuit, "tell 'em to give it to me. That'll solve the problem."

If Mother even heard him I couldn't tell it. "That's *not* what I meant," she said, sort of snapping as she flicked a couple of looks my way. "I'm sure she's a nice girl. And I'm not saying for one minute that *my* son's not good enough for her or any girl."

"Well, what *are* you saying?" Zeb asked, really curious. It was clear that he couldn't understand this suspicion of money.

Mother looked at him and then back at her plate. "I don't want to see him get hurt, is all."

I looked at Zeb and he looked at me, the look saying that that wasn't much of an answer. But we didn't say anything.

Soon, as if sensing that she needed to explain, Mother added, "I just think people are happier when they stay with their own kind. I'm sure there are some fine people who live on the Hill. Rich people too. But they're not like us. Money changes people. And even if your girlfriend doesn't care about such things, you can bet her parents do. And she will too, sooner or later."

I hardly knew what to say to all that. I knew better than to ignore her when she spoke in that tone of voice. She didn't use it often, but I'd learned that when she did she was usually right. Still, I didn't know exactly what she was trying to tell me. I just knew it was a warning of some kind. And, anyhow, I was just dating Cherry, wasn't I? Where was the harm? "We just like each other, Mother," I said, crossing my fingers. "It's nothing serious. Besides, she's going away right after graduation, and I'll probably never see her again."

"Hell, boy," Zeb said. "Don't let the rich ones get away. Anybody can marry a poor girl."

"Oh, hush, Zeb," Mother said, plainly tired of his foolishness.

I left the table to get ready for my date.

Cherry and I went to a drive-in movie that night and spent the whole time making out. I never did know what movie was playing, and if Cherry had any interest in the film you couldn't have proved it by me. Fifteen minutes after we got there, parking on the back row, the windows were fogged up, and two hours later, just before we left, we looked as if we had been in a fight. Her blouse was wrinkled and hanging out, with two or three buttons open, and her skirt looked more like an accordian, with horizontal folds all down the front. We found her sweater wadded up and stuck down in the car seat, and one of her penny loafers on the floorboard in back. Then there were her face and hair: no lipstick, raw and swollen lips, and hair that looked more in need of a rake than a comb. I must have been a sight too, because the moment we saw each other when the lights came on, we started laughing.

The next night, we dropped the pretense of going out somewhere and drove straight to a place to park, a dirt road I knew out in the country west of Augusta, near but not too near some farms and ending at a fenced pasture.

On our first date alone Cherry had let me put my hand under her bra. On following dates, against feeble resistance, I had gone on to unhooking it and finally to opening her blouse or raising her sweater to expose her naked breasts. Getting under her skirt had been a lot harder to do, but lately I'd been doing that too, though not with the same degree of success. Cherry loved petting, it seemed, and welcomed my hands all over her, but try as I might I could not get her out of those panties or even get my hand underneath them. Not so much as a finger.

Oddly I didn't try as hard with Cherry as I had with other girls. She had a way of making it seem that I could go ahead if I really insisted, that she herself would like nothing better, but that we really ought not to and that we both knew it, and that if I really cared for her I wouldn't. So I hadn't. I knew Johnny would laugh at that. And Zeb? Heck, Zeb would hoot. But I doubted that they had ever cared for a girl the way I cared for Cherry. Besides, she wasn't like Patty Wilson or Austin, or any other girl I had dated. She was more like Dianne Damico: quiet, thoughtful, considerate of others, nice. And she trusted me.

Still, I would have been lying to say that I didn't want to fuck her. I *ached* to fuck her—and believed that I would; it was just a matter of waiting until she flung herself past that last barrier of Catholic guilt. And I felt that barrier falling that very night when she looked up at me after an especially tender kiss near the end of another hot petting session and said softly, "I love you, Benny."

But where, oh, where was my brain when I needed it? Why couldn't I be Joe Cool or Mr. Suave when the situation cried out for it? Did I look soulfully into her eyes and say, "And I love you too, my darling, my pet"? Did I say, "Don't move, my love; I want to gaze into your eyes and commit this moment to memory, the night you first said you loved me"? Oh, no. Not Benny Blake, Boy Wonder of Senior English. Showing total surprise and idiotic delight, I said—no, chirped, "You do?" I winced, but it was too late. *Most uncool,* I could hear Johnny saying.

But Cherry just sighed, looked at me again and said, "I do," in a way that said, "I'm surprised too, but there it is, and I'm not going to fight it."

"That's wonderful," I said, meaning it, "because I love you too." A sarcastic voice inside me said, "Why don't you just go ahead and say, 'Golly, gosh, and gee whiz' and get it over with, Dumb Ass?" But I ignored it. I didn't feel the least bit cool and suddenly didn't care. I was saying exactly how I felt, without thinking how it sounded, and it felt good. And Cherry certainly didn't seem to mind. She smiled and said, "Say it again," and I did. And when I did she gave me a kiss that burned a brand on my heart, and then a look that I knew I would carry in my mind for years, like a cherished and worn photograph in a wallet.

Then she sat up straight and smiled, alert, eager. "Now for the really big news," she said. "You're invited to our house tomorrow for brunch."

That *did* floor me. To her *house*? *Tomorrow*? And what on earth was brunch?

"We'll eat around noon," she added. "Come at 11:30. Can you?"

I wanted to stall, to find out more about all this, but Cherry looked so excited, so pleased, that I couldn't disappoint her. "Sure," I said. "But why? I mean, what's this all about?"

"Well, I've told them so much about you, they want to meet you. And of course I *want* them to. And there's not a lot of time left before I have to leave for the mountains."

That reminded me. "What'll we do, with you away for so long?" The thought filled me with dread. I was wondering, too, *how* she had told them so much about me; as far as I knew, she didn't know that much. As always, I'd been careful to say little on that subject, and to my great relief she had not shown much curiosity. She had asked me once what my mother was like, and I told her. "I know I'd like her," she said. And she had asked what my room was like, and I described that too: records, a record player, two Picasso prints, a typewriter, and books, books and more books. It could have been a room anywhere.

"I've already asked them to let me transfer to Agnes Scott, in Atlanta, if not after the first semester, then next year." With you in Athens, we could see each other every weekend."

I squirmed a little. I *had* told Cherry I was going to the University of Georgia; I just hadn't said when. She was going off to some ritzy girls' school in Virginia, so I hadn't thought it mattered. "Did they say you could?"

"They didn't say yes, but they didn't say no, either. Besides, Agnes Scott is a good school, and it's for girls only too, just like Sweet Briar, you know, so Mother can't argue with that. And if I know Daddy he'll want me closer to home." She squeezed my hand, excited about her plans. "Oh, Benny!"

I smiled, but my thoughts were turned inward. It was all coming together for me now. Their little girl suddenly wanted to change their well-laid plans and they wanted a closer look at the boy who was causing all this. Well, that was understandable, I reasoned. And, what the heck, I didn't have two heads, did I? True, I didn't know one fork from another, but neither did I go at my soup as Zeb did his, like a man trying to beat it to death with his spoon, *bang, slurp, bang, slurp,* and finally giving up and drinking from the bowl. Besides, I had sense enough simply to watch what others did and follow their lead. I made a mental note, though, to find out what the hell brunch was.

"I think it's when you combine breakfast and lunch into one meal," Mother said. "It can be a late breakfast or an early lunch, or both. Why?"

I told her I was just curious. I didn't want to tell her I was going to brunch at Cherry's. I'd get one of two reactions, or maybe both: disapproval, which seemed likely after what she'd said at supper the day before, or a string of instructions on how to act. I went to ten o'clock mass at St. Jude, then killed some time riding around on the Hill, and arrived at Cherry's house with about three minutes to spare.

Cherry met me at the door, opening it before I could ring the bell, and greeted me all smiles and girlish excitement. She looked terrific in a yellow pullover sweater with a white dickey, a small yellow bow in her hair, just over one ear, and a gray full skirt. Taking me by the hand, she said,

"Come on," and led me inside to a room that I took to be their den, on the back of the house.

Mr. Ashford, seated in a large easy chair, put down his newspaper as we entered and got up smiling to shake my hand. "So this is the fellow we've been hearing about," he said after Cherry introduced us. Mrs. Ashford was nowhere in sight, but I heard dishes rattle in a nearby room, so I guessed she was busy in the kitchen. "Cherry tells me you're going up to Georgia," Mr. Ashford said, smiling. "I'm a Yale man myself, but we won't hold Georgia against you. Will we, Cherry?"

We all laughed and sat down, Cherry and I on a couch, Mr. Ashford in his easy chair. I had caught glimpses of him a couple of times in calling at the house to pick up Cherry, but had never seen him close up. He was short, with a medium build tending toward plumpness, but he moved gracefully, almost prissily, and something made him look sleek—the smooth skin, the manicured nails, the brown hair flecked with gray and every strand in place—something, maybe all of that. I figured him for a just-so man and not as soft as he looked.

"What will you study?" he asked, pulling his trousers legs from beneath him, smoothing them, pinching the creases. "Know yet?"

"Law, I think." It wasn't too big a lie. It did have some appeal.

"Oh," he said. "Your father a lawyer?"

"No, sir," I said. "My dad's a career man in the army." That was true, and I often used it to avoid saying who Zeb was and what he did for a living. "Officer," I added self-consciously, knowing it mattered. And he *was* a warrant officer, so I didn't feel it was too big a lie. But I saw the next question coming—where was he stationed?—and headed it off. "He's in Japan right now. Mother and I don't go with him overseas anymore. She feels it's more important to have one place to call home, especially with me in school and everything." My father was in Japan, all right, the last I had heard, but the rest was lies, and I was a bit

150

shocked to see how easily they came to my lips. I didn't *like* lying, but what the hell was I *supposed* to say? "I'm just a poor boy from Milltown, Mr. Ashford, the son of lintheads. My mother and stepfather work in the mill, and we don't have a pot to piss in. Oh, we're not starving or anything like that; we're just, uh, run-of-the-mill poor. Ha, ha. College? No, sir, I won't be going. Can't afford it. High school's the end of the line for me. I'm only messin' around on the Hill 'cause I'm trying to get into your daughter's pants. Any advice?"

Cherry and I were holding hands, down between us, sort of hidden from view, and I noticed all at once that our hands were wet with sweat. Mine, no doubt. I had to do something to stop all those questions. "What line are you in, sir?" I asked.

"Fertilizer," he said, showing some interest. "Agri-Grow, Inc.?" he prompted. "That's us."

I said I knew the company. It was downtown, or at least part of it was, in an old section of Augusta, back by the levee. Looked like it had been there when the first settlers arrived: a sleepy-looking building you could easily overlook in passing, a small, old-fashioned sign over the door, a wrought-iron balcony sticking out over a brick sidewalk.

"I majored in business. Banking. But I always knew I'd go into fertilizer."

He seemed to want to talk. I did my best to encourage him. "If you don't mind my saying so, sir, that's what I would have taken you for, a banker."

He smiled, pleased, I thought, and said, "Well, I do have other interests, and banking is one of them."

Cherry spoke up. "Daddy's being modest, Benny." She looked at him, smiling. "Everybody knows he runs the bank."

I said no, *I* hadn't known.

"Riverside National," he explained, and then looked at Cherry. "And I *don't* run it, Sugarpuss, I just—"

"He just tells the people there what to do," Cherry said. She gave him a teasing look and went on. "He practices at home on me: Cherry, do this; Cherry, do that. And then he takes what he's learned to the bank and tells *them* what to do."

"No, Honey," he said. Then he looked at me. "Women! Where *do* they get these ideas about the real world? I'm just one member of the bank's board."

"He's chairman," Cherry said flatly, acting put out with all his modesty.

"Congratulations, sir," I said. I *was* impressed. Riverside National was the biggest, oldest bank in town and one of the oldest in the state.

He shook his head as if to say, "It's nothing," and tried again to get on with his story. "As I was saying, the fertilizer business was my first love and still is. My grandfather started the business, and I practically grew up in it. I used to troop through the yards with him, holding my coat sleeve or whatever over my nose—it was all natural then; nowadays it's chemicals more and more—and my grandfather would tease me. 'Bill-boy,' he'd say—my name is Billings, but he called me Bill-boy. 'Bill-boy,' he'd say, taking a deep breath and savoring it, 'you ought to try this; it's not bad at all once you realize you're smelling money.'" His face colored a bit, as if he realized his story might sound boastful to a stranger. "Of course, in those days he was the only supplier around; nowadays it's very competitive."

I couldn't think of anything to say to that, so he turned the subject back to me. "Cherry tells me you have a car."

I was thrown for a moment, but then I saw that he meant my very own car and I realized what Cherry must have thought: who else *but* a teenager would own a crate like that? Oh, well; my mother had a saying: "In for a penny, in for a pound." So I said, "Uh, yes, sir. Bought it, uh, last summer and fixed 'er up." *Je-sus!* I told myself, *I've GOT to do something about this lying.* It was getting easier and easier. At this rate my next confession would run longer than *War and Peace*. Priests would have to hear it in relays and hold intermissions. And how could I ever untangle all this with Cherry?

152

But Mr. Ashford had his own uses for this information. "See, young lady," he said to Cherry, "there *are* people your age who do for themselves, who can save instead of spend."

Cherry just looked at me and beamed, and somewhere in the house I heard a phone ringing. Seconds later Mrs. Ashford swept into the room. "Bill, that was Mother on the phone. She's fallen again and can't get up. We'll have to go over and help her." She looked at me, flashing a smile that looked artificial, and raked me from head to foot with those cold gray eyes. "You'll have to excuse us. Welcome, by the way." Then she turned to Cherry. "Honey, it's all ready. Table's all set and everything. You and, uh, your friend just go ahead without us. No need to let it get cold."

"Oh, Mother," Cherry said in disappointment. "Well, is Grandmother all right?"

"I think so." She looked then at her husband, who was pulling on a light coat and feeling about with his free hand, for car keys, I guessed. "She's not hurt, Bill; she just can't get up by herself." Then she looked at me. "She's alone on weekends." She bent down to kiss Cherry on the cheek. "Now don't wait for us, Hon; you never know about these things. But I'll call if I see we're going to be held up long." She picked up a purse from somewhere and followed her husband out the back door, saying over her shoulder to me, "Do come again. Sorry."

After a moment, Cherry turned to me and said, "Daddy likes you. I can tell."

"Well, I like him," I said. "But the one I really like is that daughter of his. What a honey." Next thing I knew, we were kissing, kissing and falling over to lie on the couch, the kisses getting hot in hurry. I stopped only once, to ask, "Anybody else here?" She smiled and nodded no, and in no time at all I had my hand under skirt.

I never did know how much they saw. Only a moment before, I had Cherry's skirt rucked up nearly to her waist, and my hand, in plain view, was massaging her cunt. She still had her panties on—that hadn't changed. But to her mother and father we might as well have been fucking.

"Cherry!" her mother said, gasping. She had come into the room the same way she had before, which I guessed was from the kitchen. And when I looked up, Mr. Ashford was standing about two steps behind her, looking gray and grim.

Where in the hell had they come from? How much had they seen? All I could remember was suddenly hearing sounds in the next room—footsteps?—and scrambling madly with Cherry to sit up, to straighten clothing, to hide what we'd been doing.

"Mother," Cherry said weakly, looking flustered and guilty as sin. She was still patting her hair into place and otherwise straightening up as if somehow we still had a chance to fool them.

I had no idea how *I* looked, but I knew it wasn't good. Too, the air around us was thick with the smell of sex, and I wondered if Mr. and Mrs. Ashford could smell it. Worst of all though, like some idiot, I said to Mrs. Ashford, "I hope your mother wasn't hurt."

If looks could kill, I'd've been struck dead on the spot. All she said was, "Bill?"

He stepped forward, and for a moment I thought he was coming to get me. But he stopped in front of his wife and said to me, "I think you'd better leave."

Still the idiot, I said, "Well, yeah, I gotta be goin'."

"Just leave," he said, this time meaning business.

"Daddy," Cherry said in a weak sort of plea.

"We'll deal with you later, Cherry. Tell your friend here goodbye."

She gave me a stricken look and her pretty face tightened in tears. She fell on her knees to the floor, covering her face with her hands, and lowered her head to the couch. I heard her sobbing until the front door closed behind me and shut off the sound. The walk to my car was the longest I had ever taken, and I did not realize until later that parked right behind my car was her parents' car.

For some reason they had come back into the house through the front door, a simple thing I had never expected. I drove home in a daze, except for the times I was mentally kicking myself in the ass. When, oh, when would I ever learn?

I drove home and went straight to my room and closed the door, saying I had homework to do and, no, I didn't want any lunch. Mother gave me one of her X-ray looks, but she didn't say anything.

I sprawled on the bed and tried to think, but two minutes later I was on my feet again, pacing. Was that the end for Cherry and me? What did her folks say after I left? How much had they seen? Why had we been so stupid? Even if they let us see each other again, how could I face them? The embarrassment of it all just kept knifing deeper and deeper into me, making it impossible to stay still, impossible to think. I needed somebody to talk to.

A minute later I was going out the back door, yelling toward the kitchen on my way out, "Goin' to Johnny's." Taking a shortcut through backyards, I got to Johnny's in no time and uttered a prayer of thanks when I found him at home alone. Mr. and Mrs. Kelly had gone to visit relatives, and Johnny, on the couch in his living room, was reading the Sunday paper.

He gave a little whistle of alarm when I got to the part about getting caught, but his general reaction disappointed me, at least at first. He thought it was funny; I didn't see a damn thing funny about it.

"Well, I feel for you," he said. He was still on the couch, sitting up; I slumped in a nearby chair. "But it is kinda funny: Cherry Ashford? Who blushes if anybody says boo to her? And there she is, spread out on the couch with her skirt up over her head—"

"Not over her *head*," I groaned, wishing he'd take this seriously.

"—and in walk Mommy and Daddy, who think their little girl is some kind of Virgin Mary—"

"She is a virgin."

"—and there *you* are, your hand buried up the elbow in her crotch—"

"We were *petting,* just petting."

Johnny laughed. "Why didn't you pull out a plum and say, 'What a good boy am I'?"

With that, he fell over onto the couch laughing. Soon, in spite of myself, I laughed too, but when we stopped I said, "Look, I *like* this girl." I almost said "love," but I wasn't ready to tell Johnny that yet.

"I know you do," he said. "It'll all blow over."

I asked how he figured that.

"Well," he reasoned, "they couldn't have seen *too* much. In the first place, you weren't doing that much. In the second place, you got out of there alive. Naw. When they cool off, they'll see that they were young once. And, hey, Cherry didn't get here through another immaculate conception, did she? It could've been worse, much worse, and that's what they'll wind up telling themselves. You'll see."

"I don't know," I said. "Think I should call her? And what if one of her folks answers the phone?"

"I'd give it a little time, if I were you. Besides, you'll see her at school tomorrow."

"What if she avoids me?"

"Why should she? It was as much her fault as yours. Maybe more. You couldn't be expected to know how her parents come and go, how long they were likely to be gone, stuff like that. Could you?"

"No, but I can't blame Cherry either. You just don't know her. This girl hasn't been around much. She's innocent about a lot of things."

"Ain't they all." Johnny shook his head. "Innocent's one thing, Benny; retarded's another. And she *ain't* retarded, is she? Hell, you don't have to be experienced to know how long it usually takes to run over to Grandma's house and back, or that people coming through the front door can slip up on you. And she *damn* sure knew that Mama and Daddy wouldn't take kindly to catching her with a boy's hand buried in her pussy; but, my god, she was layin' there with that thing shinin' like a harvest moon."

This wasn't getting me anywhere and I didn't like talking about Cherry that way; I changed the subject. "You go out with Patty last night?"

"Friday night. Took Harriet out last night."

"Harriet Pringle?" I couldn't believe my ears.

He nodded and smiled.

I couldn't figure it. "How'd it go?"

"Fine as wine. She was nice as pie—and so was I."

"But why? I thought you didn't like her."

"I don't. But I'm not through with that bitch yet."

"Oh," I said, as if, aha!, I understood. But I didn't. What the hell was he gonna do, take her off and strangle her? "How'd that come about—the date, I mean? You didn't mention it Friday."

"Didn't call her 'til Friday afternoon."

"You mean she didn't already have a date?"

"She had a date. I told her to break it. She said okay."

I stared in amazement. "How do you do it?" If I had tried that with a girl, she would have hung up on me, probably after a fit of laughter.

Johnny smiled. "I'm learning, Ace. Women like a mean sonofabitch."

Jesus H. Christ! I thought. If that were true, I really *was* doing it all wrong. What was more, I didn't think I could ever do it right. I didn't want to be mean to girls; I *liked* girls. I wanted to be nice to one, and have one who was nice to me. Like Cherry. It didn't pay to be *too* nice, of course. I had learned *that* much. But mean? There wasn't a mean bone in my body. Suddenly my life stretched out before me like a long, lonesome road. I'd never, ever understand women. Success with 'em just wasn't in the cards for me. Was something trying to tell me something? Was all this leading me to the priesthood or something? Was I another Paul, and was my long, lonesome road another road to Tarsus? I truly wondered. Everything inside me rebelled at such a notion. But hadn't Paul fought it too? A crazy headline flashed on the screen of my mind: GOD CALLS BEDEVILED TEEN TO PRIESTHOOD. Yeah? Well, Teen replies, "Sorry, wrong number." Damned if Benny Blake was going to live a life with no pussy, stuck away in a world without women. Jesus and the Twelve Apostles could ambush me along that long, lonesome road, but, goddamit, they'd better bring a lunch if they hoped to drag *this* boy off to the priesthood, or anywhere else where there were no women. But, Christ Almighty, when was it all going to make sense to me?

"Where'd ya'll go," I asked. "Not back to Jenine's, I hope. Or to the Barnyard."

Johnny laughed. "Give me credit for *some* sense. Actually, we didn't do much of anything. Dropped by Teen Town. Danced a little. Went to the Varsity. Had a long talk. Then we parked on the Hill and made out awhile."

How was it, the making out, I wanted to know.

"Fine. She's not as hot as Patty, but she knows what that thing's for."

I was impressed. "Think you can get in her pants?"

"Got my hand there, and my dick ain't all that far from my hand."

Gee, I thought; for me it was a thousand miles.

"But she probably *won't* go all the way," he added. "She's smarter than Patty and she really is saving it, I think."

"Then what's the point?" I asked. "You don't like her and you don't think she'll fuck."

"Oh, she'll fuck; they'll all fuck. The question is: *who* will they fuck?"

"Ah, so!" I said, but I really didn't see at all.

"It's the challenge," he explained. "That bitch thinks I'm not good enough for her, but for some reason she likes me. I'm gonna make her *really* like me—and then dump her, 'cause *she* ain't good enough for *me*. Let her see how it feels. And who knows? Along the way I just might get into her pants."

I couldn't see that. It seemed like a lot of trouble for nothing and pretty underhanded too. I made a mental

158

note never to cross Johnny and changed the subject. "What's the latest on Dianne?" I figured Harriet might have told him.

"She's still *down,* Jack. Hasn't gotten out of bed since Thursday except to tinkle. She loved her brother something fierce, Harriet said. And they're thinking now that she might not go back to school, not even for the finals. Doctor said she needs a long vacation."

"Holy smoke!" I said. And then: "Speaking of vacation . . ."

"No sweat," he said, raising a hand that said don't worry.

"It's not that far off," I cautioned. "What? Three weeks? Four?"

"No sweat."

I left Johnny's house feeling a little better about the situation with Cherry. It had helped some just to talk about it. But I couldn't bring myself to believe that I had nothing to worry about, that it would all blow over soon, as Johnny had said. Every time I tried to make myself believe it, the scene in Cherry's den would play again in my mind, as if to say, "Thou fool." That look on Cherry's mother's face. The look on her father's face. Maybe worst of all, the look on Cherry's face: heartbreak and total humiliation. She might not want to see me again even if they let her.

I didn't go straight home. I struck out walking, and just walked and walked, my mind churning faster than my legs. I thought and thought and thought about it until I realized that like a dog chasing its tail my thoughts were just running in circles. Suddenly I felt worn out. But I also felt that a kind of fever had broken. I wasn't over it yet, whatever it was that had me in its grip, but it had done its damndest and pulled back. I could breathe easy for awhile. I started for home, thinking, what the hell, I'd know *some-*thing the next day just from the way Cherry acted, and of course she'd probably tell me the whole thing. I looked at the sun—it was still high in the sky—and guessed at the time: about one-thirty or two. That made tomorrow morning seem a long way off, but there was nothing to do but wait—that and avoid my mother, whose radar was probably already picking up signals as I got closer to home.

But I got lucky for once. The house was empty and a note stood propped against the face of the clock on the mantelpiece in the middle room. "Son," it said, "we've gone to see your grandmother and maybe over to Lenny's. Love, Mother. P.S. Your dinner's in the oven and on the table." I whistled in relief. Lenny was one of Zeb's brothers, and I knew that if they went by there, Zeb would get involved in a poker game and they wouldn't be home before dark.

I went into the kitchen and peeped into the oven, and then under a white cloth draped over food on the table, and suddenly I was ravenous, hungry enough even to eat fried chicken. I didn't like chicken any way you could cook it—Mother said I was the only southerner in history who didn't like it—but I fell on it like a starving hound, wondering idly what they'd had for brunch at Cherry's. After eating I went to my room, closed the door and read until around seven, when I fell asleep. I never knew what time Mother and Zeb got back.

Chapter Eight

I got to school early Monday, earlier than I had ever gone before, and waited outside Cherry's homeroom. And waited. And waited. I could see inside her room, and the minute hand on a clock up front, one of those minute hands that jumped instead of crawled to the next minute, finally hit eight forty-five, setting off the bell, and I had to leave or be late myself. I knew Cherry's schedule, so I figured I'd catch her after her first class.

But she wasn't there either—or I had missed her again. But that didn't seem likely; I had raced to the room at the sound of the bell, and the room was only down the hall and around the corner from mine. I asked a couple of people I recognized if Cherry had been in class. They didn't seem to know for sure one way or the other, but I went to my next class feeling hope leak out of me like air from a tire.

I couldn't meet her other classes. They were too far away. But when the bell rang for lunch I hurried down to Cherry's homeroom and caught the teacher, Mr. Sifford, just as he was leaving. Cherry was absent, he said.

"Gee," I said, fishing for information, "I hope she's not sick. We're working on a project together and time's running out."

"Sorry," he said. But that was all he said.

Then, coming out of the lunchroom I saw Harriet Pringle on her way in. Trying to act casual, I said as she passed, "Where's Cherry today?"

I couldn't tell whether Harriet snubbed me or just didn't hear me, but she marched right past without saying anything.

Now I was really getting worried. Puzzled too. I didn't believe for a minute that Cherry was sick. Was she too upset to come to school? Too ashamed? Was she mad at me? Was that the message in the way Harriet had acted? And, holy Christ, had she told Harriet all about it? Everything?

I walked about in the halls for awhile trying to figure it all out, but found myself going in circles again. Then I had an idea so good that I cursed myself for not thinking of it earlier. I'd call Cherry at home.

I hurried upstairs. There was a phone booth just across from the office, put in, I guessed, to keep students from tying up the school's phones. But somebody was in the booth.

I waited for what seemed like a year, though a clock on the wall said it had been only four minutes, but finally the phone was free. I put a nickel into the slot, heard it drop, got a dial tone and dialed. The phone rang and rang, but nobody answered. I tried again, just in case I'd dialed the wrong number, but again it rang and rang. "Damn!"

I went outside to meet Johnny on the front steps. He was sitting in our usual spot, unwrapping a stick of Dentyne.

"Where you been, Ace? Been waitin' for you. Have some." He held out a stick.

I hardly saw it. "Cherry's not at school. Did Harriet say anything to you about it?" I sat down beside him.

"Haven't seen Harriet. I let 'em look for me, Ace." He smiled and put the pack of gum into his shirt pocket. When I didn't smile back, he said, "Relax. Girls are always missing school. That time of the month maybe."

"Maybe," I said, but I didn't think so.

"Was Damico here today?" He knew we had a Spanish class together.

"No. Think I heard somebody say the funeral was to-day."

"Well, like I said yesterday, she might not come back at all."

But I didn't have time for Dianne Damico's problems. "Yeah, things are rough all over."

Johnny nudged my shoulder with his. "Cheer up, lad. 'It's always darkest just before dawn', you know."

"Where'd that saying come from? For me, it's always darkest just before it gets darker."

"Naw," he said, smiling. "You just worry too much."

He was right about that. "What've you got to be so happy about?"

"Me? I decided when I was five years old to be happy. Just make up your mind to it. Worry won't get you anywhere anyhow."

He was right about that too. "Okay," I said, giving him a big, silly grin, "I'm happy. You happy? Gee, we're both happy. Isn't that a happy feeling? Makes me even happier. What did you do with my gum? I'm so happy I could chew gum." He handed it over. I shucked off the wrapping and stuck the gum into my mouth. "Let's just sit here and chew the hell out of this gum and get happier and happier, okay? Ummm! What a happy taste. What a happy day."

When I quit cuttin' the fool, he said, "You know, McNulty was right; you are crazy as hell."

"Yeah, but I'm happy. Made up my mind when I was eighteen to be happy, and goddamit, I'm gonna be happy if it kills me. You hear me?"

He shook his head. "For once, McNulty was right."

By Monday night even I was beginning to think McNulty was right— or would be very soon. Starting when I got home from school, I called Cherry's number every thirty minutes until eleven o'clock, but the phone rang and rang, and I was going out of my mind. Where in god's name could she be? Why didn't *some*body answer the fuckin' phone? Tuesday was worse. She missed school again, I still couldn't find out why, and there was still no answer when I phoned her house. Even Johnny got curious and tried to help. He ran into Harriet at lunchtime, accidentally on purpose, to see what he could get out of her, but he came up empty.

"If she knows anything, she ain't talkin'," he reported.

"Did you get the *feeling* she knew anything?"

"Yeah, I did. But it was *only* a feeling. She wasn't *giving* away anything."

"No, but it tells me something *is* up, Ace." I nodded toward the phone booth, where we had agreed to meet after his talk with Harriet. "There's still no answer at her house, and I just now called for her father at both the fertilizer place and the bank— just to see what they'd say, mind you. God knows I don't wanna *talk* to him. Woman at the fertilizer place said he's out and won't be in today. At the bank, they said about the same, and when I asked if he would be in tomorrow, they said they didn't know."

He shrugged his shoulders. "Maybe there was an emergency of some kind. Maybe that grandma was hurt worse than you thought."

It was possible. I hadn't thought of that. But I had my doubts. If that were it, I reasoned, *some*body would have answered the phone by now. "Maybe," I said.

At nine o'clock that night, when there was still no answer at Cherry's, I told Mother I had run out of typing paper and asked if I could use the car to go get some.

Zeb, who was listening to the radio, feet propped up on a chair, simply reached into his pocket and handed me the keys. But Mother, who was ripping the hem out of a skirt, looked a bit suspicious. "Is this for that term paper you've been working so hard on?" she asked a bit too casually.

"Yes, ma'am," I said. "That and other things." My excuse for staying in my room so much lately had been that I was doing a term paper and studying for finals—another of those lies I was getting so good at telling.

"Where can you get paper at this time of night?" It was a good question and she knew it. Few stores of any kind stayed open after nine.

"Don't know if I can," I said, stalling. But then I remembered a sort of all-purpose store, up by the Varsity, that stayed open late. "Guess the Fat Man would be my best bet."

"Okay," she said, biting a thread. But I saw her glance at the clock on the mantelpiece and I knew I'd have to haul ass. Ten or fifteen minutes later I was turning onto Lakeshore Drive to drive by Cherry's house.

The house was dark. It sat on a corner, so I was able to see nearly all around it, but there just wasn't a light anywhere in it. That surprised me. It shouldn't have, I realized, but it did. Where on earth could they be?

I drove by one more time, just to make sure. And that time I even pulled into the driveway around back to let my headlights play over the house. Nothing. Their car was gone and the windows on the rear of the house just stared back at me like big ghostly eyes.

When I got back home, Mother and Zeb had gone to bed. I put the keys on the mantelpiece, tried Cherry's number one more time, and then went to bed myself.

Dianne Damico came back to school on Wednesday, pale as a sheet and moving as if in a coma, but Cherry was still out and there still was no answer at her house.

Feeling desperate, I marched into the office at lunchtime and asked about her. I said I was a good friend and that I had heard she was ill.

The lady at the front desk, which was actually a long counter, looked at me and smiled, and took a clipboard from a big nail in the wall. "Let's see," she said, checking the top page and then flipping it over. She flipped that one over too and then said, "Ah! Cherry A. Ashford. Withdrawn. Monday." She looked up as if to say, "Sorry."

"Withdrawn?" Suddenly I felt light-headed and for the first time in my life knew what it must be like to faint.

165

"Yes." She turned the clipboard around so I could see for myself. "So you must have heard right."

"Ma'am?" I was staring at the name, wondering vaguely what the middle initial stood for. It annoyed me that I didn't know. Anne? Angela? Hell, maybe it was new; maybe it was her scarlet letter, given to her by her folks after Sunday.

"I said you must have heard right: that your friend was sick," the lady was saying.

"Oh. Yes, ma'am," I said. "Well, thank you."

"Withdrawn!" Johnny gave a little whistle of surprise and said, "What do you make of *that?*" He sat on the school steps as I slumped against the railing.

"I don't know," I said, "but whatever it is, it ain't good." I thought for a minute and added, "What about finals? What about graduation?"

"Oh, she'll graduate," he said.

"Without taking finals? How?"

"Well, first, you don't know that she didn't or won't take 'em by some special arrangement. Next, she's got a straight A average and might have exempted everything anyhow. But, most important, she's got a rich daddy, and rich daddies can work out things that poor daddies can't."

It made sense. "Think she'll show up for graduation then?"

"I wouldn't bet on it, Benny. If they'd let 'er show for that, she might as well come on to school."

That made sense too. I sighed and sat down beside him.

"What the hell'd you do to that girl?" Johnny asked. "You sure you told me everything? 'Cause this sounds like they caught you dickin' her or something."

"Naw, man," I said wearily. "I *told* you what happened. And what did *you* say? 'Don't worry; it'll all blow over.' Well, it blew over, all right—like a friggin' hurricane—and blew her away with it."

"Sorry, Ace. I really am. But it didn't sound like that big a deal to me."

166

"It's all right," I said. "Hell, I didn't think it was *this* big either."

"There still could be another reason, you know. Could've been anything."

"No. It was what happened Sunday; I feel it in my bones."

"Well, what next?"

I sighed. "Oh, who knows? Who cares? I'm happy—that's the important thing. Made up my mind at eighteen to be happy. Fact, I'm now in my third day of happy and I've never felt happier. Hallelujah!"

Johnny smiled. "That's the spirit, lad." Then, as if motioning to someone, he called out, beckoning with a finger. "Over here with that net, boys." Pointing to me, he added. "Here's your man."

My classes after lunch dragged so badly that I cut the last one and headed for home. I needed to be by myself anyhow, and in leaving early I could walk home alone and even have some time to myself before Mother and Zeb got in from work around three-thirty.

But the walk home didn't help. I got there feeling loaded down with more questions than I could carry, and I was barely through the front door before I was dialing Cherry's number again.

When a voice said, "Hello," I was too surprised for a moment to speak. But soon I said, "Mrs. Ashford?"

"Yes. Who's this?"

I took a deep breath. "May I speak to Cherry?"

"I'm sorry. Cherry's not in. Who's calling, please?"

I braced as if expecting to be hit, and made myself say, "Benny, ma'am. Benjamin Blake." Then my words poured out in a rush. "Look, Mrs. Ashford, there's been a terrible mistake. I don't know what upset you Sunday, you and Mr. Ashford, but Cherry and I weren't— That is, we—I mean, I don't know what you think we were doing, but I'm sorry if you think we were doing *that*. I mean, Cherry wouldn't. *I* wouldn't. I respect Cherry too much and, besides, I wasn't raised that way."

I guess I'd still be talking if she hadn't cut me off. But it was just as well; I was running out of lies. Coolly, ever so coolly, as if she hadn't heard a word I said, she told me again, "Cherry's not in," and added, "Benjamin, is it?—as if she had no idea who I was—"Cherry is out of town on an extended visit. Try again in, oh, September."

"Sep—!" I caught myself and didn't finish the word. So it was *that* way, I told myself. Trying to be just as casual and off-handed as she was being, I said, "Could you give me her address, then? I know she'd like to hear from me."

"Cherry is going to be traveling about and for the fore-seeable future won't have a fixed address," she said, still cool as you please. "But if you'll mail your letters here to the house, I'll see that she gets them. Do you need that address?"

"No, ma'am," I said, defeated for the moment, but seeing that I wasn't the only one who could lie with ease. Then, afraid she'd hang up if I didn't keep talking, I said, "Cherry's not ill, is she?"

"She's fine. I'll tell her you asked."

"Is she going to miss graduation?"

Deliberately misunderstanding, I thought, she said, "She'll miss it terribly, especially saying goodbye to all her friends. But I really must go now."

"Don't hang up!" I said. "Please! You've got to tell me—" But she was gone and I was talking to a dial tone. I lowered the phone to its cradle and sat there staring at it as I turned over and over in my mind what Mrs. Ashford had said. I looked in, at, over, around, under and through her words, thinking, I supposed, that if I held them just so, up to the light in just such a way, that I'd see something there I hadn't seen before. But no matter how I turned them or how hard I looked, their message came out the same: my girl was gone, gone for good, and I'd play hell finding out where.

I lay in bed that night thinking it was over and telling myself to forget Cherry and move on. I even went to sleep and got up the next morning thinking it was all settled. But when the city bus that I often rode to school left the stop at Riverside High, heading up the Hill, I was still on it.

I didn't know what I was going to do. A part of me that I barely recognized seemed to be running the show, with the rest of me just along for the ride. But I got off at the stop closest to Cherry's house and walked straight to it, barely noticing what an absolutely beautiful day it was: clean, bright, fresh.

Mrs. Ashford looked very surprised when she answered the door, but she recovered quickly and called back into the house, "Billings." Telling me to wait there, she pushed the door nearly closed and turned away, saying as she went, "It's that boy."

Next thing I knew, Mr. Ashford, wearing a coat and tie, and smelling of aftershave lotion, loomed in the doorway. "What do you want?" he said. He sounded short and looked put out, but I had the impression that he thought he'd overdone it. At any rate, he repeated in a softer voice, "What do you want?"

I felt like saying, "Gee, I don't know. I'm just as surprised to find myself here as you are." But I blurted out the simple truth instead: "I want to know about Cherry—the truth."

The last, the part about the truth, stung him, I thought, but he looked at me as if gauging how much he should tell and said, "All right." He stepped out onto the porch, pulling the door to behind him. "The truth is that Cherry can't see you anymore."

"Where is she?" My tone of voice, demanding, surprised me.

But it didn't faze him. "To tell you where Cherry is would defeat our purpose in sending her away."

I couldn't argue with that. "What did we do that was so terrible?"

"It wasn't so much what you did as what you might have done. We felt that certain precautions were in order. You understand?"

I did, but I didn't want to accept it. Feeling cornered, I

said the first thing I could think of that might make him see things my way. "Cherry's in love with me. Doesn't that matter to you?"

He smiled. "It matters more than you know. But Cherry's young—young and inexperienced."

"And I love her." I was snapping at him now and feeling foolish because of it, but I couldn't seem to stop.

He smiled again, making me feel more foolish. He had the upper hand and he knew it. "And what can you offer her?"

That surprised me. Hell, I wasn't talking about marriage, just love. "Sir?" I said.

"Let me be frank, Benny. You asked for the truth and you're old enough to hear it. You have nothing to offer my daughter. She's young and, I admit, spoiled, and doesn't understand these things, so we must protect her until she does."

What the hell was he talking about, I wondered. "But we love each other," I said. Why couldn't he understand that?

"Let me finish," he prompted. "I don't want to hurt your feelings, Benny, but I've found out some things about you since Sunday. I don't enjoy prying; it was my duty to Cherry."

He stopped there, hoping, I guessed, that I would see what he was getting at. But I didn't. "Found out what? Where?"

"I had a long talk with the principal about you."

I was thrown. "Mr. Thompson?"

He nodded. "I also talked to the good priests at St. Jude."

I still didn't see it coming, and it must have shown on my face.

He acted a bit awkward and said, "Benny," as if I were a keen disappointment to him. "Must I say it? Can't you *see*? Girls like Cherry don't marry boys like you. Oh, once in a blue moon it happens, but even then—"

"You mean I'm not good enough for her." Suddenly I felt helpless, defeated, angry, and I silently cursed a world in which roses could bloom, birds could sing, and the air smell so fresh while a rich man stood on the porch of his fine home and told me I was nothing.

He seemed self-conscious and looked away. "I'm sure you're a nice enough boy, Benny. Nobody I talked with said you were bad—a little mixed up, maybe, but not bad."

"Just poor—was that it?" I couldn't help myself; I wanted him to say the worst so I could hate him that much more.

"Well," he said, looking about, hedging.

"Was it 'poor as a churchmouse'? Or just 'dirt poor'?" Bitterness had made my anger ice cold.

He turned a shade cold himself. "Just that you're a Milltown boy. And that your parents are millworkers."

"You sure they didn't say lintheads?"

He looked at me again. "I'm sorry if I've hurt your feelings. But I had to put Cherry first. And now . . ."

He motioned toward the door with one hand and stuck out his other for a handshake.

I looked at the hand and then at him. I wanted to spit on it. Then I turned and walked away.

I caught a bus back down to the school, dropped by the office to report in, and went to wait outside Johnny's first-period classroom. He did a double take when I told him where I'd been and what had happened. "You're braver than I am, Jack," he said.

I wasn't brave and I knew it. "Yeah, well, 'Jack fell down and broke his crown,' remember? No, I just had to get some answers or go crazy."

We walked through the halls to his second class, math, and stood outside the door. "Any idea where she might be?"

I told him about the aunt in the mountains and said that if I had to guess, I'd guess she was there. "But I don't know the aunt's name. Don't even remember the town. North Carolina's all I know. So I can't even write her."

"Maybe she'll write you."

"Doesn't know my address." I thought of all my effort to hide where I lived. Served me right.

"Well, listen," Johnny said. "You want Dr. Kelly's advice? Forget Cherry. Get a date and go out with me and Patty tonight."

"Naw. Thanks anyway. Besides, I don't know anybody to ask and it's too late anyhow."

"Ask Dianne Damico. You'll see her next period, won't you? And if she can't go tonight, ask her for a date tomorrow night. You can go out with me and Harriet. You and Dianne ought to be a good match; she's just come from a funeral and you look like you're on your way to one."

I knew it was good advice and that he was trying to cheer me up, but I had no interest in dating. None in Dianne, either. "Naw," I said. "See you later."

I told my mother that I had to study for finals all weekend, and since that wasn't a bad idea anyhow, I made a stab at it and found that it helped get my mind off my troubles. It was hard at first to concentrate, but I got better at it as I went along, and by the time Saturday night rolled around, the emotional siege had begun to lift and I felt better than I had in a week. I was even glad to see Glenn, who dropped by around ten o'clock, and tried to kid with him a bit, but I soon saw that something was wrong.

"Same old thing," he said, sighing wearily. "Dad's had a few, and Mom's raisin' the roof. I just had to get out for awhile." He nibbled on a fingernail and fixed me in a sidelong glance. "How about you?"

We were sitting at the kitchen table, sharing a Coke on ice. Mother and Zeb had turned in early. "Oh, if you mean Cherry, I'll get over it." I tried to sound more unconcerned than I felt. The last thing I wanted was to discuss Cherry with Glenn.

He didn't believe me, though. He caught my eyes with his and said, "Take my advice, Benny: that's one girl you'd better leave alone. Her dad is a big, big man in this town.

Fool around with Cherry Ashford the way you did with Austin, and he'll land on you like a ton of bricks."

I wanted to say more, but it just wasn't worth it, so I smiled and said, "No danger of that; I can't even find her." I couldn't resist adding, though: "Haven't heard where she is, have you?"

He was nodding his head to say no, when the phone rang. I hurried to the next room to answer it before it woke up Mother and Zeb—and nearly dropped the receiver when I heard Cherry's voice on the line.

"Benny!" she said. "Oh, thank God."

"Cherry! Where are you?"

"I can't talk long, Benny, and I have to talk softly. Can you hear me?"

"Yes, yes." I was having to strain, but I could hear her. "Where are you?"

"I'm at home. I had to come back to pack. I'm going to Europe early. Daddy's taking me, making me go. Oh, Benny, I don't want to go."

Europe hardly registered in my tumbled thoughts. "Where on earth have you been?"

"At my aunt's, in North Carolina. We just got back today, and we'll be leaving tomorrow. Our flight's at four."

"Where in Europe? Give me your address there." Europe? I thought; Jesus Christ! Why not the moon?

"I'll give it to you later. I have to get off the phone now. Can you meet me tomorrow?"

What a question. "Of course, I can meet you. But where, what time tomorrow?"

"After church," she whispered. "We're going to Mass at noon. Don't come to church! Meet me after Mass in the schoolyard at St. Agnes, by the basketball court. I'll say it's such a nice day I want to walk home. They'll let me."

"One o'clock. St. Agnes. I'll be there."

"Bring me your address too. I have to go now."

"Wait!"

"I have to go. Someone's coming!" I love you, Ben—"

The line went dead, and I knew someone had cut us off. Damn! Damn! Damn!

I put the phone back on the hook and looked up to see Glenn standing in the doorway. "That was Cherry," I said, simply. "She's home."

He shook his head as if to say there was no hope for me. "Don't say I didn't warn you," he said, moving toward the front door and fishing car keys from his pocket.

"No sweat," I said. "It's all over but the shouting."

"The shouting may be the worst part," he said. Moments later he was gone.

I came wide awake at seven-fifteen feeling like warmed-over death. I didn't know how much sleep I'd gotten, but it couldn't have been much. My plan had been to go to the ten o'clock Mass at St. Jude, eat breakfast out, and then drive to the schoolyard to wait for Cherry, but I decided to go to Mass at eight o'clock instead. More sleep was out of the question, and I felt that if I had to hang around the house for two hours I'd go crazy. Bounding out of bed, I threw on some slacks and a shirt. Mother was still in bed when I got ready to leave, but Zeb, an early riser, gave me the car keys, and soon I was on my way.

I could have strangled Glenn on the spot. He caught up with me after Mass, and we stood around on the backside of the church talking until Father Brady stepped out of the rectory and called to me. Right away I smelled a trap, and the look on Glenn's face told me I was right: he had set me up for that talk with Father Brady. "You bastard," I said.

He began backing away. "See you later," he said and then broke into a run toward his house.

I turned back toward the rectory. Father Brady was waiting. "Won't take but a minute, Benny," he called. "Come on in."

"Could we make this kinda quick, Father?" I said when I reached him. "I was supposed to go straight home, and Mom'll be upset." Now I was even lying to priests, but I didn't care. He shouldn't have trapped me that way, I told myself.

With his arm around my shoulder, he led me into the rectory and into a conference room that looked old-timey, with the kind of furniture—tables, chairs, hatrack, lamps—that I'd seen in the homes of old people. "Take a seat," he said, pointing to a chair at the side of a long wooden table in the middle of the room. He sat down at the end of the table, adjusted the folds of his cassock, folded his hands in front of him and said with a smile, "There now."

Father Brady was a slight, balding man with watery blue eyes in a washed-out face. Like many of the priests I'd known, he spoke with an accent I couldn't place. But this was no time to be trying to figure that out. I braced myself, wondering just what Glenn had told him and cursing myself for having shot off my big mouth to him in the first place. But what kind of guy ran tattling to priests anyhow?

I waited, and when Father Brady still didn't speak I squirmed in my chair. I had some time to kill before meeting Cherry, but this was taking all day. "Look, Father, I don't know what Glenn told you—"

He raised his hand to stop me. "He told me you're his best friend. He thinks a lot of you."

I wondered if I'd heard him right, but something told me to shut up and listen.

"Benny," he said, "many fine Catholic families have problems that they hide from the world outside. Things they're ashamed of."

God in Heaven! I thought. I wasn't the best Catholic around, and I'd be quick to admit it, but I wasn't *that* bad.

"And when those people cry out to us in their hour of need, we must as good Catholics answer."

My need, I thought, had been for a piece of ass, not a sermon. What the hell had Glenn told him?

"And your friend needs you now."

My friend? This wasn't making any sense at all.

"Will you do it?"

I felt stupid and I knew I must look stupid. "Do what, Father?"

"Glenn's family has a problem. He needs your help."

"My help, Father?" I wasn't feeling any brighter, but I said, "Of course. Of course, I'll help."

He gave a big smile. "I knew you would, Benny. There's a good boy—and a good friend too."

Was that it? Could I leave? I took a deep breath. "Uh, exactly what is it Glenn wants me to do, Father?"

"He must take that family problem I spoke of to a sanitorium—a place for the treatment of alcoholics. He wants you to go with him, but he was ashamed to ask you himself."

That floored me. I knew Glenn's dad liked his whiskey, but an alcoholic? Good lord! "Of course I'll go. Where is it?"

"It's down the country a ways. Near Savannah."

I wondered why so far. Savannah was down on the coast, a good 100 miles away. But it didn't really matter. Obviously they had their reasons. "Well, fine, Father," I said rising. I was sure my mother would let me go. "Just tell Glenn to give me a call when he's ready."

"Oh, he's ready now. He's waiting. I said I'd send you right over."

That knocked me back into my chair. "Oh! Now? Today? Well, gee, Father, I'd like to help out, but—" I stopped there, groping not only for a good excuse, but for understanding too. This just couldn't be happening. I couldn't *let* it happen. "Oh, no, Father. Any other time. *Any* other time. I'd have to ask my mother. I couldn't just take off like that. Besides, I'm studying for finals—school, you know. Sorry, Father. I really am. And now I really have to run. I'm late as it is. I'm sorry."

But all he did was smile. "I've already talked to your mother, not twenty minutes ago. Very understanding woman, your mother. And gracious. She knew you'd be only too happy to help out. She told me too that you'd been studying for days, so don't worry about those final exams. Don't worry about the car, either. She said they

176

have another key and will pick it up if they need it. Glenn told me it's out back here, so don't worry." He stood up. "And now I imagine Glenn will be ready to go." With his hand he made a quick sign of the cross. "God bless you, Benny." He left the room.

I left it too, in a state of shock. I went out the door of the rectory, down the steps, and out to the curb and just stood there, looking across the street at Glenn's house, and then up at the sky, noticing for the first time that it was overcast. The way the sky looked was how I felt: gray, gloomy. Was I really going to do this? Was I going to leave Cherry waiting in that schoolyard, waiting and wondering what on earth had happened to me, and maybe never see her again? Everything inside me cried out no. I felt sorry for Glenn, and he *was* a friend, I guessed, but this was asking too much. It wasn't fair. It just wasn't fair.

I looked down the street at the car and was very tempted to go to it, get in it and just drive off. Worry about the consequences later. I even reached for my keys and took a step or two in that direction. But just then Glenn appeared on his front porch, caught my eye and waved frantically for me to come.

I looked at my watch. Mass had ended earlier than usual and it was now only two or three minutes after nine. If we hauled ass I could make it back in time to meet Cherry after all. It would be close, but she'd wait as long as she could, I figured. I looked at my car one more time, and then at Glenn, who was about to have a fit for me to come on. Cursing under my breath, I ran toward him.

"We're coming out the back door," Glenn said. He pointed to the alley alongside his house. "Go around back, please, and get the car started." He tossed me some keys, and I headed down the drive, but he stopped me before I really got started. Leaning over the porch rail, he caught my eye and said, "And, Benny, I don't know how to thank you."

That made me feel a little guilty, so I just waved as if to say forget it and went on down the alley. The Pontiac was parked near the back door, the front end aimed toward the street. I got in and started her up, and seconds later Glenn opened the back door on the passenger side. "Watch your head," I heard him say. I looked around and got the shock of my life. The passenger was Glenn's mother. My lips began to move as I whispered, almost without knowing it, "Hail, Mary, full of grace; the Lord is with thee. . . ."

Glenn jumped in beside me. "You drive, Benny. I might have to . . . to tend to Momma."

Again I didn't know what the hell was going on, but I was getting used to that feeling. I eased down the alley to the street and turned left.

"You know the way to Savannah, don't you?" Glenn asked.

I nodded and headed east. Soon we were leaving the city behind and running into the rain. But at least we were on our way. Now if we could just make some time.

In the rearview mirror, if I cocked my head just so, I could see Mrs. McNulty. She hadn't spoken a word, but just sat there, pale and drawn, huddled inside a light green coat, looking out at the rain. Glenn, sunk in his seat, wasn't talking either, so I just drove.

We'd gone about fifteen miles in silence when a small, dry voice from the back seat said, "Glenn." When he didn't answer, the voice said again, "Glenn."

Glenn didn't look around, but said, "What, Momma?"

"Stop the car," she said, and I knew then she was drunk.

Glenn sank lower in his seat and said in a mechanical voice, "Can't stop, Momma." He began to bite his nails.

About five miles on down the road, when the rain, heavier now, had lulled me into a kind of mental blank, Mrs. McNulty suddenly leaned forward and said, "Glenn, stop this car."

Glenn didn't look around. "Can't stop, Momma. You know that."

Lord, no! I thought. We gotta keep rolling. I glanced at my watch, but the time didn't even register.

Mrs. McNulty sat back. "Turn around, Glenn. Benny, turn this car around. I want to go home."

I almost said, "Now you're talkin', Momma," but Glenn said, "Goin' to the hospital, Momma. You agreed to go, remember?" Now he was gnawing his nails. I caught a glimpse of his fingertips; they were ragged and raw.

The woman grumbled a bit under her breath, but went back to staring out at the rain. I looked at her in the rear-view mirror. Her hair, a rich dark brown flecked with gray, was pulled back in a bun, making her face look even sharper. I guessed her to be about 40, but she wasn't aging well. Crow's-feet dug at her eyes, and wrinkles around her mouth made her lips look stitched or something. In spite of it all, though, she held herself in a proud way that said, "Drunk or sober, I'm somebody." I had to respect that, but she was about as warm as a year-old grave, so I had always steered clear of her.

But I soon saw that this wasn't to be one of her proudest moments. Suddenly she sat bolt upright, raised her fists and screamed, "God damn it, stop this car! Stop it this instant!" She lunged forward and started slapping at Glenn's face and head, yelling, "Stop it! Stop it! Stop it!"

I nearly jumped out of my skin when she screamed, but all in all Glenn stayed pretty calm. He dodged the blows as best he could and then said, "Watch it, Benny; I'm going over the seat." He clambered into the back, the heel of his shoe hitting the side of my head as he squirmed to get on over and at the same time ward off her hands. "Sorry," he said, but I wasn't hurt.

When he got back there, he set in to calm her down, and for awhile it worked. "I'll just stay back here," he said when she quieted down.

We passed through Waynesboro, a small country town southeast of Augusta on a ridge up from the river, and headed out through gently rolling farm country and pine forests. It was still raining, but we were making pretty good time. Then, about halfway to the next small town, Sylvania, Mrs. McNulty started again. "I want a drink," she said. "Stop and get me a drink."

"This is Sunday, Momma."

179

She leaned forward against the back of my seat and edged toward me. "Benny will get me a drink; won't you, Benny?"

I said, "I think this is a dry county, Mrs. McNulty." We were out in the middle of nowhere anyhow.

"No, no," she said, sort of laughing. "I can get a drink here. I can get a drink anywhere. Stop at the next filling station. Or store. Stop anywhere."

Glenn raised his voice a notch. "Dry county, Momma. There's no whiskey for miles around."

She turned on him viciously. "You shut up!" she spat. "I want a goddam drink. Who are you to tell me I can't drink?" She turned back to me, put her hand on the back of my neck and said in a sweet slur, "Benny'll get me a drink. Benny knows how to treat a lady; don't you, Benny?"

Glenn leaned forward, put his hands on her shoulders, and said gently, "Momma, please sit back. We'll be there soon and you can ask the doctor for a drink."

She jerked away from him. "Momma, please; Momma, please," she mimicked. "You're just like your father. Just like him. Well, both of you can go to hell. You hear me? Hell!"

The look on Glenn's face said he'd already been to Hell, but he didn't say anything, just tried again to get her to sit back. But this time she got violent, slapping at him first with her left hand, and then turning and going at him with both hands. He shielded himself from her blows, but the more trouble she had hitting him, the madder she got. I was trying to watch both the road and the fight, and not doing a good job at either, so I slowed almost to a crawl and called, "You all right, Glenn?"

"Don't slow down, Benny!" he shouted. "I don't know how long I can hold her."

That turned out to be not long at all. I had gunned the Pontiac back up to fifty and was going for sixty, when all of a sudden Mrs. McNulty turned from Glenn and started climbing into the front seat, saying over and over, "Gonna stop this car, you hear me. Gonna stop this car."

Glenn sprang forward and grabbed the leg that was still in back, but she jerked it loose and kicked him, and next thing I knew I had a crazy woman up front with me, her skirt nearly up to her waist, and reaching for the steering wheel.

I tried to fend her off with one hand, but it was impossible to do that and drive too. Fortunately, Glenn was helping out again, leaning over from the back, with his arms wrapped around her neck, trying to pull her away from me. But she was stronger than she looked. Grunting and groaning and jerking this way and that, she kept breaking his hold and grabbing at the wheel again, clawing at my hands with her fingernails and trying to pry my fingers loose. By now I had slowed to about twenty miles an hour, but it was still scary to be in a moving car that was weaving all over a rain-slick road.

"Stop this car!" she screamed at me. "It's my fucking car, so stop it. I didn't give you permission to drive."

I was stunned to hear Glenn McNulty's mother talk like that, but foul language was the least of my worries. Finally, I got my right hand up and on her shoulder, and shoved with real force. It drove her away, but Glenn, still hanging onto her, was pulled half way over the back of the seat. Next thing I knew, he was in the seat between us—but upside down.

I put on the brakes, but Glenn yelled, "Don't stop. Keep going."

Somehow he managed to right himself and plop down between us, which at least kept her away from the wheel. But she had another trick up her sleeve. I felt and heard a whoosh of air and looked quickly to my right. She had opened the car door about two or three inches and was looking at us with a malicious smile on her face. "Stop or I'll jump," she said, both hands on the door.

My foot came off the gas pedal as if I'd stepped on a rattlesnake. I believed she'd do it.

Glenn braced as if he'd been shot. "Momma, oh, Momma," he pleaded, "close that door!" He grabbed her arm, but she was still able to open the door wider and lean out a bit. "Slow down, Benny. Slow down!"

We were already slowing, but I braked the car to a stop. We were on a long, straight stretch of highway, with no cars in sight in either direction and no sign of a farmhouse either, and it was pouring rain. I checked my watch and squirmed in my seat. This was costing precious time.

Mrs. McNulty opened the door all the way and started to get out. "Gonna find me a drink," she said.

"Momma," Glenn said, sounding desperate, still holding on, "if I give you a drink, will you get back in the car?"

She smelled a trick. It was written all over her face. But she was interested. "You hiding something?" she said. "You hiding something from your mother?" She looked at him as if she were a cat and he were a mouse.

He still had hold of her arm. He was taking no chances. But he said, "Get back in the car and I'll give you a drink. You're getting wet anyhow."

She swayed a little and shook her head in a big no. "You give me the drink first."

Uh, oh, I thought. She wasn't going to fall for it, and the minutes were ticking away.

Glenn said, "I'll *show* it to you. How 'bout that?"

Her look said she was willing to think it over.

"Deal?" said Glenn.

She licked her lips and shook her head.

"Benny," Glenn said. "Reach under your seat and hold up that bottle."

Still thinking he was bluffing, I leaned down and felt around under the seat—and pulled out a half-pint of Jack Daniels.

"Just let her see it," Glenn said.

I held it up and she licked her lips some more and reached out for it.

"Uh, uh," Glenn said. "You get into the back seat, and *then* I'll give it to you."

"The whole thing," she said, raising the ante.

Glenn hesitated. "The whole thing," he said.

She nodded and got out, and he slid out behind her, still

holding on to her arm. They climbed into the back again and Glenn closed the door and locked it. Both were soaked to the skin, but they seemed not even to notice. Keeping his eye on his mother, Glenn held out his hand for the bottle. I gave it to him and started moving again, eager to make up for lost time. We had hardly hit second gear when I saw in the rear-view mirror that Mrs. McNulty had the bottle turned up to her lips and that nearly half of the whiskey was gone.

About thirty miles east of Sylvania the rain stopped and the land began to level off. I eased the speed up to 65, and soon we were driving across low, flat country where water stood in ditches on both sides of the raised roadbed, and every now and then a swamp loomed around us. Savannah couldn't be much farther, I told myself, and Mrs. McNulty was still quiet. I felt as if I'd been holding my breath for an hour.

She remained calm, though, and a few miles on down the road, Glenn leaned forward and said, "You'll soon hit some railroad tracks, Benny. About half a mile past them you'll see a Shell station on the right and a road off to the right. Turn there."

That surprised me. We were still ten or fifteen miles out of Savannah and passing nothing but an occasional gas station or grocery store. The land was higher here, but not much more than pines and wild undergrowth surrounded us. Sure enough, though, just beyond the Shell station was a road with a sign on the corner saying: Hospital. Underneath the letters an arrow pointed down the road.

Soon Glenn pointed to a gravel-covered driveway and told me to turn in. From the road, I couldn't see anything but more pines, but before long we pulled up in front of a low-slung building and stopped.

"We're here, Momma." Glenn opened his door to get out.

"No!" Mrs.McNulty said—and when she said it I braced for another fight and looked at my watch. It was already past eleven-thirty. But she sat up straight, held her head high and said, "I'll go in alone or not at all. Get my suitcase and put it on the steps, and then get back in the car."

I handed Glenn the keys, and he got out and went to the rear of the car. Getting her suitcase, he put it on the top step of the hospital and got back into the car, this time up front with me. "Okay, Momma," he said, turning. "Give me a kiss."

With great and deliberate dignity she stepped out of the car. "Kiss my ass," she said and slammed the door. As soon as she reached the bottom step, the doors of the hospital swung open and a man came out, got her suitcase and waited to escort her inside. She took his arm and never looked back.

We watched until she got inside and the doors closed behind her, and it was then that I realized Glenn was crying. He was on the side nearest the hospital, and I couldn't see his face, but I heard the sobs. Still looking away he handed me the keys. "Let's go," he said. Ten minutes later I was streaking up the highway for home.

It rained on us, poured, nearly all the way back, and try as I might I couldn't make good time. I kept looking at my watch and checking the mileage, but no matter how many times I figured it, the verdict was the same: I was going to be late. My only hope was that Cherry would wait.

Glenn didn't speak again until we were almost home. He just sat looking out at the rain and chewing his nails, tears rolling down his face. I hadn't minded the quiet. My thoughts, for the most part, were on Cherry anyhow, and when they weren't I was thanking my lucky stars that no such curse as alcoholism had settled on my family. The McNultys might be a lot farther up the social ladder than we were, but what good was that if your home life was hell on earth?

When Glenn finally did speak, we had just passed through Waynesboro. "Benny," he said, "you won't say anything to anybody about this, will you?

"Not if you don't want me to."

"Not even to Johnny?" He had nearly stopped crying.

"Not even to Johnny." I meant it too.

"And I really appreciate your help in this. I just couldn't ask you myself."

"No sweat," I said, feeling a little sick. It was closing in on one o'clock and we were still a good twenty-five minutes from home. I nudged the speed up to seventy. "Your dad should've done this chore, though. This isn't something a son ought to have to do. I mean, look at you: you're a nervous wreck."

"You should see him," he said softly. "He's not a strong man, anyhow. And he worships my mother."

"I really feel for you, Glenn. I never dreamed your mother would come out that door this morning. Talk about shocked. I thought your dad was the problem drinker."

Glenn sobbed once and I thought he was going to break down again. But he fought it and somehow got control. "That's what we *want* people to think." He looked at me, eyes red, face swollen. "That's why you mustn't tell, Benny. Please."

"Gave you my word, pal, and I meant it."

"You know how people are. If a man has an alcohol problem, people tend to overlook it. But if it's a woman—"

"I understand. You got my word." I hesitated. "You can tell me to butt out if you want to, but does this kind of thing happen often?"

"She's been in the hospital before, twice, if that's what you mean. But it's all been in the past year. She didn't drink at all until Perry went off to school. Since then, it's just gotten worse and worse." He spoke even more softly. "Perry's always been her favorite, and he comes home less and less."

That struck me as odd. I could see *celebrating* because Perry left—but *sorrow*? "Maybe it's something else. The change of life, maybe." I didn't know squat about the change of life, but I knew it was a big, big thing with women and that lots of them went kind of crazy when it happened.

"No," Glenn said. "It's me."

"You?"

"Yes, me." And now he was crying again. He pulled out a handkerchief and wiped his eyes and blew his nose. "God's punishing me for my sins."

"Naw," I said, hardly able to believe my ears.

"Yes, He is, too. I *try* to do right, to be a good Catholic, but I'm always backsliding."

"Glenn, nobody's perfect, you know. Surely—"

He wasn't even listening. "I'll just have to do better, that's all. And I will!" he said, crying harder, leaning his head against the dashboard. "I will!"

"I know you will," I found myself saying. "Don't cry, Glenn. It'll be all right. Everything will work out fine."

"Pray for her, Benny. Pray for her."

"I will, buddy, and that's a promise." What the heck, I thought; if anybody could get through to God I ought to be able to; He hadn't heard from me in a month of Sundays. He had probably put all his switchboard angels on notice: "If Benny Blake should happen to call, put him straight through. Should be good for a couple of laughs."

Soon we were on the outskirts of Augusta, but it was already one-fifteen. If I drove all the way to Glenn's house to get my car, and *then* drove to St. Agnes, I might as well not go at all. He was quieter now, crying softly, so I said, "Glenn, I hate to bring this up now, but do you mind dropping me off on the Hill? I'll hitch a ride later to pick up my car."

Staring straight ahead, his cheek glistening with tears, he said so softly I had to strain to hear him, "Won't do you any good, Benny; she's not there."

"What do you mean?"

He broke into new sobbing, buried his face in his hands and said in a muffled tone, his words thick with saliva, "I told, Benny; I told. I heard you on the phone and I told.

186

Oh, God, I told!" He took his hands from his face, sat up, and whirled on the seat to look at me. "But I did it for you, Benny. You *have* to understand that."

Glenn's words bloomed in my mind like an ugly flower, and for a moment their horrible meaning short-circuited my anger. He really believed I was bad, believed it so strongly that he betrayed me. Betrayed me to save me. He had hurt me, hurt Cherry. To save me. Screw friendship. Screw love. Screw dreams. All that mattered was some wrong-headed, pig-headed, royally fucked-up belief that somebody else's morals, namely mine, needed help. And all to save me. Great God! I thought; what a twisted grasp of goodness. No wonder he was a miserable creature; he had been born in the wrong place *and* time. Salem, 1640— that was where he belonged.

I was madder than I'd ever been, but it was cold anger, not hot. And the deeper it chilled, the colder it got. "Who'd you tell?" I asked. We had come to Central Avenue, about halfway up the Hill. I turned right, heading downtown.

He slumped back against the door, but he was still looking at me, trying to gauge my reaction, I figured. "Father Brady," he said.

"And, of course, Father Brady, seeing his Christian duty, called Mr. Ashford and told him."

"Yes," he said. It was almost a whisper.

"And this whole trip was a set-up, to make *sure* I didn't get to Cherry."

"No, no," Glenn said. "That was a coincidence. I *did* need help, and Father Brady knew it. So when you showed up at eight o'clock Mass—"

"Father Brady decided to kill two birds with one stone."

"Something like that."

"How efficient. How morally efficient. Surely goodness and mercy will follow you and Father Brady the rest of your lives."

For a moment Glenn said nothing, but, then, in a tiny voice he asked, "Do you hate me?"

I weighed the question. "Hate you? No, I don't hate

187

you." Hate, to me, was a big emotion; Glenn was too small a target for it. "But I sure as hell don't like you very much."

"I did it for you Benny; I really did."

I sighed. "No, you didn't, Glenn. You did it for a reason I don't understand at all. It's people like you who pave the road to Hell with good intentions. Your notion of goodness is ass-backwards. So screw you, McNulty; a friend like you I can do without."

He started shaking his head before I was even finished. "You just don't understand. You just don't understand."

But I did understand. I sure as hell did. God save us, I thought, from the do-gooders who meddle in our lives because we don't understand.

I stopped the car at the entrance to Glenn's driveway and got out. The old Chevy was still sitting there, and without saying goodbye or even looking back, I started toward it, feeling in my pocket for the keys. I'd gone only a step or two, though, when I heard somebody call my name. Father Brady had seen us drive up and stepped out on the rectory porch to hail me. "Benny," he said, "could you come over a minute? I need to talk to you."

I think it was that innocent lilt in his voice that did it—that and the way he seemed to assume that all he had to do to meddle some more was call out and I'd come running. I looked at him, and then looked all around me. In the gutter on his side of the street I spied a broken brick, walked to it and picked it up. Flipping it lightly in my right hand, I looked up at him—the porch was little more than a high stoop—and said, "You want me, Father? Okay, here I come!" Then I threw the brick as hard as I could, aiming it straight for a big window just to his left, one of the windows of the room in which we had talked. It was an old window, the kind with only two panes, and the brick hit right in the center of the top one, making a hellacious noise and spraying glass in all directions. A perfect strike!

Glenn who had witnessed the whole scene, yelled my name and streaked across the street toward Father Brady, who just stood there as if he'd heard the first clap of thunder on Judgment Day. I walked calmly to my car, cranked it up and drove away.

Don't ask me why I drove to St. Agnes schoolyard anyhow. I knew Cherry wouldn't be there, hadn't been there. But somehow, in looking out over that empty schoolyard, I felt closer to her. It made no sense, I knew, but it made about as much sense as anything else did in my life lately. It didn't make any sense, either, to drive by her house. All I needed at this stage was to have her father spot my car and call the police. But I did it anyhow. Heck, the police were probably already looking for me. I could hear the bulletin crackling on police radios at that very moment: "Be on the lookout for Benjamin Blake, who's wanted for vandalism and terminal stupidity. You won't have any trouble spotting him; he's driving a junkheap on wheels." I could see the next day's headline too: "Teen Stones Priest; Says, 'I Did It and I'm Glad'." So what did I have to lose?

Didn't do me much good though. I saw the Cadillac there, but that was all I saw, and after one more trip around the block, I left. I felt sure Cherry was inside, but there was no way I could get to her. She'd have to contact me—and she would if she could, I believed. Might've already tried. I looked at my watch—two-thirty—and headed for home to wait by the phone.

I fully expected to walk into a nest of policemen waiting for me at home, or at the very least, a motherly hell-raising that would peel paint off the walls and put me on restriction until I turned twenty-one. But to my enormous relief, all was normal on the homefront. Incredibly, Father Brady had not called about the incident, and neither had Glenn. That floored me, but it really didn't matter. I still wasn't sorry I did it, and if I had to take the consequences, I would. Besides, I had another phone call on my mind, and when Mother said nobody had called, I sat down to wait for it.

189

I waited in vain. The minute hand on the clock moved as if mired in molasses, and I stared at the phone as if I could will it to ring. But it did not ring. And finally I knew it was not going to ring. Both my watch and the clock on the mantel said it was too late for her to call. It was three-thirty; she'd be at the airport by now and in thirty more minutes fly out of my life. My heart sank and I slumped deeper in my chair, mentally cursing Father Brady and Glenn. I had them to thank for this.

But a moment later I sat up with a bolt. I hurried around the house looking for Mother and Zeb, but couldn't find them. When I spotted them at the back fence, talking to neighbors, I yelled from the back porch, "Be back soon," and dashed for the front door. The keys to the car were still in my pocket, and in no time at all I was racing toward the airport.

Augusta's airport was a nice one. Located about fifteen miles south of town, it looked more like a country club than an airport, but it stayed pretty busy, mainly shuttling passengers to Atlanta, and I wondered if I'd be able to find a parking place close to the terminal. It was already three-fifty, and I was still a good five miles away.

That old Chevy was never the same after that drive. Feeling as if I were riding a plow horse in the Kentucky Derby, I gunned her through two stop signs, three red lights and over one curb, and when I got onto the highway running out to the airport, I put the gas pedal to the floorboard, and then tried to push it through. Honking my horn and blinking my lights, I wove in and out of traffic with a disregard for life and limb, mine and everybody else's, that I'm sure lives on in the lore of other drivers who saw me that day. But at four minutes till four, I roared up to the front of the terminal, slammed on the brakes and was out of the car and running toward the entrance before I even realized that I had left the car sitting there, right out in the street, door open, motor still running.

A few people near the entrance stared at me, wondering what the hell was up, but I paid them no mind. I dashed through the swinging doors, skidded to a stop, and looked up and down the length of the building. The terminal was small enough that I could sweep the whole area in a glance, but all I saw was people behind counters. At the rear of the building, though, through big plate-glass windows and another set of swinging doors, I spotted people standing about, as if waiting to see friends or relatives off on a trip. Hurrying closer I spied, out on the field, off to one side, the tail section of a big plane. It had to be Cherry's flight; no other planes were in sight.

I ran forward, but as I got closer my heart nearly stopped. I could see that most of the passengers had already boarded and that most of the other people were moving back toward the terminal.

I must have looked like a madman as I burst through the swinging doors and ran down a walkway toward the field. A policeman standing at the end of the walk yelled, "Hey!" and tried to grab me as I swept by, but all he grabbed was air. When I hit the sidewalk leading to the boarding gate, though, I saw that a security guard was shutting the gate. And looking beyond him, toward the plane, I saw Cherry and her father waiting to board. They were last in line—a very short line, and getting shorter as I got closer.

"Cherry!" I yelled at the top of my lungs. "It's me, Benny."

By this time, people were gawking at me and ducking out of my way—everybody, that is, except the security guard and the cop; the cop was now chasing me, shouting, "Stop! Stop!" and the security guard, looking startled and confused, stood his ground nevertheless.

As soon as Cherry saw me, she tried to run to meet me, but her father grabbed her and held her, and tried to hurry her aboard the plane. I could see that she was crying, but I also saw that there was no way I could get to her. I slammed against the closed gate and yelled so Heaven and half of Hell could hear me: "Cherry, I love you!"

About that time, the cop caught up with me, grabbed me by the arm and fought for breath to speak. But I beat him to it. Pointing toward Cherry, I punched at the air and shouted, "That girl is being kidnapped! Do something!"

The cop darted a look at the plane, where Mr. Ashford was all but pushing Cherry up the steps as she fought to break away, and then he looked at me. Confused, he tried to ask about three questions at once, but merely sputtered, so I screamed, "That girl is my sister and she's being kidnapped. Can't you see she doesn't want to go? Stop him!"

The cop might still be standing there if the security guard hadn't spoken into a microphone and put the flight on hold. I didn't hear what he said, but it was quickly obvious that that plane wasn't taking off until he had found out what the hell was going on. Seeing that, the cop said to me, "You wait here," and told the guard to open the gate. Seconds later, he was standing at the foot of the boarding stairs, one hand on his gun, ordering Mr. Ashford and Cherry to come on down. When they did, he led them away to the terminal, going out by another gate, and soon another cop, this one a sergeant, came and took me inside too.

It was some time before they let me see Cherry. They made me wait outside the office of the airport manager while the sergeant, a big barrel-chested man named Wallace, used the office to talk to Mr. Ashford and Cherry. Finally, though, the other cop, a sandy-haired, consumptive-looking guy named Compton, came out and waved me inside.

The first face I saw as I walked in was Mr. Ashford's, and it didn't look a bit more pleasant than it had that day in Cherry's den. Cherry, however, seated on a couch next to her father, jumped to her feet and ran to hug me. She was weeping quietly and I felt the dampness of her cheek on mine.

"Over here," said Sgt. Wallace. Seated behind a big desk, he pointed toward a chair near one corner of it and wagged his finger. I sat and Cherry went back to the couch. For a moment or two the room was silent, but then Wallace said, looking straight at me, "Did you know this man, Mr. Ashford, was Miss Ashford's father?" Wallace had a deep bass voice that seemed to start somewhere around his colon and use the rest of his body as an amplifier.

"Yes, sir."

"And don't you know, too, that kidnapping is a very serious charge?"

"Yes, sir."

Do you realize you held up a domestic flight?"

"Yes, sir."

"And that you created a situation where somebody could've gotten hurt?"

I hadn't thought of that one. Still I said, "Yes, sir."

He slapped the desk top hard and boomed, "Then why in the name of God did you do it? Did you think it would be great fun to run through the airport like a hare-brain scaring the wits out of everybody? You some kind of practical joker? Tell me."

I was so scared I was shaking, but I said simply, indicating Mr. Ashford with a wave of my hand, "They—the Ashfords—wouldn't let me see my girl." I pointed toward Cherry. "They sent her out of town to keep us apart and now they're sending her to Europe to keep us apart. Wouldn't even let us meet today to say goodbye."

Wallace looked flabbergasted. "You did all this to say goodbye to a girl?"

"Not just any girl. My girl."

Wallace sat back in his chair and shook his head. The look on his face said, "Youngsters nowadays are going to Hell in a taxi cab, and right here before me is the ding-a-ling who's driving." He pulled off wire-rim glasses that fit his big face so tightly they left red indentations along the sides of his head, and he sat there a long time rubbing his eyes and massaging the bridge of his nose. Finally, he put the glasses back on and said, "I oughta put you *under* the jail, you know that? Lucky for you, Mr. Ashford here says he'd rather not press charges."

"I don't want any favors from him," I said. Maybe I was being foolish, but I meant it.

Wallace said, "A false charge is serious business, son, and a false charge of *kidnapping* ain't funny one bit."

"Cherry's of age, eighteen, and he was taking her away against her will. If that's not kidnapping, what is?"

Mr. Ashford moved forward on the couch. "Now see here, boy . . ."

"No, Daddy," Cherry said, putting a hand on his arm.

Wallace looked at me and then at Cherry, and then at Mr. Ashford. "Boy may have a point there, Mr. Ashford." He stood up. "Tell you what, though: the more I hear, the more I think we got a domestic situation here. I think I'll just go outside and smoke a cigarette, and see if you three can't hash this out between you." He looked at me. "But I warn you. I'll be right outside that door, and if I hear any commotion in here, I'm gonna come back in here and we'll all take a ride downtown and see if we can't settle it there. Understood?"

After the sergeant left, neither of us spoke for awhile. At first, Cherry started to get up and come to me, but Mr. Ashford put out a hand to stop her, urging her to be patient, so she waited. Finally, Mr. Ashford, looking at me but addressing Cherry, began to speak. "Cherry, do you love this boy?" he asked.

"I think so," she said. "Yes."

"Do you know anything about him?"

"What is there to know?" she asked. "We went to school together. He's Benny Blake. His father's an army officer. He's going to Georgia to become a lawyer."

"Did he tell you all that?"

"Well, yes." She was clearly puzzled.

Mr. Ashford shook his head as if to say that Cherry

would never make it on her own in this world. "The only thing that's true there is his name."

Cherry looked at me, but said to him, "I don't understand."

"I did some checking, Honey," Mr. Ashford said; "he's a Milltown boy. Did you know that?"

"Well, no," she said, "but it makes no difference."

"And he's not going to college. His parents are too poor to send him. A year from now he'll be working in the mill. Is that what you want for a boyfriend, a millhand?"

"I *am* going to college," I snapped; "I just don't know how yet. I *won't* be a millhand."

He ignored me and patted her hand. "Honey, nobody from Milltown goes to college. They're not like us. College is for people like you, people of breeding, people whose parents can afford to send them. Why, that one outfit you're wearing cost more than his parents make in a month."

I looked at her clothes, surprised to hear that a single outfit could cost so much. She wore what appeared to be a simple sun dress of royal blue jersey with a white bolero jacket and blue high-heels.

"But, Daddy," she said, showing her impatience that he could be so dense, "you can *fix* all that. Give Benny a job at the bank. He can work there all summer. Then lend him the money to go to college. He can work at the bank every summer to pay off the loan, and he'll also be building a career, a respectable career."

"Hold on there," I said, getting to my feet. "I don't want any favors from him, and certainly not charity. I'll make my own way. And the last thing I want to be is a banker. No thanks."

"You see, Honey," he said, raising his hands in a show of helplessness; "even if I were willing to do that, he's not. You can't help these people. Oh, every now and then one of them makes something of himself, but look at this one: a "C" student at best; he was lucky to get out of high school."

Cherry turned on the couch to face her dad, "But,

Daddy, I love him. You just don't know him; he's very intelligent."

"Okay," said Mr. Ashford, slapping his thighs and rising; "if you want him so badly, take him. I guess you'll just have to learn the hard way. You don't want to go to Europe? Don't go. I won't send you to college either. From now on, you get nothing from me but meals and a roof over your head. And tomorrow morning you can start looking for a job, become self-supporting. Might as well find out right away what your new life will be like. See lover boy there anytime you please; just don't bring him to *my* house. You want him, you got him. Marry him, for all I care."

"But Daddy—"

"'But Daddy,' nothing," he said. "If you're determined to sink from your rightful station in life, go on and do it. But I won't *help* you do it. And don't come crying to me when you find out what a mistake you've made."

Cherry ran to me sobbing, hugged me and buried her face in my chest. Mr. Ashford looked at us, made a scornful face, and started to walk out of the room.

I panicked. I loved Cherry and wanted her with all my heart, had been through hell to get her, but I couldn't ask her to give up everything for me. I had nothing, *nothing*, but love to offer her in return. I couldn't even marry and support her. She *needed* her father and would be unhappy without his love. She also needed to go on to college. Nobody, I felt, should pass up an opportunity like that. *I* could get to college on my own, I believed, but a girl like Cherry? And where would a girl like her find a job? Why, she'd wind up clerking in a dime store. I had to think fast. Mr. Ashford was already opening the door to leave.

"Wait!" I called. "This has gone too far." I braced myself and told a whopping lie: "I like Cherry a lot, but I . . . I don't love her, and it's time I told her that." She stiffened in my arms and pulled away, her eyes searching my face for understanding. I held her at arms length and said, "Gee, Cherry, I never meant it to get so serious between us.

I was just foolin' around. I couldn't settle down to one girl. Everybody who knows me knows that. I mean, I like you 'n' all that, but—"

"Oh, Benny," she cried, a look of horror on her face. "How *could* you?" She started to sob and turned to her father, who opened his arms and took her in. When I left the room, he was patting her affectionately and saying, "There, there, baby girl, it'll be all right. Daddy was just upset."

Outside the office, Wallace and Compton were waiting. "It's all settled," I said. "Can I leave?"

Wallace gave me a measuring look. "Well, there is the little matter of your car. It's against the law, you know, to leave a running car unattended, and in the middle of the street, at that."

Compton stepped forward, waving a piece of paper in his hand. "Got the ticket right here, Sarge."

Wallace took it and said with a knowing look, "On the other hand, seeing as how you walked out of there alone, it could be that you've had enough things go wrong for one day." He held out the ticket and tore it up. "One of the skycaps parked your car. It's outside at the curb. Keys are in it."

"Thanks," I said, and left. I couldn't get out of there soon enough.

Johnny's eyes just got bigger and bigger as I told him that night what had happened—everything, that is, except about Glenn's mother. We were sitting on his front stoop so we could talk in private—Grace and Mr. Kelly were back in the kitchen—and Johnny said, "Boy, you sure know how to liven up a lazy Sunday afternoon, don't you? Tell you what: when you get your next Sunday afternoon all planned, count me out of that one too. You're lucky you ain't in jail tonight. Or the morgue. No. You belong in an insane asylum. You *got* to be crazy as hell, stopping a plane like that. I won't even mention accusing Billings Ashford of kidnapping his own daughter. He's a big man in this town, Benny. Why, he could swat you like a fly. Believe me, *no* girl is worth all that."

I hadn't yet told him the part about giving up Cherry just when I had won her. And when I did tell him, I didn't tell the truth. He'd only shake his head and laugh. I told him instead that Mr. Ashford offered to drop all charges if I promised to stay away from Cherry and that I accepted.

"*Now* you're being smart," Johnny said elaborately. "There are plenty more fish in the sea."

"Yeah," I said, looking away so he couldn't see my face when I said it. "Easy come, easy go."

Part 3

Chapter Nine

Mother said, "I'll be glad when you *do* go on vacation. I'm tired of seeing you mope around here like a sick cat." She was sewing again and I was slouched in a chair staring glumly at my right foot as if I'd never seen it before. Zeb had gone over to his sister's house.

I didn't say anything, but Mother wasn't any more tired of it than I was. Graduation had come and gone, and I'd hardly been out of the house since then. I had hoped against hope that somehow Cherry would get my address and write to me, but day after day passed with no letter, and now, after nearly two weeks, I knew none was coming.

"This is the second Friday night in a row you've stayed home," Mother said, looking up between flurries of stitching, "and you stayed home last Saturday too. Don't tell me nothing's wrong."

I could tell she was winding up for a real fuss and wondered how I could head it off. "Cherry's gone for the summer," I said, "and I don't know anybody to ask for a date. That's all."

She waited just a second too long for it to be a casual thought. Also, she tried a bit too hard for nonchalance. "Ask Inez."

I figured two could play that game. Very casually I said, "Mother, I think Inez has a boyfriend. I think somebody told me that. I forget who."

"No, she doesn't. Her mother works next to me in the weave room, and she was telling me just today that Inez hardly even dates."

"Maybe *that* was it. Somebody said Inez *doesn't* have a boyfriend, the idea being, I think, that Inez doesn't like boys."

Mother was sewing faster again. "Humph. Inez doesn't go out with just anybody. That's what *that's* all about. Somebody's just jealous and spreading malicious gossip."

"Gee, maybe so."

Her hands stopped moving and she looked at me. "So why don't you ask her?"

I looked at the clock. It was eight-thirty. "Oh, it's much too late."

Mother gritted her teeth. "Not for tonight, Benny—for another night. Ask her for tomorrow night."

"Well, I'd have to ask her no later than tonight, and she's probably not home."

Keeping her eyes on her lap, Mother said, "Well, you won't know until you call, will you?"

I felt trapped into making the call, but I still wasn't worried. No seventeen-year-old girl in all of America was at home at eight-thirty on a Friday night in June, and even one who just happened to be home then would already have a date for Saturday. Cocksure, I got up and went to the phone, looked up Inez Crowe's number and dialed it.

That's how I wound up with a date with Inez Crowe the very next night.

Inez hadn't been in the car five minutes before I knew I could make time with her on the first date. It wasn't that she seemed easy or anything like that. I was pretty sure Inez was a virgin. Word got around in Milltown about girls who put out. It was that she really seemed to like me and wanted me to like her.

To my surprise, I did like her, a lot better than I had thought I would. With no adults around, she didn't seem so prim and proper, so grown-up and serious. She talked and laughed easily, and seemed perfectly natural, though a little on the quiet side. She looked good too. A brunette, she was slender and shapely, about 5-feet-4, and had striking green eyes that seemed to take in everything while holding back just enough to make you wonder.

She agreed that it was too nice a night to go sit in a movie, so we went to the Varsity, ordered Cokes, and just sat and talked for awhile. She would miss high school, she said, but she was ready to get on with her life. She wanted to land a job as a secretary, right there in Augusta, and get married one day and have two or three children. That didn't sound very ambitious to me, but in a way I envied people like Inez, people who seemed content with the ordinary. It certainly made life simpler than my way made it. But I knew not to get into all that with Inez. Tell her I wanted to go to college, wanted to get out of Milltown, and she'd think I was putting on airs. People in Milltown didn't got to college, and if they got out of Milltown it was only to go to prison, the cemetery, or some other Milltown. So when Inez asked about my plans, I just said I was thinking of joining the Navy—"but not any time soon." I didn't want her to think she was wasting her time dating a guy who'd be gone next month or something.

But it probably wouldn't have mattered if I'd said I wanted to move to Atlanta and be a pimp on Peachtree Street. Underneath all this talk, something was going on between me and Inez that soon had us talking but not listening. As usual I was a little slow on the uptake, but as I became aware of this something, it felt like a spark trying to jump a gap, and when we looked into each other's eyes again, we made contact. She handed me her Coke, half-finished, and I flashed my headlights for service. As soon as the boy took away the tray, I left looking for a place to park.

Inez Crowe turned out to have the softest lips I ever kissed, and maybe the hottest mouth. She knew *how* to kiss too, so well, in fact, that she soon had me wondering how fucking could be much better.

I aimed to find out, though, and before long had my hands under the pullover top, caressing her naked back and opening her bra. It took a while before she'd let me raise it above her tits, but she finally gave in and laid her head back against the seat as I bent to suck the nipples.

When she moved her hand to my head to stroke it as I sucked, I put my left hand on her knee and began to sneak it under her skirt. She stiffened right away, closed her thighs tightly and gripped my wrist with her right hand.

I went back to kissing her, moving my hand to her breasts, and her kisses got hotter and hotter. So a moment later I slipped my hand under her skirt and got about halfway up before she stopped me.

It was quite awhile before she'd let me move it farther up, but I could tell she was weakening. Then, during an especially hot kiss, she relaxed her grip, so I pushed, her thighs opened, and suddenly I had my hand on her crotch.

Something was wrong though. It didn't feel like anything I'd felt before, and it was several moments before I figured out why: Inez was wearing a girdle.

I couldn't imagine why. Inez was as slender as a sapling. But the garment itself proved a much bigger mystery. I could find no snaps, no zipper, no ties—no opening of any kind—and it fit her so snugly that I couldn't even slide a finger under the thing. That was frustrating, but it didn't worry me too much; if Inez had put the damn thing on, I reasoned, she could certainly take it off.

But I soon saw that Inez was not going to help me. From the waist up she was a writhing, hot-to-trot female, lashing me with her tongue to new peaks of desire. But from the waist down she was as passive as a cow. She had opened her thighs; the rest was up to me.

I tried going in from the top, where the material was a bit more flexible. But about an inch below her navel my hand stuck as if caught in a vise and could go no further. Next, I hit upon the idea of rolling the girdle down from the top. But that merely made the material that much stronger.

I cursed my luck. God in His infinite mercy finally sends

me an apparently willing female, but she arrives wrapped in rubber, stuck fast in a goddam innertube. This was more like changing a tire than making out.

By now I was good and frustrated, and trying to get Inez to be just a little helpful. With any kind of cooperation, I figured, I could get both hands on the top of that girdle and shuck it off— if in the process I didn't slingshot her into the next county. But gentle hints and finally pleas for *some* assistance met with nothing but an occasional moan.

"Could you lift just a little?" I whispered.

"Ummm, ummm."

"Shift just a bit this way," I urged.

But Inez didn't move below the waist, and I soon saw that she had a defense that was even better than the girdle: as long as she *sat* on her cunt, nobody was going to get into it.

I gave up. I was sick and tired of whipping myself into a sexual frenzy with girls and getting nothing out of it but nutache. I was tired of the whole routine: dating, Teen Town, the Varsity, parking, petting. It wasn't getting me anywhere, and suddenly it all seemed pointless and silly. I had Inez home by ten-thirty and went on home myself. Next day, when Mother asked me about the date, I told her Inez was nice and that I liked her, but that in the future I'd prefer to pick my own dates. Mother never mentioned her again.

It was a real disappointment, but Johnny said that was the best he could do. He could go to the beach for a long weekend, but not for a whole week. Grace wanted him out looking for a job, and Mr. Kelly was backing her up. We had also planned to hitchhike to save money, but both Grace and my mother insisted that we take a Greyhound bus instead.

We got to Savannah around noon and out to Tybee Island about an hour later, and went looking for a place to stay. The rooming houses seemed overflowing with teen-

205

agers, but we soon found a room upstairs in a weather-beaten two-story house. The house didn't overlook the water, but it was right in the middle of things, and our room looked out over a porch to a backyard with an alley that ran down to the beach front. We unpacked and got into our bathing suits, and then went walking to have a look around.

Savannah Beach was mainly a weekend vacation spot popular with Georgians because of its wide sandy beach and, in spite of the state's blue laws, the Sunday sale of alcohol and the presence of slot machines. Most of the island was residential, with many of the owners renting out rooms and apartments, but clustered along the waterfront in the middle of the island were bars, beachwear stores, a small hotel, hotdog stands, restaurants, a shooting gallery, a bingo parlor, and a nightclub or two. Then, jutting way out into the water was a combination pavilion and fishing pier.

The pavilion, with games of all sorts, various concession stands and loud music, was easily the most popular part of the island. If you hung around for awhile anywhere near the pavilion, you'd eventually see nearly everybody who was at the beach. And that is where Johnny and I were standing, munching on french fries from cone-shaped paper cups, when Johnny, looking up the street that led down to the waterfront, said, "Your eyes are better than mine. Is that Dianne Damico up yonder?"

I looked up the street, but didn't see anybody I recognized.

Johnny said, "She just went into a store, Young's, I think. Let's stroll up that way."

Young's was a department store specializing in swimsuits, beach towels, suntan lotion, souvenirs—anything you could want for a beach vacation—but it sold other goods too, even furniture, and over the years had grown to a sprawling operation with entrances on three different streets. "We'll never find her in there," I said.

"We're not doing anything anyhow. Let's go. I need some suntan oil anyhow."

We didn't spot Dianne, and after about thirty minutes we gave up. "Maybe it wasn't her," Johnny said, "but I heard she might be down here."

"We'll see her sooner or later if she is. But then what?"

Johnny smiled. "Well, I'd sure like to see her in a bathing suit, wouldn't you?"

"I'd rather see her *out* of it," I said.

"If she's in one, most of her *will* be out of it."

We laughed, went back to our room to get towels, and then went down to the beach, where we stayed until it was nearly dark. After cleaning up, we went out to eat and then strolled around for a couple of hours, mainly looking at girls and batting the breeze. Around eleven, though, we both felt tired and decided to turn in. We wanted to get up early anyhow and go swimming as the tide was coming in.

Shortly before dawn I awoke to the sound of an angry voice, a woman's voice, coming from the room directly below. I lay there for a moment, listening, trying to get my bearings, and soon realized that Johnny was awake too. I turned to lie on my back and said, "What was that?"

"Some woman's giving her old man hell. It's been going on for an hour. Don't see how you slept through it."

I yawned. "What time is it?"

"About four. They came in about an hour ago and have been at it ever since. Or, rather, *she's* been at it. Haven't heard a peep out of him."

"What's it about?"

"I don't know, but whatever it was, she sure as hell didn't like it. She'll let up on him and then start in again, and she just gets louder and louder."

As if on cue the woman began again. "You did it, didn't you, Rufus? Didn't you?"

If Rufus answered, we didn't hear him, and after a moment, she added, "I know you did it, you sonofabitch, you bastard."

Johnny and I couldn't help laughing. The woman spoke with a country twang, the man's name sounded hickish, and we both imagined a hatchet-faced old crow from the

207

sticks giving her poor henpecked husband, suffering and silent, a down-home tongue-lashing.

We heard nothing for a moment or two, but she soon started in again. "You went off with that woman, didn't you, Rufus? You fucked her, didn't you? Just left me there at the party and went off and fucked her." Apparently she got no answer, for after a long pause she screamed in a shrill voice. "Didn't you?"

We heard a low rumble that must have been Rufus' reply, but we couldn't make out what he said. We could make out what he did, though: he slapped the hell out of her. The sound of flesh meeting flesh snapped in our ears like a pistol shot.

"Ouch!" Johnny said softly.

"Damnation," I said. "He really let her have it." Suddenly the quarrel wasn't very funny to either of us.

"You did it, Rufus," the woman screamed; "you fucked that bitch, that whore, and I know it."

All we heard in reply this time was a *ka-whop*. He had hit her even harder, judging by the sound of the blow.

I looked toward Johnny and he looked toward me. The first light of day glowed dimly in the window beyond him, and I could see that he was getting as concerned as I was.

"That guy's not foolin' around," he said.

"You can say that again. She must be a tough old bird, though; have you heard her cry out?"

"No, but, hell, she may be out cold after that last one."

She wasn't. "Rufus," she screamed, "you dirty sonofa-"

He hit her before she could finish, and when she opened her mouth to try again he hit her again, the blows echoing like rifle reports.

I winced at the sound of each one and stiffened as though bracing to get hit myself. Again Johnny and I exchanged looks, this time serious ones. Clearly the fight should be broken up, but were we the ones to do it? I had been cautioned all my life against interfering in a domestic quarrel. Where the devil was the landlady? What about other tenants? Surely nobody close by could sleep through this ruckus.

But the fight went on, and the next slap was followed by the sounds of wrestling: scuffling feet, grunts and groans, upended chairs, furniture being bumped, glass breaking, bed springs squeaking, and finally a blood-curdling noise. "Ahhhgggggh." It was the sound of someone strangling, a scream being cut off at the windpipe and drowning in saliva, a sort of tortured gargle being snuffed out. And then the woman's voice, quick and panicky, cut through the gray dawn like the squawk of a parrot. "Rufus! Rufus!" she gasped. "You're killing me! You're killlliing meeee."

Johnny and I bounded out of bed at the same instant. I grabbed my blue jeans off the arm of a chair near the bed, jumped into them in record time and, while snapping them on and zipping them up, fished about on the floor with my bare feet for my penny loafers. By the time I found my shoes and got them on, Johnny was dressed and waiting by the door. I hurried toward him, but stopped to listen when he raised a hand and pointed toward the floor.

The bed springs squeaked again and I thought I heard feet hit the floor, but otherwise it was quiet below. I gave Johnny a questioning look, but he extended his hands, palms up, and shrugged his shoulders. Jesus, I wondered, was the woman dead? I tip-toed over to Johnny so we could talk, but just as I reached him the woman spoke.

"You tried to kill me, Rufus." Her tone was matter-of-fact. Rufus said nothing that we could detect, and soon the woman said again, a bit louder, "You tried to kill me." A moment passed in which, again, we heard Rufus say nothing, and then we both jumped as she screamed at the top of her voice, "You tried to kill me, Rufus! You fucked that woman, you sonofabitch, and you tried to kill me!"

I braced for the blow and it was quickly delivered, followed by sounds of more scuffling.

I'd heard enough. "Johnny," I said, "see if you can find a cop. I'm going for the landlady, or anybody else who can help."

Johnny flew out the door and down the back stairs. I grabbed my tee-shirt, pulled it on and raced down the stairs too.

As I got to the bottom of the stairs, I heard the woman scream, "You're pulling my hair out," and then more urgently: "You're pulling my hair out!"

I looked around at nearby buildings, saw nobody, and then ran up the alley toward the front of our house. I took the front doorsteps in one leap, bounded across the porch and began banging on the landlady's door. No one came to the door and I heard no movement inside.

Racing back to the sidewalk, I looked up and down the street. It was deserted. Cursing under my breath I decided to run up to the intersection to look for help, but I hadn't taken two steps when a man's voice brought me up short.

"She don't stay there at night, Sonny. Rents out her rooms and goes and stays with her daughter."

"Uh, where's that?" I was looking all around. I still hadn't seen him.

"Up here," he said.

I scanned the porch of the house next door and finally spotted him, standing behind the screen door. He was nearly invisible in the gray light of dawn.

He went on talking. "It's on the other end of the island. Too far to walk."

Something in his manner made me reluctant to ask for his help, but I did it anyhow. He certainly looked big enough to help. "There's a big fight going on next door." I pointed toward the house. "I think a woman's life is in danger."

The man smiled. "Yeah, I been listening to that. Somebody sure is ketchin' hell." He wore only trousers and a sleeveless undershirt, and he stood there, hands in his pockets, and rocked back and forth on his heels, completely relaxed.

I approached his front steps. "I don't think you understand," I said, trying to keep my voice under control. "I'm staying upstairs over them, me and my friend, and her husband is beating her something awful."

"Well," he said slowly, still smiling, still rocking, "that's *their* business, ain't it?"

In his words I heard the voice of Zeb: "You interfere in a fight between a man and his wife and they'll both jump *you*. You can't win." But surely there were exceptions. I decided to try again. "Yes, but—"

"Me, I mind my own business and let others mind theirs. Ain't no skin off my nose if a man wants to beat up his old lady. Cops'll take care of that."

"Where can I find one?" I was nearly frantic to get moving, to *do* something, and the man was clearly a waste of time.

He smiled. "Doubt you'll find one this time o' morning, but you could check down around the lifeguard station. The police have a little office there."

"Thanks," I said. I knew the place and knew that Johnny would have gone there first, so I turned and ran back down the alley. I hoped as I ran that I'd see Johnny coming from the other direction, either with help or without it, but he was nowhere in sight. I'd have to go in there myself and do what I could to break up the fight.

I stopped at the foot of the stairs to listen for sounds of more fighting. Hearing nothing, I scurried up the stairs, taking them two at a time, and rushed into our room to search for some kind of weapon—anything that might serve as a club. There was nothing in the room itself, but when I looked inside the closet, I found an old mop, brought it out into the room and broke off the handle by pulling on one end while I stood on the other.

I liked the length of it. I could defend myself without having to get too close to old Rufus. Gripping it with both hands I swung it like a bat a couple of times. I liked the heft of it, and the way it swished through the air was satisfying too. I started toward the door.

Just then, I heard the *blam* of a screen door below. Puzzled, I hurried to our door to look out and saw over the porch railing a man walking toward a car parked in the yard. The back of his head was balding, so I guessed his age as thirty-five. He was shorter than I had pictured him, about 5-feet-8, but he was built powerfully, especially in the shoulders. Those shoulders could pack a wallop, I decided.

He strode across the yard, got into a dark gray Oldsmobile and started the engine. But as he was backing away to pull out of the yard the door below slammed again, and a second later a woman walked out into the yard, moving toward the car. I nearly dropped the stick in my hand. She was, from the back at least, the most voluptuous woman I had ever laid eyes on, and she was naked except for a pair of panties.

I must have been hypnotized for a moment by the sight of her as she tripped daintily through the sand, jiggling here, swaying there. Nearly as tall as Rufus, she had shoulder-length sandy blonde hair and a slender frame that flared at the hips into a magnificent ass and then flowed downward into long, shapely legs. At any rate, next thing I knew, Rufus was stuck in the soft sand of the yard, and the woman was trying to open the doors to the car, getting to each one a fraction late, it seemed, as Rufus frantically reached around to lock them.

I eased out onto the porch and moved to the railing, wondering what the woman would do next. For a moment or two, she beat on the window of Rufus' door with the heel of her fist while he sat gunning the engine, spinning his wheels furiously, spewing sand and getting nowhere. But then, when he stopped for a moment, she climbed onto the hood of the car and sat there, knees up, her hands locked around them, looking as calm as if she were sitting on the beach and watching the waves.

That didn't last long though. In an effort to dislodge the Olds from the sand—and maybe out of spite too—Rufus began to rock the car back and forth, throwing it first into forward gear and then quickly into reverse. The sudden lurching to and fro jerked the woman this way and that on the hood, tossing her about, arms and legs flailing, as if she were a rag doll caught on a shuttle.

Somehow she hung on, but I just knew she would be

hurled off at any moment and hurt, if not killed, so I headed toward the stairs hoping somehow to get her off that car safely.

By the time I reached the yard, Rufus was really gunning his engine, still rocking back and forth in the sand, but making headway. I saw that he might pull free at any time, and just as I headed for the car, he did, coming out backward and swerving as the rear tires danced around searching for solid ground. At that instant the woman flipped over backwards off the hood, on the side away from me, and disappeared from sight.

I yelled, "Stop!" and broke into a run, fearing that she had somehow rolled underneath the wheels, but when I raced around the front of the car, I saw her kneeling on the ground, a grim look on her face, clinging with both hands to the base of the car's radio antenna. Apparently this woman didn't know the meaning of give up.

Rufus rolled down his window, cursed at her and yelled, "Let go that antenna, you crazy bitch. Let it go or so help me god I'll drive off anyway. We'll see how long you can hang on then."

The woman tightened her grip and spit like an angry cat. "You go to hell, Rufus."

With that, Rufus flung open his door, flew out of the car, and grabbed her hands, trying to pry her fingers loose. When that didn't work, he kicked her on the leg and cocked his fist to strike her on the head. That was when I swung the stick with both hands with all my might, aiming for his head and hoping to knock it off. I missed his head. The stick slammed across his shoulders and broke neatly in half, and the lick seemed to do no more than get me his attention. He stared at me and blinked, obviously puzzled to see me there. But then, with a look of complete frustration, he let out a roar and backhanded me across the face, knocking me to the ground.

It is true that one sees stars when struck such a blow. I saw a whole galaxy, and when my eyes began to focus after a few seconds I was astonished to see the rear end of the Oldsmobile moving away from me and to find the woman bent over me, cooing.

"Did he hurt you?" she asked, the twang in her voice softened with sympathy. She was kneeling on one knee and cradling my neck in the crook of her arm.

I felt my jaw with my hand and moved it around a bit. "I don't think so. But what about you?" I shook my head to clear it.

"Never mind about me. You're bleeding, but I think it's just a scratch. His ring probably cut you there." She traced the wound with a finger and then showed me the blood on it. "Come on," she urged, trying to help me to my feet; "I'll wash that for you and put something on it."

I must have been groggier than I thought, for it was only as she was trying to lift me that I realized I was face to face with a woman who was all but naked. One of her breasts, in fact, was dancing right in my face, the nipple not more than an inch from the tip of my nose. Embarrassed, I glanced at her face to see if she had noticed, but she seemed completely unself-conscious. I saw for the first time, though, how pretty she was—hazel eyes with flecks of honey in the iris, a small turned-up nose, and small, white, even teeth that bit into a full lower lip as she strained to lift me. I got to my feet, still a bit wobbly.

"Hold on to me," she said, looping my arm around her neck and putting one of hers about my waist.

After a couple of steps I saw that I could walk just fine without assistance, and I told her so, but she merely shushed me and kept on walking toward the house. It felt so good to have her next to me that way, rubbing up against me as we walked, that I just kept my mouth shut.

We got inside her apartment and she sat me on the foot of the bed. "Lay back if you want to," she said.

I didn't want to. I couldn't take my eyes off her. She started toward the bathroom, which was just off the bedroom, but caught herself and walked to the closet instead.

A moment later she was pulling on a short, thin, pale blue housecoat and tying it at the waist. I wondered why she bothered; I could see right through it, and besides it only made her look sexier.

She went into the bathroom and came back with a damp washcloth. Placing a hand under my chin she lifted my face and dabbed gently at the scratch. "There now," she said; "does that hurt?" I said, "Uh, uh," and she dabbed some more and then looked at the wound closely. "It's not deep. It'll heal up just fine in a few days."

She went into the bathroom again and returned this time with a bottle. "This ol' alcohol is all I've got." She wet a facial tissue with some of it, warned me, "This'll sting," and patted it along the scratch. When I flinched, she leaned closer, pursed her lips and blew on it. Her nearness made me forget the sting.

She straightened up, studied her handiwork and said, "There, that ought to do it," and for the first time I saw her smile. Lord, she was pretty.

Shifting her gaze to my eyes, she said, "That was a brave thing you did, and you just a boy."

I spoke before thinking. "I'm not a boy."

Her eyes locked with mine again, and I knew she was looking at me, really looking at me as a person, an individual, for the first time. Her hands moved to my shoulders, and her eyes raked slowly down my body and then back up again. Finally, her fingers kneading my shoulders gently in a show of affection, she cocked her head and said in a quiet voice, "My mistake; you're obviously a man." She leaned forward and kissed me on the cheek, right on the scratch. Standing straight again, she added, a wistful look in her eyes, "It's been a long time since a man, or anybody else, stuck up for me, tried to protect me. Thank you."

I didn't know what to say, and, if I had, couldn't have said it. My mouth was dry, my tongue was tied, and my thoughts were skittering this way and that, some disappearing before I could seize them, others colliding with each other in total confusion. And when at last I *could* speak, I didn't say at all what I wanted to say. "How old are you?" I asked, clenching my teeth too late.

She laughed. "Twenty-seven. And you?"

"Twenty-one." She gave a doubtful look and I added quickly, "Well, almost."

"Truly," she prompted.

I blushed. "Eighteen. Going on nineteen."

She smiled. "Where'd you come from anyhow?"

"Augusta."

She laughed and poked me in the shoulder. "No, silly; just now."

"Oh." I nodded toward the ceiling. "I'm staying upstairs."

"Ummm," she said, looking thoughtful. "Then I guess you heard all that."

I nodded yes. "He your husband?"

She made a face, "He is, but he won't be for long. I warned him last time about fooling around and I meant it."

I glanced at the door anxiously. "Will he come back here?"

"No. He'll go on home, get drunk and stay over at his mama's place a couple of days. Then he'll come around, beggin' me to forgive him and take him back. I been through this before."

"Where's home."

"Statesboro. Know where it is?"

"Sure." It was a small county-seat town in south Georgia, about 60 miles from Savannah.

Suddenly, with an elaborate show of exasperation, she said, "I haven't even asked your name."

"Benny," I said before thinking. "That is, Ben."

"All right. Ben." She stuck out her hand for shaking. I took it and she said, "I'm Peggy. Peggy Bowles. Soon to be Peggy Andrews again."

I knew the next question was none of my business, but I

had to ask it. "Does he do that often—beat up on you, I mean?"

"This was the first time. And the last. Oh, he's threatened before, but he's basically a coward. He wouldn't've hit me this time if he hadn't been drinking. And guilty."

Suddenly it dawned on me that she didn't look nearly as battered as I had thought she would. One side of her face was red and a bit swollen, a scuff mark sat on her cheekbone, and a necklace of faint bruises ringed her neck, but otherwise she appeared unmarked. "You know, you're lucky; we thought he was killing you down here. We could hear the blows all the way upstairs."

She waved a hand, dismissing my concern. "Ah, he was only slapping me—not that it didn't hurt, 'specially when he hit me in the face, but that didn't happen but once. Knocked me awinding though. Made me mad too. The other licks were on my, uh, behind or somewhere else. They hurt though; they weren't love taps. One of 'em nearly broke my arm. It went dead for a few minutes." She frowned and began to massage her left arm, just below the shoulder. "Only time he really scared me, though, was when he strangled me." her hand moved to her neck. "I thought he *would* kill me then. I've never seen him like that before."

"Are you sure you're not hurt?"

"Oh, I'm fine. Just real tired. Haven't slept a wink, you know." She turned the left side of her face toward me. "How's it look?" But before I could answer, she walked over to the dresser mirror to see for herself. "Um," she said, moving her head this way and that, "a little makeup ought to hide the damage." She turned and smiled brightly.

"What will you do now?" I said. "I mean, how will you get home and all?"

"Buses run there every day," she said, unconcerned. "As for now, I looked forward to coming to the beach and I'm going to enjoy it— right after I get some rest."

I figured that was my signal to leave, so I got up, saying, "Good. Maybe I'll see you around."

"I hope so," she said, walking up to me and kissing me on the cheek. "And again, Ben, thanks."

I hadn't been back in our room five minutes when Johnny showed up. He had been unable to find a policeman and finally had given up.

"They say there's a cop on duty here at night, but I'll be damned if I could find him. Guy at the bus station said he's probably shacked up somewhere. I even tried to find out where, but if anybody knew they sure as hell weren't telling me." He pointed toward the floor as he crossed to the bed and sat on it. "What happened down there? Did he finally kill that bitch?"

"Naw. He left just after you did. It's all over." Something kept me from telling him what had happened. Peggy was not a bitch; she was warm and kind and good. But I felt that if I told him what had happened, it wouldn't come out sounding that way; she would sound cheap and crazy and common, and Johnny would laugh at her. I just kept quiet about it all and was glad he showed no further interest.

Johnny lay back on the bed, his head on a pillow, hands clasped behind his head. "Hey, guess who I ran into," he said, a big smile breaking over his face.

I gave him a puzzled look and sat on my side of the bed, at the end.

"Dianne Damico," he said beaming. "That *was* her yesterday. She's down here with her big sister. Staying at the Sand Castle—you know the place. Ran into her—Dianne, I mean—down by the pavilion. She likes to walk on the beach early in the morning."

Something told me there was more. I was getting to where I could read Johnny pretty good. I just waited.

"I told her we'd see her tonight. There's a dance at the pavilion, and she said she'd be there."

That sounded like a date, but I didn't mention it. "How's she doing?" I asked.

"Seems quieter than before, and a couple of times there I thought she wasn't quite with it—sort of off in another world. But, let me tell you, she *looks* better than ever. Nice tan, and had on white short-shorts and a white tee shirt. Man, oh, man!"

"Tough, eh?" I had a mental picture of her in that outfit.

"Lemme tell ya. All that meat—and no potatoes."

I couldn't resist. "Are you the potatoes? Is that what you have in mind?"

He smiled. "Well, I certainly wouldn't mind—"

He saw the look on my face and stopped. "Hey, if *you* want to go after her, be my guest. There are plenty more out there."

"No. It's not that."

"It's *some*thing," he said.

There *was* something, but I didn't quite know what, and besides it was really none of my business. Still, I owed him an explanation. Haltingly I said, "It just seems a little unfair to move in on her when she's just getting over her brother's death. I don't know. It's like taking advantage." I was no longer looking at him, but I could tell he was offended.

"People die every day. Life goes on. Besides, it's been—what?—a month now."

He was right, of course, and I knew it. Or at least part of me knew it. I had this ridiculous picture in my mind of a grieving, defenseless, pitiful girl who wanted to be a bride of Christ, and here was my best friend, caring nothing at all for her feelings, circling like a shark, closing in for the kill. Lamely I said, "But this girl wants to be a nun."

"Yeah," he snapped, "and *I* want a twelve-inch dick. What's that got to do with anything? She ain't a nun yet, is she? She wasn't struck dumb with grief, was she? She can still say no, can't she?"

I stared at the floor for a minute, thinking. He was right. I was being silly. Besides, it was no skin off my nose. I smiled, reached over, and grabbed his shoe and shook his foot. "You're right. If she doesn't want guys sniffling around, she ought not to wear short-shorts and tight tee shirts. I just have this thing about nuns, but it's silly. I'm getting worse than Glenn. What do you say we hit the beach?"

"Now you're talking," he said, rolling off the bed.

Five minutes later we were riding the waves.

That night, after a supper of fried shrimp, hush puppies, and iced tea, Johnny and I went to the pavilion. The dance was just getting under way, but the place was already crowded with teenagers. A five-man band was playing "Glowworm," and several couples were dancing, but most people were milling about or standing in clusters at the edge of the dance floor, talking, laughing, having fun. I scanned the crowd, but saw only a couple of familiar faces, and they belonged to people I didn't really know. I figured that most of the teenagers there were from Savannah, which would explain how they all seemed to know each other. That was all right with me. Savannah had some good-looking girls, I knew, and they seemed better able to let go and have a good time than Augusta girls did.

Johnny nudged me. "You see her?"

"Who?" I said. Then realizing that he meant Dianne I scanned the crowd again and said, "No."

But just as I said it she came up behind us. "Looking for me?" she said, sipping from a paper cup.

I turned and saw that she had meant that for Johnny. "High and low," he said, to which she gave a shy little smile that made me say to myself: *Uh, oh.*

She was wearing yellow shorts and a long-sleeve tee shirt with blue and white stripes, and smelled faintly of soap and suntan lotion. She looked terrific, and even her clothes seemed to know it: they hugged her curves as if it were a privilege to be worn by such a body.

"You know Benny," Johnny said.

"Hi, Benny," she said warmly. "How'd you do in Spanish?"

"C," I said, "and glad to get it. You made an A, I hear. Congratulations."

"School's over," Johnny said. "Let's dance." He took her hand and headed for the dance floor. "Here," she said, handing me her cup as he whisked her away. "Hold this."

The band was playing "You Belong to Me," a nice slow number, and I watched them as well as the other couples dance. The floor was crowded now, and somebody had switched off the brighter lights, to make things more romantic, I guessed. Then, without thinking, I took a sip from Dianne's cup and nearly lost my breath. It had looked like plain Coke, but it was laced heavily with whiskey.

I didn't say anything about it when they got back, but it preyed on my mind. The young people I knew did not drink, and certainly not whiskey. Oh, occasionally somebody, usually a guy trying to act like a big shot, would show up at a party drinking beer, but in general drinking just was not done, especially by nice girls like Dianne. Was that how she was coping with her brother's death, I wondered. Or was it just her way of saying, "I've put high school behind me; I'm grown up now"? Either way, it was troubling. It didn't jibe with what I knew of her or with my idea of how a girl going off to be a nun should be acting.

I shouldn't have let it, but it put a damper on my evening, and when Johnny finally grabbed us a booth that was coming vacant I just sat and, for the most part, watched him and Dianne dance. I might as well not have been there anyhow, for as the evening wore on they grew more and more involved in each other. Every now and then, though, Dianne would excuse herself and go over to another booth to visit briefly with friends, some people I'd never seen before, and each time she came back her cup was full again. I also had begun to notice a slight slurring of her words and maybe a little slowness in focusing her attention when spoken to. It was barely noticeable, and I might have overlooked it altogether if I hadn't known she was drinking. But finally, when she paid another visit to her friends, I said to Johnny, "She's drinking, you know."

I though he'd be surprised, but he said, "I know," and smiled like the cat that ate the canary.

"Johnny," I said, trying to shame him.

"She's a big girl, Benny," he said coldly and looked away.

"She's a *vulnerable* girl, Johnny."

His temper flared. "Hey, what are you—her guardian angel or something?"

"No—"

"And when did you get to be such a knight in shining armor?"

"I'm not, but—"

He leaned across the table. "Look, Ace, if you think I'm gonna pass up a chance to fuck Dianne Damico, you got another thought coming. I'd give my left nut to fuck her, and if you had any sense, so would you. I gave you first shot, remember?"

"Yeah," I said, getting sarcastic myself, "first shot at a crippled bird. Thanks, but no thanks."

He sat back. "Have it your way—but spare me this holier-than-thou shit."

I looked at him. "You really gonna do it?"

"Do it?" he said, looking amazed. "Does a dog eat meat? Fuckin' A, I'm gonna do it. In fact, I was just about to ask you to go play bingo or something for a couple of hours so I could take her up to our place."

"No way. If you do it, you'll do it without *my* cooperation."

He looked astonished. "You really mean that?"

"Johnny, the girl is confused—"

"You're the one who's confused."

"She's obviously still not over her brother's death, and on top of that she's drinking."

"What does that matter to you?" he demanded. "What is she to you?"

I wanted to say, "She's a human being." I wanted to say, "What really matters to me is my opinion of *you*." I wanted to say all that and more, but I knew it would sound namby-pamby. So I said, "So Johnny Kelly fucks a mixed-up girl who's drunk. Big deal."

He leaned across the table again. "Listen: I'd fuck Dianne Damico if she was dumb, deviled, crippled and blind. And so would every other guy here tonight. And so would you if you had any damn sense."

I started to say something, but he raised a hand to shush me. "She's coming back," he said.

Her cup was full again and now she looked noticeably tipsy to me. She tripped getting into the booth and spilled some of her drink. I looked at Johnny as if to say, "See," but he was paying attention to her.

"Where's big sister tonight?" he asked.

"Big sister had a big date," she said with a dazzling smile, her full lips parting to show perfect teeth. "She went to Savannah and won't be back until late." I noticed with relief that Dianne still sounded reasonably sober. Maybe my mind had played tricks on me. Or maybe she was just one of those people who could hold their liquor. But when she and Johnny went off to dance again, I sniffed her drink and sipped it, and found it still heavily laced with booze. Sooner or later it had to get to her.

When the song ended and they got back to the booth, Johnny surprised me by saying they were leaving. "We're gonna walk on the beach awhile, and then I'll take Dianne home."

"I'll just wait here for you," I said, hoping he'd take the hint. "It's only ten o'clock. You'll be back in fifteen or twenty minutes, won't you?"

"Naw, I think we'll be longer than that," he said. "You sure you wouldn't like to go play bingo or something?"

"No," I said, seeing that he was going to go through with it, one way or another. "I'll just walk on back to the room. I'm kind of tired."

"Later," he said.

"'Bye, Benny," Dianne said. "Good to see you."

I let them get nearly out of the pavilion before getting

223

up to go, and when I got to the front steps they were still in sight, apparently headed for the Sand Castle, a rooming house near the pavilion where Dianne was staying. I watched them for a minute or two and decided that Dianne was definitely tipsy. Not falling-down drunk, or anywhere near it, but she wasn't walking right, that was for sure. They had an arm around each other's waist, which was to be expected, I knew, but she seemed to be leaning on Johnny for support. Then, just as I was about to head on back to the room, I saw her sag momentarily against Johnny as if she had tripped. Johnny steadied her and they went on. I shook my head and started back to the room.

But I hadn't gone twenty steps when I whirled and started after them, breaking into a run because they were now out of sight, swallowed up by darkness. As I got near the Sand Castle, though, I saw them in the glow of an outside light. They were on the porch, moving toward some stairs. "Johnny!" I called.

They stopped and waited.

I had no idea what I was going to do or even what I *could* do. I stopped at the steps to the porch and said with ragged breath, "Can I see you for just a minute? It's private."

He said something to Dianne that I could not hear and she pointed a finger upward, as if giving directions, and then went on up the stairs. "Night, Benny," she called.

Johnny came to the edge of the porch. "What is it? Forget your key?"

"Uh, no," I said. "Actually, I wanted to, uh, try one more time to get you, well, uh, to leave Dianne alone—at least until she's sober."

He cocked his head in a show of exasperation. "Look, Benny, this has gone far enough."

"Actually that's what I was thinking too," I said, wondering what I could say to make him see. "This isn't like you."

"No, Benny; this isn't like *you*."

"Johnny," I said, "the girl is drunk."

"That's *her* lookout."

224

"You don't mean that. This is a girl we know, a girl we went to school with. She's not some whore."

"One," he said, counting on a finger and making a great show of patience, "she is not drunk. Drinking, yes, but not drunk. Two, I know she's not a whore, and I haven't treated her like a whore. Three, this may come as a surprise to you, sonny boy, but a drink ain't gonna kill Dianne, and a fuck ain't either. Now if you'll excuse me, I got business upstairs." He turned to go.

I jumped onto the porch and grabbed his arm. "Wait! What you say may be true, but this is true too: Dianne hasn't been the same since her brother died. Everybody knows that. You do too. And you're taking advantage of a girl who's still in shock."

He jerked his arm away. "And you're taking advantage of my good nature. Good night."

He turned to go again and I grabbed him again. But this time he whirled and brought a flying fist with him, hitting me flush on the temple and ear, and knocking me down the steps. I landed in the yard on my ass and elbows and lay there looking up at him, stunned more by the fact that he had hit me, *could* hit me, than by the blow itself. "You hit me," I said, realizing as I said it that I sounded like a ninny.

"I warned you," he said, glaring at me from the porch, clenching and unclenching his fists.

"No, you didn't," I said.

"Well, I'm warning you now. Get off my back. You're not me and you're not my conscience, and all this bellyaching over a little piece of ass is ridiculous. No wonder you can't get any pussy. You can't even decide if you really want it: yes, no, maybe, what if, how come, supposin' this, supposin' that. Shit, by the time you make up your mind, the girl's home in bed, fast asleep. You're worse than Glenn; at least he *knows* he doesn't want it." He looked at me scornfully for a moment. "Catholics!" he spat. "You can't even beat your meat without thinkin' the Devil's got you by the balls. Well, I got news for you and the whole damn Catholic Church: pussy is more powerful than all of you put together, and a damn site better too. Wise up. Grow up." He turned and marched up the stairs.

I got to my feet slowly, brushing sand off me, and walked on back to the place we were staying, Johnny's words ringing in my head— especially the part about me and Catholics. I didn't like it worth a damn, but there was some truth to it, I had to admit. My ear was burning too from the blow, and when I felt it I saw that it was bleeding a bit. Damn! I thought: first it was a fight a month; now it was one a day. And on top of that, one of them was with my best friend. I just wasn't living right.

Just as I got to the bottom of the stairs leading up to our room, somebody called my name. It startled me, because I hadn't seen anybody around as I came down the alley and through the yard, but I soon realized that it was Peggy.

"Over here," she said. "I'm on the porch. I *thought* that was you, but I wasn't sure until you started up the stairs."

It was dark as pitch near the house, and I had poor night vision anyhow, but when I stepped up onto the porch, following the sound of her voice, I saw her outline. She was sitting in a swing at the darkest end of the porch.

"Reach inside the screen door there and turn on a lamp," she said, "and then come join me."

The lamp was a small one, but it helped a lot, throwing a soft light through the door and a window near the swing. I went over and sat down beside her, realizing as I did how tired I felt. But I was glad to have company, especially hers. Her smile was as warm as her voice, and she looked beautiful. She was dressed as if she had been out—a white, filmy short-sleeve blouse, a straight skirt that looked pink or peach, and white high-heels. She looked fresh and cool, and smelled faintly of soap and powder.

"High-heels at the beach?" I said.

She laughed. "Yeah. I just felt like dressing up. Dressing up and going out. Being good to myself, you might say. So I took a long bath, got dressed, and went out and treated myself to a good meal down at the Brass Rail—just me,

myself, and I. Got back about an hour ago and been sittin'
here ever since, contented as a sow. But what about you?
What's a boy your age doing at home alone on a Saturday
night at the beach?"

I sighed. "That's sort of a long story."

She looked at me. "Well I'm not going anywhere; are
you?" Then her smile faded and she leaned closer, peering
at the side of my face. "Benny, you're bleeding." Self-
consciously I wiped at my ear with my fingers, but she said,
"Wait," and reached into her purse and got out a Kleenex.
She touched it to her tongue to wet it and then dabbed at
the blood. "Just a scratch," she said, "but your ear's all red."
She leaned back a moment. "Say, is that part of your long
story?" She went back to work on my ear.

"Yeah, guess it is."

She was still concentrating on my wound. "Were you
helping another damsel in distress?"

"That's what *I* thought; *he* thought I was sticking my
nose where it didn't belong. And I guess he was right."

She looked at me again. "Was that it, really? I was just
teasing, you know."

"You hit the nail on the head."

She smiled, wet the Kleenex again, and put it to my ear.
"Well, what *is* this thing with you and fair maidens? Are
you the Purple Avenger or something? Augusta's answer
to Sir Galahad?"

I scoffed. "I'm Augusta's something or other, but I'm
damned—I mean 'darned'—if I know what." I made a
mental note to watch my language. I knew it had gotten
awful lately, and now, around Peggy, was a good time to
clean it up some, I figured.

"There," she said. "The bleeding's almost stopped. Hold
this Kleenex to your ear for a few minutes. That should do
it. Now, back to the mystery of Benjamin Blake." She put
her hand on my arm. "But first I'm going to get us a tall
glass of iced tea. Fresh-made. Want lemon?"

I said I did and she got up and went inside. Minutes
later she was back. "Here," she said, handing me a glass

and then sitting beside me. "Now tell me that long story."

I set out to tell her a *short* story, just about Johnny and Dianne, and how I'd wound up getting knocked on my rear end again. I wanted to keep it brief so I wouldn't bore her. Besides I didn't particularly want to hear all that crap again. But as I told the story, it turned out to have more roots and runners than a grapevine, and by the time I finished I'd told her nearly my life story, it seemed: all about my troubles on the Hill, all about Cherry, all about Austin, all about Johnny, all about Glenn—heck, even about Inez Crowe, the latex virgin. It must have been near midnight by the time I got through. Peggy and I both had drunk three or four glasses of tea, each of us had made a couple of trips to the bathroom, and the evening air had turned from balmy to chilly. But she had listened very closely to every word, it seemed, and wouldn't let me stop until I'd told it all. Now that I had, I felt in a way like the Ancient Mariner, but I also felt oddly cleansed and refreshed. "You must be bored stiff," I said, "I'm sorry, but you did ask for it."

She smiled. "I'm stiff all right, but it's from sitting."

I thought that was my cue to leave, so I said, "What you need is a good night's sleep. That's what I need too."

She gave me a solemn, thoughtful look. "No. No, Benny, that's not what you need. It's not what I need either." I looked at her, puzzled, waiting for her to explain. Instead, she said, "Come with me. I've been meaning to put some alcohol on that scratch."

"Oh, it's all right," I said. "You must be tired of doctoring on me anyhow."

She stood up. "Don't argue with the nurse, Benny. Right this way." She took my hand and led me inside. "Close the door, please," she said over her shoulder. "It's turned cool."

I closed the door and waited. Soon she came back from the kitchen with a basin of water and a washcloth. She put them on a table by the bed, pointed to the bed and said, "Sit," and then went back into the kitchen. This time she came back with a bottle of alcohol and some cotton, went over to the window and pulled the curtains closed, and then came around to where I was sitting. "Can't be too careful with scratches in hot weather," she said. Putting down the alcohol and cotton, she snared the washcloth from the water and wrung it out. Placing her left hand under my chin, she turned my head to the side and gently put the warm cloth to my ear. "Do you mind if I tell you something about girls, Benny, about all females?"

I could feel her breath on the side of my face. "I wish *some*body would," I said. I wished too that she wouldn't call me Benny.

"Now don't get your feelings hurt, but women aren't pieces of meat. They're just like you, except that they're made different, and you're not a piece of meat, are you?"

I wasn't sure what she was getting at, but I nodded.

She continued. "Sure, girls want you to think they're attractive—but not just because they've got breasts and a vagina, and maybe a pretty face. A girl wants you to see her as a whole person, to like her for *who* she is, not *what* she is."

"But—"

"Let me finish." She dipped the cloth in the water again. "Now, I *know* that you do like girls—and respect them. You proved that with me. You proved it with Dianne. Seems that your problem comes when you get romantically in-volved. You start thinking of sex, and pretty soon that's all the girl means to you."

I didn't like hearing it, but she was right. I told her so.

She soaked the cloth again. "But that's not unusual in a boy your age," she said. "Once you get some experience you'll be fine."

"But, Lord!" I said wearily; "how long do I have to wait?"

"Oh," she said, dabbing the warm cloth to my ear, "you never can tell about such things." She dropped the cloth in the water and said, "Now for the alcohol." She got the bottle and cotton and sat on the bed beside me. "Scoot down a bit and put your head in my lap. No. Wait a minute." She stood up, handing me the alcohol and cotton. "I don't want that stuff to spill on my skirt. It's new." She reached to her side, undid a button, pulled down a zipper and stepped out of the skirt.

My eyes got wide and time stood still for a moment. But she was so matter-of-fact about it that I felt guilty for looking. I was just a boy to her, a friend. Taking off the skirt meant nothing. Besides, she still had on a slip.

She folded the skirt and laid it carefully over the back of a chair, paying no attention to me, and then turned. As if having a second thought, she said, "Don't want to get it on this slip either. It's silk." Hooking fingers in the waist band, she pulled off the slip and put it too on the chair.

Now, from the waist down at least, she wore only white panties, stockings and high-heels, and suddenly my cock was stiff enough to hang a coat on. I couldn't help it: I was staring.

She turned to walk toward the bed, saw the look on my face, and stopped. "Benny," she said, laughing a little, showing surprise. "It's nothing you haven't seen before. In fact, it's less."

I felt my face burning. "Sorry," I said and made myself look away.

In a bright voice, she said, "Panties are new too. What do you think?"

I looked and she did a slow turn, inviting me to examine them. I tried twice to speak and couldn't, but finally said in a squeaky voice, "Nice." I cleared my throat and said again, "Nice," and then held my breath.

But as quickly as that, the show was over. All business again, she came to the bed, took the alcohol and cotton, and sat down. "Wouldn't want to get it on your shirt, either. Take it off."

I stood beside her on trembling legs and fumbled for buttons before I realized I had on a tee shirt. I pulled the tail out of my blue jeans and hoisted the thing over my head. While my eyes were covered, I felt a hand on my hip, and then another on the front of my jeans. I froze.

"What's this, Benny?" She sounded surprised, curious, innocent. "It feels swollen. Do you hurt there too?"

I pulled the shirt all the way off and looked at her hand on my crotch. When I saw it there, my dick gave a lurch. But I could not speak.

She reached for my belt and unbuckled it. "This looks much more serious than a scratch, Benny. I'd better have a look at it."

She unsnapped the jeans and lowered the zipper, and then gripped the cloth at the hips to tug the jeans down. Soon they were puddled around my feet and I stood there in jockey shorts. She pulled those down too and said, "Step out." I did and she studied my cock for a moment, and then said, "Um, this may be a bigger problem than I thought. I'm putting you straight to bed." Her voice had gotten low and kind of husky. She got up, pulled down the covers, and said, "In you go."

Moving like a robot, my mind a blank, I took off my shoes and socks and got into bed. Shy, still embarrassed, I pulled the sheet up over me. Peggy turned off the light, and for a moment I couldn't see her. But soon she was at my side, sitting on the edge of the bed, and as my eyes adjusted to the dark, I saw that she was taking off her stockings. That done, she turned toward me, one knee touching my side, and said, "Don't want to wrinkle this blouse either." By now I could see pretty good. Light from somewhere in the alley leaked through one window, and moonlight filtered through the top panes of another. Peggy slipped the blouse off, hung it on a bed post behind my head, and then unhooked her bra, slid it down her arms and hung it on the post too.

She looked so pretty, like a vision glowing faintly in the moonlight, but close, warm, attainable, that desire and longing shot through me like lightning. But I could not move. Move? I could barely breathe.

"And now," she said, taking hold of the sheet at the top, "Let's see what we're up against here." Edging toward my knees, she pulled the sheet down slowly, up and over my cock, and dropped it on my thighs. Gently, she cupped my balls in her left hand and began to massage them. Leaning closer, she took my cock in her right hand, moved it this way and that, as if examining it, and then looked up at me. "No telling when a swelling like this will go down, but I'll do the best I can. Do you think a kiss would make it well?"

I tried to say something, but a sound like gargling came from my throat. And that turned into a moan as she lowered her head, put her lips to my cock and then flicked it with her tongue.

The feeling was heaven and hell at the same time, and part of me, maybe my cock, wanted to just lie back and float away on waves of pleasure. But I had to get this woman in my arms, had to feel her against me, taste her lips, smell her, eat her up if I could. With a groan that nearly became a scream of desire, I leaned up, grabbed her by the arms and hoisted her up to face level, turning as I did so that suddenly she was beneath me. She hit the bed squirming, kissing, writhing, clutching, her hands all over me, her legs opening, the panties gone. My cock felt her moist cunt, nudged open the lips, and I plunged it home so hard it took her breath. "Oh, Benny," she moaned, grabbing me by the ass to hold me in, to hold me still. "So good," she whispered, moving her hips in a gentle circular motion for awhile, and then in a sort of lazy-eight formation. Between gasps of pleasure, she kissed me all over the face while I nibbled at her neck and shoulders, and rubbed my face in her hair.

Soon I started moving my hips too, following her lead, and I quickly got the hang of it. The idea, it seemed, at least with her, was sort of like a game of tag. She'd move it around while I tried to hem it in and tag it, and every time I tagged it she'd grunt or moan with pleasure, and then move it again. I didn't care what it was called; it was absolutely the best thing I'd ever felt, better by far than I had even imagined—and different too. It was a feeling simply beyond description, and something Johnny had said flashed into my mind; this *was* powerful stuff. I didn't know if it was more powerful than Catholicism. Actually the comparison seemed absurd. But I knew *I* would never feel guilty again for wanting sex. The Vatican just didn't know its ass from third base.

Peggy was now quickening the pace, and I picked it up too. She also stopped moving her hips in circles and began to heave them straight at me, urging me deeper and deeper into her. Gone now was any notion of play; this was serious business.

I gripped her tighter, noticing a film of sweat between us, and hammered my cock home again and again and again. Suddenly she convulsed, cried out, and froze except for violent trembling, and when I felt her cunt spasm around my cock, I slammed it in one more time and damn near shorted out my brain, so good, so intense was the pleasure of coming in my first woman.

Before long, I rolled off her and lay on my side, looking at her. She lay so long with her eyes closed, one arm over her forehead, that I thought she might have fallen asleep. Finally I said, "Peggy."

"Um," she moaned.

"You asleep? Am I supposed to leave now?"

She turned to me quickly, searching my face with her eyes. "No!" she said. "Whatever gave you *that* idea? I was just floating and dreaming. No. It was wonderful! You're not going anywhere, at least until seven o'clock or so. My bus leaves at eight." Her eyes widened. "You don't have to go, do you? I mean, might as well stay here as go upstairs."

"No, I don't have to go. Don't *want* to go. This is the best place I've ever been."

She laughed and kissed me on the cheek. "Besides, that swelling has gone down, but something tells me it's only temporary. No, Mr. Blake, I'm afraid this treatment might take all night." She reached for my cock, pulled me down beside her, and kissed me.

It did take all night, all of a wonderful night, or most of it, and during it Peggy taught me many things, things that would leave me forever in her debt and her in my memory. I don't know when we drifted off to sleep, but she woke me at seven with a kiss. "Ben. Ben, honey. Wake up."

I opened my eyes, yawned and stretched. I felt like I had just closed them, but the memory of the night before made the loss of sleep seem like nothing. Peggy was already dressed and nearly ready to go, it appeared, so I rolled to the side of the bed and reached for my jeans, still on the floor.

"I see that swelling has gone down," Peggy said. She stood in front of a dresser, putting on lipstick and watching me in the mirror.

"Yeah. Your treatment certainly did the trick."

She turned and curtsied. "You were good medicine for me, too. In fact, the best."

I blushed. "You really mean that?" I zipped up the jeans and got my shirt.

She walked over to me. "I certainly do, Ben Blake, and don't you ever forget it."

"Not likely, ma'am, not likely—and thanks for calling me Ben." I pulled the shirt over my head.

She regarded me closely. "Yeah. Suits you better. More grown-up. Besides, you earned it."

She smiled and I felt a stab at my heart. "Do you have to go?"

She kissed me lightly on the lips. "Yes. There's a little boy at home—my mother's keeping him for me—and he'll be wanting his mommy."

"Will I ever see you again?"

"You better," she said with a pretty pout, followed by a smile. "Heck, if you were about five years older I'd take you with me."

"Give me your address."

"Why, of course," she said, looking amused. She went quickly to the dresser, picked up a sheet of paper and handed it to me.

I saw that she had already written her name and address on it. I smiled and thanked her, and folded the paper and put it in my pocket. Then I stood there, thinking of a thousand things to say, but saying none of them. Feeling awkward, I looked about for my shoes and socks.

I put them on, watching as she primped in the mirror again, and it struck me that for the first time in my life I knew what mysteries lay beneath the clothes of a fully dressed woman. It felt mighty good to know that, and even better to realize that knowing didn't spoil the pleasure. If anything, it made it nicer. So many things, it seemed, weren't all that good when you got past the pretty wrappings—like a Christmas present that turned out to be a dud: handkerchiefs from your Aunt Pauline or something. But, Lord, I could unwrap something like Peggy every day for the rest of my life and never get tired of it.

She turned from the mirror, ready to go. I stood up and walked to her. "Kiss me goodbye," she said.

"It'll smear your lipstick," I warned. As much as I wanted to kiss her, she looked so pretty I hated to mess her up.

"That's another thing, Ben," she said, tears coming to her eyes. "With girls, do more kissing and less thinking."

I blushed and said, "Yes, ma'am," and then she gave me a kiss so sweet it made me ache.

"And another thing," she said, leaning away in my arms, locking my eyes with hers: "your friend Johnny was right. You're *not* him. Just be yourself. That's plenty good enough."

We kissed again. Pulling away, holding her hands, I looked hard at her face, hoping to print a picture of it in my mind forever. Then I turned and left, wanting to get out of there before the tears came.

Johnny wasn't in the room, and the bed had not been slept in. That surprised me, but it shouldn't have; I'd been awake most of the night and hadn't heard him come in. It all meant to me that he had spent the night with Dianne, and though that whole thing no longer seemed the big deal that it had the night before, I still didn't think it was right. It made me think that Johnny cared for no one but himself. It still hurt, too, to think that he would hit me. I couldn't imagine a situation in which *I* would hit *him,* and that said to me that he didn't like me as much as I liked him. Get in his way and he'd knock you down, no matter who you were. Peggy was right: I wasn't like Johnny. Getting what I wanted mattered a lot to me, but if I had to be *that* way to get it, I'd rather not have it.

Suddenly I was glad Johnny was still out. I didn't feel up to facing him yet. And I was especially glad that I didn't have to explain where I'd been all night. I wouldn't have told him about Peggy anyhow—that was too good to share, too special to tell to anybody who'd see it as only a roll in the hay—but at least I didn't have to make up some lies. I wasn't ready to be friends again either. That would mean I'd have to hear about him and Dianne, and I just didn't want to. I didn't know if I'd ever want to.

Before I even knew what I was doing I was throwing my clothes and other stuff into my travel bag and leaving. I left a note on the dresser, using my room key as a paperweight, saying that I'd gone home—that and nothing more—and got out of there. Starving, I walked up the alley, away from the beach, hoping to avoid running into Johnny, and found a place serving breakfast. An hour later I was on a bus headed for Augusta.

Chapter Ten

The last two weeks of June seemed to fly, but July brought a heat wave in which time seemed stuck in a puddle of melting days and sultry nights. I hadn't been back to the Hill since talking to Cherry's dad, and had no intention of going back anytime soon, but when day after day topped the one-hundred degree mark, I was tempted. All the homes I'd been in on the Hill had central heating and air. Such a home in Milltown would have been a tourist attraction. With two window units, one in the middle room and one in the living room, we were probably among the more fortunate Milltowners, but both of those units running night and day couldn't pull the temperature in either room below eighty. The house, with high ceilings and no insulation, trapped heat like an oven.

Around the middle of July I began to feel trapped in it too, but at the same time I felt myself sliding into a don't-give-a-damn attitude that made escape seem unimportant. Since coming home from the beach I'd hardly gone out at all during the day, hanging around the house in nothing but blue jeans, blinds drawn, reading. Even at night I did no more than go once a week with Glenn to meetings of the Naval Reserve, which I had joined reluctantly in my first week back from the beach, and to an occasional movie. Dating seemed too much of an effort; I didn't know anybody I wanted to take out anyhow. And I hadn't seen Johnny since the beach. He hadn't come around or called, and I hadn't bothered either. I missed him, but I just wasn't ready to see him again—and didn't know when I would be.

Glenn had talked to him. Johnny had found a job. He was an apprentice draftsman for some architect downtown. Didn't like it much, but at least Grace was off his back.

Glenn was full of other information too, and on our rides to and from reserve meetings on Tuesdays he filled me in. Rusty Brown had joined the Marines the day after graduation and was in boot camp at Parris Island, down on the South Carolina coast, near Beaufort. Austin and Holdenfelt were going steady. Chuck Conlin had been accepted at Georgia Tech. Wanted to study electrical engineering. "Good," I said. "Maybe the sonofabitch will grab hold of a hot wire while standing barefoot in a pool of water." I didn't really wish that would happen; I said it partly because of the mood I was in and partly just to get a rise out of Glenn, which in a way showed me how bored I was. Anybody could get a rise out of Glenn; all you had to do was say something unkind about somebody, something cynical about life in general, or anything in the slightest way "unChristian."

By mid-July my once-a-week meeting with Glenn had become my main source of news about the people we knew in Augusta. Even so, I listened to most of it with dull interest. I did perk up a bit when he told me that Cherry was in Europe going to school. But he didn't know what school or even what country. Big help.

He also got my attention when he said that Miss Johnson was now Mrs. Ramsey. She and the coach had eloped back in June while I was at the beach, slipping over to South Carolina one night to tie the knot. Their secret was only now leaking out.

"Lucky bastard," I told Glenn. "How'd you like to run around *that* end for the rest of your life?"

"Benny," Glenn groaned. "She's married."

"I can dream, can't I? Imagine those long, silk-stockinged legs sticking up in front of you like goal posts and you on the one-yard line. Could you score, or could you score?"

"Benny," he groaned again.

I ignored him. "I'd call a play right up the middle, wouldn't you? I'd bust right through there and stick it in the ol' end zone. Down! Ready. Set. Go! I'd light up the ol' scoreboard with a big six and then ask if she wanted to go for eight." By now I was thinking not of Miss Johnson, but of Peggy, who had taught me, among other things, that sex didn't have to be so deadly serious. It had its serious moments, of course, but it could be fun too, especially with a playmate like Peggy.

"You wouldn't score," Glenn said, scoffing. "You wouldn't even play, 'cause you're sick, sick, sick." He laughted loudly, getting a big kick out of his own joke.

I laughed too, not only because it had been a pretty good line, but because humor from Glenn, especially about sex, came as such a surprise. "Hey, you're feeling your oats these days, aren't you?"

He turned thoughtful. "Yeah, I guess I am." He looked at me as if weighing whether to say something, and finally said it. "Benny, we brought Momma home last week, and she's a *lot* better. She hasn't had a drink since that Sunday we took her down there. She's a different woman."

"I'm glad, Glenn, for her sake *and* yours." I really meant it.

The heat wave held through the rest of July and burned right on into August. The house remained an oven, but outdoors was even hotter, like walking into a blast furnace. The sun put a fierce glare on everything; tree leaves, covered with a film of dust, drooped like tongues hanging out; and radiant heat rose in billowing waves from the streets and sidewalks, making the world look slightly unreal but oddly beautiful, like a gallery full of impressionist paintings.

Much of the time, I felt the same way—not beautiful,

but slightly unreal. Something was going on deep inside me, it seemed, and all I could do was wait to see what it was. I tried to figure it out, but whatever was working on the problem didn't want my help and wasn't answering any questions either. "Wait outside," it seemed to say, disappearing behind closed doors down a dark hallway. "We'll call you when we're ready."

About the only thing that lifted my spirits was getting a letter from Peggy, who wrote every other week or so, and then writing her back. I tried to keep my letters to her light and bright, but I knew they were full of vague dissatisfaction and longing. Hers were better: caring, funny, encouraging, filled with news of what was happening in her life, and occasionally sexy in a teasing, playful way that brought back that night at the beach in a series of erotic and tender images. Especially interesting to me was that she had filed for a divorce, but that Rufus wouldn't leave her alone, so she was thinking of moving up to Atlanta to stay with her sister while looking for a job. I thought it was a good idea to get away from Rufus, but I wanted her to move to Augusta. She said she didn't know anybody in Augusta but me, but that Atlanta wasn't that far away and that I could visit. I understood and let it go at that.

Between letters from Peggy I just kept on drifting from one day to the next, and finally my mother began to worry about me. I'd been extra careful around her to act as normal as possible. I had even started going out nearly every night, mainly because I was restless, but also to make her think everything was all right. I knew she'd think I was somewhere close by. Lots of Milltown guys hung out at The Corner, which was a combination grill and pool hall at a bus stop three blocks from home. Three blocks in another direction lay Allen Park, where the swimming pool stayed open on summer nights until ten o'clock and where baseball games played under the lights might last until eleven. Too, across from The Corner stood Jennings Stadium, home of the Augusta Tigers, and I had grown up hanging around there at night when the team played at home.

But I wasn't going to any of those places anymore. At least none of those places was my destination. I'd start out walking to one of them, get there and keep on going, going nowhere in particular. Just walking. I must have walked five or six miles some nights. I made the mistake, however, of coming in later and later each time, and Mother finally nailed me. One Friday night, when she didn't have to go to work the next day, she waited up for me, and the look on her face when I came through the front door told me I was in for it.

"Well, it's about time," she said, looking at me, and then at the clock on the mantelpiece, and then back at me. The clock, a pink and white ceramic thing with winged cherubs, pointing out the time with chubby little arms, said one-thirty. Mother sat in an overstuffed chair facing the door.

"Sorry. I didn't realize it was so late."

"It's not," she said, sarcasm coloring her voice. "It's early—for you. Last night it was two-ten. Night before, it was two-twenty. Night before that, five till two. Benny, *what* is going on?"

I was surprised that she knew so precisely when I had come in. That meant that she was staying awake each night until I got home, and I knew she needed her rest. To get to work by seven, she got up around five-thirty each morning during the week. "I'm really sorry, Mother. I'm just restless, that's all." I eased into the overstuffed chair by the door.

"I'm restless too, Benny—and it's because of you. Now I want to know what's going on, what's wrong."

I saw that she wasn't going to be put off by a simple answer, so I got ready to explain it as best I could. But before I could begin she said, "Where do you go? What's there to do at this hour of the night? Everything's closed up, isn't it? Zeb said the ballgame was over three hours ago, and no movie lasts to this hour."

241

"I didn't go to the ballgame. Movie, either."

"Where, then?" she was plainly mystified, but there was also a touch of accusation in her voice. "I was taught that people out at all hours of the night were up to no good." She nodded her head once, sharply, as if to say, "And that's that."

I couldn't help it; it got away with me. "You're right, Mother," I said, throwing up my hands and then slapping my thighs. "Your son, who looks innocent and harmless by day, is actually by night a hard-bitten criminal. I'm the leader of a gang of cutthroats. Under cover of darkness we rape, plunder and pillage. We're so bad we give 'rotten' a good name. And that ain't all. We rob and steal, and then give it all back just so we can rob and steal it again—"

"Benny." She looked disgusted.

"Don't you want to hear this? Confession's good for the soul, they say." I knew I was being silly, and maybe a little mean. But when I got like this I got carried away, and the words just kept spewing out, like steam from the spout of a pressure cooker. "Now, I *like* all crime, but far and away my favorite is cattle rustling. I use a different gang for that—a band of desperadoes. I'll bet you thought this wasn't cattle country. Well, it isn't, but now you know why. I'm so good at what I do that there ain't a cow left in six counties around here. That's why I've been coming in so late. We just can't rustle up any cattle to cattle rustle any-more. It's gotten so bad that I'm thinkin' seriously of goin' straight."

"Humph! You're going straight, all right: straight to bed—but not until you tell me what's wrong. And no more nonsense. You hear me?"

"Yes, ma'am," I said. "Again, I'm sorry."

"Well, I should hope so. Now out with it."

I slumped back in the chair. "The truth is, I don't know." She looked as if she didn't believe me, so I tried to explain. "It's like I can't decide what to do."

"About what?"

"My life, I guess." She looked away as if dismissing such

242

a big to-do over so small a matter, and then looked back. I went on. "High school's over. Done. I want to go to college. Can't. Don't want to work in the mill. Won't." I shrugged my shoulders. "So what do I do?"

"What do you *want* to do? I mean *really*."

I sat forward. "All right, I'll tell you. I want to get out of Milltown—forever!" I said it with such intensity that I surprised myself and Mother too, and for an anxious moment it hung there between us, the naked and quivering truth, vulnerable but dangerous. I pushed on. "It's not that I don't love you, Mother. I do. And I'm grateful for everything you've done for me. Zeb too. But I don't want to live like this for the rest of my life. I can't explain it, but I don't belong here. I don't know where I do belong, but I *don't* belong here. I want to *do* something with my life."

Very calmly she said, "Do what?"

The answer was almost too ambitious for me to utter, but I knew I'd never find a better person to tell it to. "I think I want to write—to be a writer," I said, feeling a solid satisfaction at how that sounded. It fit. It defined. "I've wondered a long time if I could," I added. "I won't know, of course, until I try. But I *think* I can. Miss Johnson said I had what it takes. At least she said I had talent."

"What kind of writing?"

"Fiction. Books. Novels."

I could tell she was thinking that over. Then she said, "Well, I don't see why you couldn't. Lord knows, you've *read* enough of 'em." She smiled, but another thought cut it off quickly. "What do you do to become a writer?"

"Mostly, you do a lot of writing until you get good at it. That can take a long time. Miss Johnson said I needed to go on to college, and I want to anyhow."

Mother gave me a helpless look. "Well, son, you know we don't have that kind of money and no way of getting it."

I slumped in the chair again. "I know. Suddenly I felt desperate. "What if I *did* go to work in the mill—just for a year? I could save all my money and then go to college until the money ran out."

The whole time I was saying that, Mother was shaking her head. "No." she said firmly. "If you go into the mill, you'll wind up staying. I've seen it happen too many times." She leaned forward and pointed a finger at me. "Understand: I don't want you thinking you're *too good* to work in the mill. But if you can better yourself, I want you to do it." She smiled. "Beside, you wouldn't last a day in the mill."

I didn't know whether to be offended or not. "Why? You think I'm some kind of cream puff or something? You think I'm lazy?"

"No, I don't. I know better than that. But you're not the type. I can't explain it, but you're different."

This was news to me, at least coming from my mother. "When did you decide that?"

She shrugged her shoulders. "I've always known."

"Well, thanks for telling *me*," I said sarcastically. "I thought I was some kind of freak."

She looked deeply concerned. "I'm sorry, son. I didn't know you felt that way. I never mentioned it because I didn't *want* you to feel that way."

I breathed deeply and slowly blew out the air. "How am I different?" I really wanted her to tell me. *I* certainly didn't know.

She pondered a moment. "I don't know, Benny. I'm not smart enough to figure it out. You'll have to do that. I just know it's true." She sighed and made another stab at it. "You're not like any of your cousins; not like any of your friends, except maybe Johnny; not like anybody I see around here. Zeb knows it too. That's why you two have never gotten along."

"God! Maybe I *am* a freak."

"No, you're not!" she said angrily. "And don't let me hear you say that again." Then her voice and attitude softened. "These people are rough, rough and coarse—as coarse as that cloth I weave down at the mill. You're not. I don't know how that happened, but you're not. Maybe you get it from your daddy. He was different too, full of—I don't know: dreams, ambition. He was smart, even if he didn't get much schooling. Read, just like you. I always knew no mill town was going to hold him for long." She was pointing at me again. "Now don't you get it in your head that you're better than these people are." With a wave of her hand she indicated Milltown. "You're just different, not better. Some of these people are as good as they come."

I agreed and nodded my head to show it.

"But you're not one of them. I know it and I expect they do too. But as to what you are and where you belong in this world, *you* will have to find that out." She stood up. "But for now you're going to bed, and I am too."

She headed toward the door and I watched her, feeling a new respect for this woman, this woman who had quit school in the fifth grade to go to work in a cotton mill. "I stuttered then, and the other children made fun of me," she had told me once without a trace of self-pity. "So I quit going. They also made fun of my clothes; we were poor and couldn't afford better. Besides, we needed the extra pay. Times were hard then."

On an impulse, I said, "Mother, we learned in history that George Washington had only a fifth-grade education."

Paused at the door, her hand on the knob, she scoffed. "Well, I'm no George Washington, but I know this much: worry won't solve your problem, and the first two letters of 'done' spell 'do'." She blew me a kiss and went on to bed.

Ten minutes later I was in bed too and sound asleep.

I woke up the next morning to the sounds of rain and thunder. The heat wave was broken, doused with rain that fell in sheets as if poured from a great tub in the sky, rain that blew in gusts up and down the street, swirling against the house and pecking at the windows like so many tiny beaks. The air in my room felt deliciously cool, especially as I dressed, and I wondered if I had not been in the grip of some fever that had broken with the heat wave. I felt better—that was for sure—better than I had felt in weeks. I didn't know how or why, but my talk with Mother had

245

eased my worried mind. Whatever had been hard at work on my problem, deep within, had either finished, given up, or knocked off for awhile. I felt relaxed. I felt good.

The rain ended around noon, but the sky remained overcast and the air cool. Looking for an excuse to get out of the house, I asked Mother if she needed anything from the store. She told me I could pick up a loaf of bread, so off I went.

Lord's was the nearest grocery store, down from our house about half a block, so I went there for the bread, and on the way out saw Johnny coming toward the door. My first impulse was to duck out of sight before he saw me, but then I thought better of it: what the hell. He got closer and looked up. "Long time, no see," I said.

"Hey, Ace," he said, smiling. "How's it goin'? Where you been keepin' yourself?" He saw the bread in my hand. "Hold on a minute while I run in here. I'll walk back with you and then cut through your yard."

Minutes later he came out with a loaf of bread too. I looked at his loaf and then mine. "Great minds *do* run in the same channels, I see."

He smiled. "Either that or great stomachs."

We ambled back toward the house, chatting about nothing special, and then stood outside for awhile, talking more, mostly about the heat and his job. He wouldn't come in—Grace needed the bread for lunch, he said—but he asked what I was doing that night. When I said I didn't know, he said, "Why don't we go out then? Just kick around?"

I was glad to accept, said I was pretty sure I could get the car, and that I'd pick him up at eight.

We drove first to the Hill, just driving around and talking. Johnny was no longer dating Patty. Her father had grown suspicious and put Patty on a short leash. "I showed up for a date, one Saturday night about a month ago, and her old man met me at the door," Johnny said. "He was standing there with his church collar on and told me Patty couldn't go out that night or any other night with me. Said he hoped I burned in Hell, and slammed the door in my face. Pissed me off, but all good things come to an end, they say. God knows, Patty was a good thing. I felt like ringing the doorbell again and telling him, just for spite, how good his daughter's pussy was. Sonofabitch probably wants some of it himself anyhow—not that I'd blame him."

"Well, who're you dating these days? Harriet?" I figured he was seeing Dianne, too, but I didn't want to be the first to bring up her name.

"Well, I'm sort of betwixt and between. Some Harvard guy home for the summer is beating my time with Harriet—and just when I was making real headway." He laughed. "Ralph something-or-other. Know him?"

I laughed. "Sorry. I run with the Princeton crowd, you know."

He nudged my arm and gave me a knowing look. "Med student, I hear."

I rolled my eyes. "Oh, hell. Well, you can kiss Harriet goodbye." We laughed, and since he seemed in a good mood I went ahead and asked. "What about Dianne?"

He looked at me as if he couldn't believe I hadn't heard. "Dianne moved to Atlanta."

"Moved?"

"Yeah, moved—as in 'gone.' As in 'vamoosed.' As in 'left home.' Don't ask me why; I don't know. All I heard was that she moved to Atlanta to go to work."

"When?"

He turned on the seat to say this: "I know what you're thinkin', but it's not true. You're thinking that I took advantage of her, seduced her, ruined her life, and that she's now fled to Atlanta in sin and shame, right?" I started to deny it, but he answered his own question. "Right. She did come home right after I did, and moved to Atlanta the very next weekend. But I didn't have anything to do with it. In the first place, I wasn't her first. So help me, Ace," he said, raising his right hand. "In the second place, I don't even think I was her second. I don't even think I came in third. She *knew* what that thing was for and knew how to use it. She nearly fucked me into next week. That's why I didn't come back to the room that night. If *that* girl is nun material, then I'm applying for Pope."

Now I had to ask. "Well, was it any good?"

He smiled. "Fan-tastic! But weird. She goes at it with a vengeance, like a starving dog on a meat wagon. But *I* might as well not have been there. It was my dick she wanted, not me. Hell, if it were detachable, I could have taken it off, pulled up a chair, relaxed, had a sandwich, and watched. I don't think she'd have noticed the difference. She didn't fuck *me;* she just used my dick to fuck herself."

I shook my head. "That *is* weird. You reckon her brother's death just pulled all her wiring loose?"

"Don't know. She didn't mention it, and I sure wasn't gonna bring it up."

Gee, things could change in a hurry, I thought. Only a short while back, it had seemed that nothing ever changed much. We went to school, we went to parties, we went out on dates. Now, only three months later, Cherry was in Europe, Dianne was in Atlanta, Miss Johnson was married, Rusty was in the Marines, Glenn was going off to college, and Johnny was working for a living. God only knew what the rest were doing.

That's when it really hit home that high school and all that was over. Done. Finished. Gone. It was sad, in a way. Graduation had split the Class of '53 as neatly as science had split the atom, and for the rest of our lives we'd be going separate ways. But which way was I going? Here it was August and I was still riding around on Saturday night with Johnny.

Just as I was thinking all that, I found myself driving by Cherry's house. We had been riding aimlessly, up one street and down the next, passing first one house and then another where we'd attended a party or gone to see a girl or we simply knew who lived there—and all of it, the whole Hill, seemed like a place I used to know but was no longer involved in, a place I no longer needed. It was a ghost town to me, and Cherry's house, dark, quiet, sort of summed it all up. I had to get on with my life.

I turned to Johnny. "I've had enough of this. What do you say we go to the Varsity?" He said fine, and I headed down the Hill and never looked back.

The Varsity wasn't crowded. Too many people on summer vacations, I guessed. I backed the old Chevy in, back by the rear fence, and left the motor running so I wouldn't have to turn off the radio. We ordered hamburgers, french fries and Cokes, and ate in silence, looking out at the parking lot and listening to the radio. The weather was still cool, and every now and then I thought I smelled fall in the night air. I loved autumn. It filled me with a kind of restless melancholy, and I felt it stir again.

I began to twirl the radio dial. On some nights, if the wind was right, you could pick up WLAC out of Nashville, and both Johnny and I got excited when we could do that. On WLAC, "with 50,000 clear-channel watts," we were hearing a new kind of music called rhythm and blues, had been listening to it in fact for more than a year, and we really liked it. It was simple, almost primitive, with strutting pianos, gut-bucket guitars, moaning harmonicas and wailing saxophones, all laid over a bass line you could've hung the wash on. And the lyrics—sometimes funny, sometimes sad, often raunchy, but always real—were very different from the moon-June mush of Tin Pan Alley. More down-to-earth. If none of the other teenagers in Augusta liked it, or had even heard it, too bad for them. Johnny and I were used to that; we were also the only ones we knew who liked jazz.

The show we liked best on WLAC was "Randy's Record Shop," and in a moment or two of searching along the dial I got it—not the best reception, but all right. Johnny and I looked at each other and smiled, and sat back to listen. One of our favorites, "Lawdy Miss Clawdy," by Lloyd Price, was playing.

Even the commercials were good. We cracked up every time we heard the ad for White Rose petroleum jelly. Not for one second did this product try to pass itself off as a remedy "for chapped and sunburned skin." No, sir. These people *knew* what America used petroleum jelly for, and that was their message, pure and simple: "When you're up against it, friends, and the going gets rough, just slap on a little White Rose. In no time at all you'll slide right in, jam up and jelly tight."

But best of all to me, except for the music, was the feeling that the disc jockey, sitting up there on some mountain in Tennessee, could look out over the whole country and see what was going on. This was silly, I knew, but I liked that feeling, the idea that we were a nation of cities, towns and villages all *connected,* all on the same wave length, instead of scattered to hell and gone, and living in isolation out on the prairies, up in the hills, along the shores and river banks. What helped this illusion most was that people from all over the country, it seemed, phoned in requests for records they wanted to hear, and I always listened carefully to the names of places they called from. That night, in the space of an hour, calls came in from Bluefield, West Virginia; Baton Rouge, Louisiana; Cincinnati, Ohio; Roanoke, Virginia; Louisville, Kentucky; Atlanta, Georgia; Jackson, Mississippi; and Mobile, Alabama. The names were like poetry to me, but frustrating too, especially that night, for they made me wonder if I ought not to be there, in one of those places, instead of where I was, stuck in Augusta. I tried to explain the feeling to Johnny and asked if he ever felt that way.

"Well, some of the names are pretty," he said, "and I wonder about some of those cities, but, no, they don't make me wish I were there. I like it right here in Augusta. This is home to me."

It was home to me too, but I didn't *feel* at home there, and the thought made me realize that that was something else I'd been struggling with lately. It wasn't just Milltown; it was the whole damn town. But what did a person do, I wondered, when home sweet home no longer was sweet and didn't feel like home either. If a man didn't belong in the only place he'd ever known, where *did* he belong?

I didn't know the answer to that, but I made up my mind then and there to try to find out. Johnny and I called it a night around eleven-thirty, but bright and early Monday morning I walked downtown to Bell Auditorium, marched into the office of the draft board and volunteered to be drafted. A week later I got my draft notice, took it with me to my next reserve meeting, and told the officer in charge that I wanted to go into the Navy—provided I passed the physical, scheduled in Columbia, South Carolina, the following Monday. I passed and soon received a letter from the Navy telling me to report to Bainbridge, Maryland, for basic training on September 24.

My mother wasn't entirely happy about all this, but I told her, "The first two letters of 'done' spell 'do.' Well, I'm doing. Besides, it's too late to back out now."

Zeb thought it was a good idea. He'd always wanted to serve in the Army, but a curved spine from a childhood disease had kept him out. "Let him go, Janie; it'll make a man out of him."

"He's already a man," Mother said, "A fine, young man." She hugged my neck with tears in her eyes and then went into her bedroom—to cry, I knew—but after that she never let me see her sorrow again.

Johnny got off work to go to the bus station with me on the twenty-third. Mother and Zeb had to work, so he volunteered to drive me down to the Greyhound terminal. We got there around nine o'clock. The bus wasn't due to leave for another thirty minutes, so we stood around outside the depot and talked, keeping an eye on dark clouds that threatened rain at any minute.

"I probably won't be far behind you," Johnny said. "I've been thinking of joining myself. Air Force. I don't like my job and I might as well go ahead and get this service thing over with."

"Let 'em draft you," I advised. "Only two years that way."

"I think I'd rather do four in the Air Force than two in the Army," he said.

"Well, whatever you do, keep in touch. I'll write first chance I get."

"I'll do it," he said. Then snapping his fingers he said, "I *knew* there was something I wanted to tell you. First, Cherry's home. Got in yesterday. Been all over Europe, but mostly in Germany."

My pulse quickened a bit when he told me, but that was the only effect it had on me. "Thanks," I said, "but that's over. I've climbed the Hill for the last time."

"Second, guess what I heard about Dianne Damico?"

"She's entered the convent after all," I said, sure that that was it.

"Uh, not quite," Johnny said. "She's a high-priced call girl in Atlanta."

"Naw!" I just couldn't picture that—though on second thought I wasn't so sure anymore.

"Guess who found out about it, or least how I heard it. Helen McIver's father. He told Helen and Helen told me. Seems her old man was in Atlanta on business, staying at this fancy hotel, and spotted Dianne in the hotel lounge. He almost didn't recognize her, he said, 'cause he remember her as a teenager. But there she was, dressed to kill and looking like a million—and obviously working. Apparently she didn't see him or, if she did, didn't recognize him. But he checked with the bellboy, and sure enough that's what she was. Hundred bucks a throw, the bellboy said. Man, I'm glad I got it before she put a price tag on it. At a hundred bucks for pussy, I couldn't afford a quick feel."

That left me feeling numb. Johnny was amused by the story, but I felt that it was a sad one. Very sad. And it wasn't because she had become a prostitute; it was because I still believed her story that she had wanted to be a nun. It was one thing not to get what you wanted in life, but to miss it by that much was a crying shame. "What do you think happened to that girl?" I asked.

Johnny said without hesitation, "Got a taste of cock and went crazy over it."

I didn't think that was it, but I didn't say so. Love in some people was a fragile thing, and if it got broken, all the king's horses and all the king's men couldn't put it together again. "You reckon she loved her brother so much that she just lost her faith when he died?"

"Don't know about that," Johnny said. "But that's about the time she lost her cherry, I hear."

I was surprised. "Who told you that?" But I answered my own question at the same time he did: "Helen McIver." We laughed. "You better marry Helen McIver," I said. "She's a goddam treasure trove of information. She could make you a fortune in the stock market."

Johnny flashed an odd little smile just as my bus was called over the loudspeakers. "Well, she *ain't* a bad lay," he said.

I was taken aback, but I couldn't help laughing. "Why you sorry rascal," I said. He laughed too.

"All aboard!" the dispatcher said.

We moved toward the bus. "Look," I said, "when you write just tell me who on the Hill you *didn't* fuck; it'll make a shorter list." I handed the bus driver my ticket and stepped up into the well of the door. "See you, friend," I said.

"Later, Ace," Johnny said.

I found a seat by a window, put my travel bag in the rack overhead, and sat down, thinking I'd wave to Johnny one last time. But just as I did, the rain swept in, and when I looked out, Johnny was running for his car. Minutes later, the bus eased out of its dock and turned down Greene Street. I took a last look at all the old Victorian homes and the huge live oaks, swaying in the wind and rain. Soon we were crossing the Savannah River on the Fifth Street Bridge, pushing into South Carolina, heading north. The river, speckled with rain, looked even muddier than usual, looked more than ever like a strong, brown god. I raised my hand in a farewell salute to it.